COLD WAR HORROR

BRIAN HUNTER

Dedicated to the very late, very great Gilbert E. Rigdon;
"Don't let the bastards get you down!"

Roadside

Séamus 'Shay' Hayes gripped the collar of his coat by its lapels. He snapped the stiff collar up in a futile rebuke against the wind, nestling his ears in its fur lining, seeking reprieve from the needling November chill. He glanced upward once more with a tired sigh, hoping to catch a fleck of starlight, but the streetlights' warm yellow glow radiated through the low fog and had the curious effect of blanketing him in a dull light from all sides. The sort of light that muffles the twinkle of the stars and hushes your voice like falling snow.

His hands darted back into the cozy map pockets, his right hand wrapping around the damp sheath of a hunting knife, and his left hand cradling the small leather-bound flask that carried the last of his particularly rare swill. He could tell by the tinny jostling sound that he had little to spare. No… he'd find some other way to fend off the cold on his long walk back out of this nameless lane and back toward the bright glow on the horizon, which he was hopeful was Portland.

With a pause, without lifting his feet, he pivoted at the hips for a final glance at the mound crumpled just outside the corner of a streetlamp's drape of light. Steam still emitted from the husk of what was once a man, rising slowly from the hot fluids spilled on the smooth black pavement below it. His mind flashed back to the moment he first saw this thing as it stood tall in the mocking shape of a man.

Shay recalled the grisly scene an hour earlier in a very different way. Shay was earlier convinced that he would be himself lying dead in a dark alley, ended by the hand of the predator he'd just slain. The thought of such a reversal, one he had experienced well more than once, brought a distinct smirk across the weathered face of this tired gent. As he turned back to face the road, he shrugged his shoulders up and forward to hide in the wooly collar against this stinging cold and fog. The only sounds to be heard were the soft clacking of his loafers and the woodland creatures scuffling about.

With a click-clack, Shay's feet met the pavement without the usual spring in his step. His head ached, and his gut was knotted, but he was *alive*. The city was waiting, and he'd never been happier to head toward home.

The road was long, a dozen miles or more, mostly downhill. The rural roads showed little sign of life, save the residential street he'd left behind after his narrow escape. His watch ticked away the minutes, two heartbeats between ticks. He could feel his pulse in his stiff hands. It was nearing three o'clock in the morning—the *witching hour*, he thought with a chuckle.

Only a few homes set back from the road had glowing porchlights; most were extinguished when their owners retired for the night. It was a common way for folks in rural towns and pleasant societies to let it be known that they were no longer to be disturbed. He remembered many a day in his youth when a neighbor would be annoyed at him for knocking on a doorway too late. He'd been a tedious young man, just a bit smarter than his peers and always too curious for his own good. At least, that was what his mother told him on no less than a dozen occasions. He'd developed a bad habit of wandering too far from home and realizing it too late, which often meant pestering a neighbor for hospitality or help finding his way home. Thankfully, a small town's folk had a way of taking care of their own.

Now, in the bleak and misty night, Shay dearly wished he were able to knock on a door, pester a neighbor, and receive a ride home. Or to the city. Or to anywhere where it was warm and dry and perhaps offered a good tea… his hands and pant-cuffs still damp with the blood of his abductor, it would be best to vacate the area without being seen, arguably better than being associated with thirteen stone of body cooling quietly in the mist. He counted his blessings for having been brought against his will to such a quiet place, such a delightfully empty spate of streets where he could soft-shoe his way out without much effort or notice. His attention waned from the walk back to memories of Ireland's dirt and cobblestone streets and many long walks home over the decades. He hadn't seen another soul for an hour, and he was now walking down roads that were lined with bush and trees rather than home and garden. The rolling hills challenged his shins, and while he could doff his dress shoes with their stiff heels, the piercing cold of this night put that idea in the bin.

At least it's a fine place for a long walk,… he convinced himself. *Could've been harangued out to the hills of Los Angeles or some other armpit.*

During his time in Oregon, Shay appreciated that the roads all led *somewhere*. Whether it was another small town, a collection of apple orchards or perhaps peaches, or even a winding road to a mountaintop, there was so much life in this state.

The hills had given way to a rather lovely view of the city. The mist extended through the city, and with this view, Shay noted that it appeared to be most dense at the distant side of town. His side of town. Finally, he trudged down streets with street lamps. Shay watched his shadow undulate in front of him. It would grow short as he walked under a new street lamp, then stretch out for meters as the last lamp's glow waved goodbye. A hundred paces along the dark, then again, he was greeted by another veil of light which sent his silhouette cast far behind. Alone, he felt as though the lights were stage lights, theater trickery to make him appear great in stature. The silence of the night pushed his mind toward such eerie thoughts.

"Ocean air brings in a deathly cold, Shay.' His mother would shake her finger at him sternly, 'and there's no sense in dyin' of a chill when you've got such fine garb ye mother has laid out. Why do you insist on going out half arse-bare for your little adventures with ye friends?" His memory, bad as it was, shimmered forth a short memory of himself as a pip, standing in his cramped home between the table and a dresser full of that woolen garb. He recalls he was wearing a scarf, a button-up shirt, and some short pants. Wasn't that enough? No, not for Ma. She was perhaps the most nurturing and loving a Ma ever to rear a child, but Shay, as a lad, knew not what a rare prize that was. The memory warmed him just a bit as the first hint of light cracked over the mountains in the East.

Another mile in, he reached his favorite stretch of Portland. The place where all the brick-and-mortar stores were bound together in blocks as the land became less affordable, and the need for proximity to the city center became a priority. Even in the mist, he could see some of the hand-painted billboard advertisements bannered across the sides of some buildings. Signs for shaving products, cola, and even a train trip on the North Coast Limited, famous for its giant potato plates. Signs lying to so many people about how a product or service would make their life so much better, telling them to "call now" or "get yours today!"

The road 'rose to meet his feet,' as the old saying goes. Quickening his pace now, his recollection of what his night still might entail flashed images of that mess he was leaving behind. The car in the middle of the street, the slumped husk... the smell of death that clung to it well before he sent it off this realm with deft thrusts of a trusty old blade. While he'd never taken the life of a man who wasn't a threat to his own, this time was... different.

As the streetlights had become frequent now, he stopped at a small park and located a stone bird fountain. Washing the knife, he shook it dry and slid it back into the old sheath, abandoning his now-stained handkerchief nearby. He felt guilty about whoever may be using the fountain next, its waters now murky with more than moss. He swiftly abandoned the park in pursuit of the streets that would take him home. He was in desperate need of a shower and a more comfortable pair of shoes.

Arriving at his building, the keys in his hand let out a rattle as he quietly and swiftly went into the breach of this warm place, closing the door behind him on its well-oiled hinges without more than a soft 'click' of the latch. He'd had plenty of practice sneaking through this door. He felt warmth against his cheeks and smelled the scent of good pipe tobacco.

Christ, home at last...

Shay loved this tired old building full of trinkets and dusty furniture. As he walked down the tread-worn wood floors of the entry hall, he passed the few small rooms on the first floor. The doors were closed, and murmurs of radios or perhaps a record player quietly filled the space between the creaks of his gentle yet hard-soled footsteps.

The building had been a small apothecary when it was built around 1905, but now, in its golden years, it had been lovingly reimagined as a small cafe. The back of the building now served as the residence of the cafe's owner, Martîn Gollack. Gollack was a retired French chef, but with a name that wasn't very French. It amused Shay to no end, as every time he'd corner the man to inquire about it, Gollack refused to answer directly. No, the septuagenarian would embark upon another misty tale about his youth, his travels in tow of his architect father, and the story would usually weave so long that Shay would run out of time before the part of the story was reached where Gollack would tell him where in the bloody hell that name came from! The man was an enigma, to be sure, but he brewed quite a cup of coffee (or even a fancy little "un café"). It amused Shay that if you ordered coffee with an accent, you'd receive a much smaller cup. However, it would be a right kick in the teeth. Frothy, nearly *chewy*.

Shay tiptoed down the hall, a hand steadying him along the beltline trim of the wall. None of the other residents would be awake, and he had no desire to change that.

The cafe's back door was the first door on the left, the prettiest door. That space had been converted into the cafe far more recently than the other units had been inhabited, and so it wore quite a fresh coat of rose-colored paint, thick and sloppily applied over the old once-white door and frame. A small sign hung off a nail, handwritten on a thin slab of fruit-crate wood and hung with twine, to remind folks the cafe was closed.

Across the hall, the other two abodes on the right were of a more lived-in character as they hadn't seen a paintbrush in some years. Gerry, also known as Gerald, was a WW1 veteran with a penchant for good cherry pipe tobacco and big-band music. It was part of his charm, and nobody ever seemed to complain about the wisps of smoke crawling out into the hallway when it was too cold for him to crack a window. No bother; Shay happened to enjoy the smell. On an occasion or two, he'd even invited Gerald up to his abode (with the pipe) in an effort to rob the old bugger of a bit of that warm, rustic smoke.

Still heading toward his private stairway, Shay passed the second door on the right. This door proclaimed its age through years of wear at two places: the original brass knob, and an ornate kick plate crowning layers of paint worn off the edge of the door near the bottom. The doorknob was nearly bare of decoration, and it had been greeted so many times by the hand of a guest... often later than society deems polite. The missing paint, however, was something less suggestive. A fat and very friendly tabby cat named Jasmine would rub against the door on her way in and out of the abode, warmly marking her territory and asking to be let in. Little Jasmine was the sole child and favorite companion of the occupant, Ginger Fisher. Ms. Fisher was a lovely woman with the brightest blue eyes and a hypnotically sultry, almost raspy voice. Ginger (perhaps not the name she was born with, but the name she carries now) had been a singer most of her life, and an entertainer. A fascinating and well-traveled gal, she would hum or sing from dawn until after dusk... just quiet enough not to bother her neighbors and just well enough to be appreciated by any whose ears were lucky enough to hear it above the frequent din of the cafe. Shay wondered if he'd ever tire of her humming. One can only drink the finest whisky so many times before one wishes for a bitter ale.

Truth be told, Shay had a slight schoolyard 'pash' on this woman. His tastes in potential partners were becoming a bit silvered. He was older than he looked. His kin aged well. It was one of the few blessings of the Hayes clan. Ginger had told Shay once, over a tea, that she'd been an exposition model in her heyday. She neglected to mention that the exposition was for the stylistically brash and chrome-laden 1930 Buick, some twenty years prior.

From his fragmented memory, once or twice, the fleeting moment when his own Ma told him, "Dear, the soul grows old as does the heart, no matter how your reflection lies. Follow that truth and don't take up kin who aren't looking to stay close." She had always been keen on Shay finding one of his lot to marry, build a family. It weighed on his heart that people had so little time, and that thought echoed far louder when he thought about Ginger Fisher.

He reached the final door in the hall and deftly opened it with his slightly bent key, sneaking up the plush carpeted stairs in the narrow stairwell. Ascending the stairs to his abode, on the last step, he reached out in the darkness to the Tiffany lamp he kept near the stairs. With a tug of the cord, the lamp shone its rays of rich, colorful light across the room.

His abode was cozy and small. Walls of beadboard and brick, flanked by oak storage shelves, were repurposed as a place for the little knick-knacks he had collected over the years. In dust and dim light, hundreds of strange little artifacts sat awaiting the touch of another curious visitor. Ivory knives from the Orient sat in rich, hand-carved stands, copper tobacco tins from Edwardian England, silly little warrior figurines from Istanbul, eyes painted crooked with bellies round, and swords waving wildly. His youthful travels were wide and far, his love of new shores and new cities one of his few remaining hobbies. He'd gotten bored with most of his little pursuits as the decades wore on, but the little shelf was a gleam in his fanciful nature.

The staircase banisters came up behind a lovely fainting chair, stitched in gold throughout a crimson-red plush weave, where he would toss his heavy coat. The fire he had left burning was now embers, so Shay went to the hearth and threw a few twigs under a good, dry split log. In no time, he'd have the place warm as a baker's oven.

Walking into the center of the room, he took a moment to stretch his arms and back a bit, the color coming back to his hands while the rattling left his bones. His favorite chair awaited him —a lovely auburn-colored wingback recliner. Its years shone in the arms and the seat, but it was worn to a perfect fit for Shay and perfectly inviting after a damnably hard night. As he leaned back, he peered out the window behind him; dawn was already approaching, with the twilight of the sky overtaken in a rich azure as the fog departed. Without a care, he closed his eyes and let the fire crackle on. The sleep was well deserved.

...

Across town, a shadow cast across the scene. The shadow, a limp and lifeless form, lay flat on the cold roadway in waning twilight. Coastal fog crept across damp, manicured lawns, and the faint hum of an electrical transformer echoed across the otherwise graven street. Still air hung heavy over the wisps of mist now crawling across the pavement and over the detritus pile of cloth, flesh, and bone, which looked grotesque against the clean pavement. A small chirp of a morning starling, the only sound joining that electrical hum in a soft symphony.

Then, a faint rustling—the scrape of a watch band against a rough road top, the scuffing of a shoe heel against the same. Nobody witnessed this creature moving with a nearly hydraulic, slow, machine-like motion. The once-limp frame of a well-built man sat straight up and stiff through the tendrils of mist. Without looking down or around, the body stumbled to its feet against the car fender, wet with condensation and harsh against its cold flesh.

That little starling let out nary a chirp now; the crisp air was disturbed with the groan and grunt of something akin to a wild predator. No animal that may fear as prey fear would now dare to evoke the interest or attention of this abomination they were now acutely aware of. No, the whole world was still, and nature held its breath in terror of the thing arising.

A mild electrical hum radiated in the air. Shoes dragged heavy and sluggish towards the source. The only other sound was a drip... plop... drip of thick, wicked bile onto the ground as whatever dark force that rose this hulk off the ground like a puppet by the strings now coaxed it toward the hum of voltage.

A few more steps, another long drag of feet now over rough rocks that lined the pavement. Through the gravel and a patch of muddy red dirt, this unseen force coerced this puppet a dozen yards and right up next to a large metal appliance. City utility markings in crisp white stood against a rich green background.

With dirty, claw-like fingers, the devil grabbed and pulled at the thin metal handle on the cover of the box. Slowly, it began to bend away from the latch under the formidable strength of this ambling ghoul. With a final slow creak, the cover flung open to reveal complex components, audibly humming and alive with energy.

The dark figure paused as if to assess its accomplishment or perhaps suss out what its purpose in front of all these brass levers and ceramic insulators might be before near-instinctively reaching into the box. One grey hand lay on a large, thick copper wire. With sluggish reach, the thing grasped the grounding cable for the panel. With a crackling din filling the air, muscles clenched and flesh seared. A percussive flash of smoke and sparks erupted from the now-smoldering conduits as hundreds of volts coursed through the filthy hands, the equipment shorting out and failing spectacularly.

The violator was thrown free, and the streetlamps cut out. Darkness enveloped all.

Moments later, a half-dozen feet away and now closer to the road, lay this once again motionless pile of flesh and bone. This thing now *lay* alive merely feet from where it had previously *stood* dead. Steam rose off the contorted face of this body as new life lurched through veins stiffened by rigor mortis, with blood dark and thick. A small gasp of cool night air. Its eyes flickered open almost as wide as could be, with its face and cheeks drawn tight in a silent scream, not of agony, but of sheer trauma to the tissues of this mechanized beast.

Peering up toward the misty sky, two dry eyes blinked as blackened, charred hands planted into tufts of wet, tall grass. Without a sound, the thing sat up straight and then expelled a breath of putrid air into the low mist. The punctures in the abdomen, the muscles around the body still clenched in recoil from such violent electrocution, neither seemed to hinder the thing limping back toward the road, toward the sedan that rested there patiently. With a slight shove, a heavy hand slammed the trunk of the sedan. Charred fingers reached to the dashboard and turned the keys. Shortly later, the flathead six-cylinder hummed to life. With head hanging low and the stench of rot lingering in the air, those charred hands shifted the car into gear.

The warm golden dawn rose over a stain on the pavement, nothing more.

Recovering

Monday, November 20[th,] 1950

Radiant white sunlight shone through the wood slats, jostling open the eyes of a weary man. Shay sat up, his sprung recliner chair meeting his posture and seating him upright. To his right, a mug still half-full of the prior day's coffee collected dust. To his left, rays of the sun warmed the panes. He squinted and turned away, rubbing his eyes to coax them to adjust to the light. His stomach growled at him, and he leaned forward, resting his face in his palms. The night's wild dreams were still swirling, cold rooms and angry throngs of dead men lurching at him. Dark, tight spaces where he couldn't move, couldn't breathe. It distressed him now still.

With a sigh, he leaned back in the chair. With a shrug, Shay downed the cold, gritty, leftover brew and set it back down on the table, regretting it as his tongue felt coarse grit. A glance at his watch told him it was about eleven. Taking it off revealed a clammy pink band of skin on his wrist, a perfect outline. It disgusted him.

In a haze, he peeled off his socks and stripped off the twill slacks along with the rest of his filthy garb. A hot shower would get his blood moving and his mind right. He turned on the water and stepped in, yelping aloud as the icy splash of water on his bare body chased him right back out, shivering.

"You look a damned fool, you know that?' he chided his reflection, 'Look at you, skin and bones now. Get some damn *meat* on ye!" It was true; he'd been letting himself skip too many meals and had not been exercising. Too many achy mornings lately for all that Army-trained routine.

Stepping back under hot water, Shay leaned on the wall of the shower and hung his head. As the hot water ran down his crown and his back, he recounted the night's turn of events. Surprisingly, his usually cloudy memory was crisp and clear at this moment.

All right, you impetuous tool. Ye did everything wrong and survived... good fortune won't last forever. Cam would be chewing your behind right now, t'be sure.

...

The prior night had begun in a rather mundane way; he'd had tea at a small steakhouse near downtown, joining a meet of the local Irish League, a club dedicated to... well, very little. In truth, it was a social club and an excuse to sing a few songs over some pints. The restaurant had booked their group in the rear half of the establishment, keeping the main dining room open for guests of all walks. After that group's very friendly invitation for all to drink and sing along, by the close of business, every man, woman, and child in the place was an Irishman in spirit. He'd spent most of the night leaning on the polished brass bar edge, simply observing, feeling a touch antisocial as was often the case around holidays.

Not yet nine in the evening, Shay had on that night wandered soberly back to his home to find a small envelope postmarked for him, no sender on the corner of the envelope. He assumed it would be a holiday card, and took it upstairs and sat to give it a look in the light. He found instead a handwritten letter, an impassioned plea for help from a person purporting to know Shay's profession as a private detective... and offering generous pay for a small job sussing out local union busting.

In his haste to earn a buck, he never considered it might lead to another case he was working on —one that his good friend and Private Investigator William Bigsby had commissioned him to take on, with little tangible progress made thus far.

William, Billy to friends, had sent Shay a dossier covering some rather dubious claims of bodies going missing from morgues and funeral homes in Oregon and Washington, only to be seen later alive and well in a state of confusion or utter aggravation. In Billy's records, multiple people claimed to have seen suspicious men lurking about and committing low-level crimes... men who resembled recently missing corpses. It all seemed a bit too fantastical for Shay, but Billy's money was as green as any, so he had taken the job a few weeks prior without much thought. Nothing significant had come of it, just some dead-end interviews and a few hastily-recorded police reports that dismissed it all as 'crackpot.'

The letter promised a fine payout for some simple reconnaissance; the choice was obvious. Shay set out in his evening finery under a stout coat to meet the sender, who was deeply concerned with preserving his local millworker's union. It had necessitated a long taxi ride to a cluster of industrial buildings on the West side, practically headed to Beaverton. Not that Shay minded the trip; it was an open invitation for Shay to visit this man's office under the pretense of "If I'm not already waiting, I'll arrive in short order. We cannot do this without your help."

"Suppose it's nice to feel wanted?" he joked as he donned his coat.

The taxi had dropped him off curbside in front of a cluster of brick and mortar buildings, stalwart thirty-foot-high warehouses, and loading docks. He saw no smoke from a chimney, no lights in the windows save a few glimmering doorway lamps some fifty yards down the walk between the rows of buildings. Like a fool, he shrugged it off. "Suppose they all look abandoned at night…" He bid the taxi driver goodnight, supposing he would find a phone if his digging uncovered little (or the man was a blowhard; it had happened before).

With his stiff soles clacking, Shay walked toward what looked like offices or a guard station. He had pulled out his cherrywood pipe from his airman's coat, striking a wood match to the bowl. The tobacco, not as sweet as Gerry's, embered under the tamp of ash and had a smooth draw. He watched the puffs of smoke from his pipe hanging in the air behind him as he walked, unintentionally mimicking a chuffing steam locomotive.

As he passed a narrow gap between one building and its furnace house, someone stepped out and heavy-handedly clubbed him from behind, the strike landing on the gumshoe's temple and sending his vision to blur almost immediately. As he fell to the ground and his vision faded to black, he recalls someone with strong hands grabbing him by the armpits and slinging him over their shoulder like a child. He'd heard the clatter of his pipe breaking to pieces on the ground as he blacked out.

After some time, several hours, judging by the cold that had set in, he awoke in the trunk of a car. His head throbbing and the exhaust gases creeping into the boot past the seals, his pitch-dark ride was unpleasant, to say the least. He was groggy and slow to come around.

The car drove for quite a while, and there was no way to decipher where he might be headed.

When his head stopped spinning, he took stock of his position. He was captive in the middle of the night, in someone's fume-filled car boot, and his only chance to escape was clear. He'd need to stop the car from where he was, trapped in that trunk. He squirmed to reach his coat breast pocket and, after succeeding, lit a wood match from its little box and took a view of his surroundings. Being built on the lanky side had its advantages, and he was able to twist and contort just enough to estimate what he could reach in that tight trunk space. As he fumbled around, he felt a few objects in reach just as the match burned out; now, all he could smell and taste was sulfurous match smoke; it would be wiser to work in the dark.

In his makeshift dungeon, Shay took stock of what his hands could reach. At his shins (lying on his side with his knees bent as a child sleeps), stretching as best he could to get them, he could feel the car's jack stand and tire iron nestled in their brackets against the inside of the fender. Behind his back, against the fiberboard backing of the rear seat, he laid his hands on the firm rubber of a spare tire laid flat... he could hear its hubcap rattling around loosely on the steel rim. He intuited it was a wide tire —some 20 centimeters —so he knew it must be a more modern automobile, likely a post-war American. He reached in front of himself and pulled up the edge of the trunk's floor liner. He'd seen in the brief matchlight that it was houndstooth vinyl-covered and rather flimsy.

Prying the trunk's floor liner back despite his body weight holding it down, Shay got under the edge and found what he'd been looking for. The cloth-wrapped wiring loom for the tail and brake lights laced between his fingers. Having a great thought, he knew if he reached back a bit further, he would strike gold. With all his ability in the small space, Shay reached down and wriggled loose the tied-down tire iron. Its heft in his hand, he thought about using it as a weapon. "Got to get the damn lid open first..." he thought as he used its bladed hubcap-removing end to stab into the fiberboard trunk liner. With a bit of leverage, he was able to make a hole in the fiberboard, where he pried and pulled until he could fit his hand through. Smashing his knuckles on the rusty metal trunk floor underneath, he wriggled and reached around and found what he was looking for: the wire that ran from the taillight wiring harness to the sending unit submerged in the fuel tank. One tiny little wire, limp and soft. Silly, considering its importance.

He wrapped the wire around his now-bloodied knuckles; with a gentle tug, he yanked the wire clean off its terminal on top of the fuel tank. Now, he knew the driver would see the car's dashboard gauge showing it was empty, no matter how much fuel was in the car. He drew his hand out of the floorboard, then, with another wrap-and-tug, he ripped the taillight wiring harness clean out of the bulb sockets on one side of the car. Contorting to reach further up the wiring harness, he yanked the wires from the other side of the car's taillamp housing. He knew he'd need to work fast if he wanted time to act when his abductor stopped to check the vehicle. He supposed that at night, either the driver would notice the lights out (as the taillights' shine could be seen in the rearview of any car) or stop for fuel. Now, he waited.

Come on, you son of a bitch. Pull this car off the road and come say hello!

He waited; he counted. Two minutes rolled past. The counting helped him stay calm. Five minutes. Ten. The counting was no longer keeping him calm.

Okay, change of plan. Looks like you're going to make me do this the hard way. Fine.

Taking a breath and relaxing his back, he used his knees against the inside of the trunk lid to push himself somewhat clockwise; now, the car's jack was within reach. It took him a minute or more and a good bit of painful skinning of his knuckles to release the metal spring that was holding the jack against the wall of the trunk, but then, having released it, he knew what he would do. He pulled the heavy steel jack post up between his legs and wedged it between the trunk floor and the lid; it stood straight up in front of his chest. As a bumper jack, the ratcheting portion would only lift the jack's head so far. He'd need a wedge. With an uncomfortable twist, he reached back and snatched that hubcap off the spare tire. Placing it on the lip of the bumper jack's raising point, the heavy steel hubcap could act to transfer the lifting force from the lip of the jack to the underside of the trunk, or so he hoped.

You'd better be ready, you fool. Heaven knows where he's taking you…

With some effort, he slipped the tire iron into its place in the jack mechanism, where it became the jacking handle. With the limited range of motion he had, he jacked that goddamn trunk lid up with all his might… and felt the hubcap bend.

Stay stiff, you little tin shit…

He cranked down on that tire iron again, and the jack creaked and groaned… the trunk lid relented! He saw a bit of light and felt a breeze of cool air at the sides, where it was bowing. This sent a wave of relief into the man, not to mention clearing out some of the exhaust fumes. "Ah, thank Christ…" he mumbled. Using all the strength he had in his shoulders and chest, he pumped the jack handle another four times. The deck lid bent further, but the latch held. "No worries, almost there!" he assured himself. He pulled the tire iron out of the jack and shoved the flat end into the trunk latch.

"Okay, you bastard, this is for all the beans…" he grumbled aloud.

Bracing his feet against the fender and his back against the spare tire, he used every bit of strength to twist that tire iron back toward his chest. The latch snapped, and the trunk lid shot open, sending the jack stand tumbling out onto the street and making an awful clatter. He could feel the car lurch, immediately slowing down from highway speed. He took a breath of air and grasped that tire iron, knowing he'd be a dead man if he tried leaping out of a fast-moving car.

Wait for it to slow, just wait…

As he sat up on his heels in the trunk, the lid banging against the back of his sore skull, he gripped the tire iron firmly, ready to escape.

To his credit, that was a good plan. Yet, his captor was no slouch either. To his surprise, the car, which had been slowing down, came to a skidding, abrupt stop, which sent Shay tumbling back into the trunk and ruining his plan to leap out and leg it. By the time he'd regained his footing, there was already a shadow of a very sizable man stepping up to the semi-open trunk.

Quick to his reflexes, Shay sat half-upright and swung the tire iron wildly. It made a hard, very dense 'thudding' as it struck the assailant's face. He leaped out of the trunk at this moment, but he realized his prior head injury had him a bit wobbly on his feet, and he was not going to get far by legging it.

Instead, Shay had stopped just aside the trunk and reached into the front map pocket of his thick coat. Feeling double-lucky, his hand clasped around his lucky knife, which he withdrew from its leather sheath in a quick motion. The tire iron's blow that would topple nearly any man had barely slowed this bastard. In the moonlight, Shay saw the face of his assailant, collapsed on one side. It was a stout strike, yet despite the damage, the man's hands raised and grasped toward Shay in a slow but determined manner.

Shay ducked the slow grab, of course, and countered with a few swift swishes of his razor-sharp knife. He felt the blade slash through coat and flesh, nearly to the bone, on the arm and back of this menacing beast. His heart skipped a beat as the man turned toward him again, making no sound and lurching forward with clutching hands outstretched.

Grabbing the knife by the hilt and aiming it downward, Shay leaped forward between the arms of the man while he swung his hands downward. It was a direct hit; the blade sank into the chest of the man just above the collarbone. The heavy arms clasped tight; he was now in a dance of death with this juggernaut as its bear hug crushed the wind out of Shay. He switched his hands, one pushing away the pulped face of the towering man as the other wrenched the knife out of his chest. Shay knew he'd held little air left to finish his attack, so with his last strength, he jabbed the blade down again into the neck of his attacker, quick as a prizefighter and maybe a half-dozen times. The man, nee brute, relaxed its grip and then stumbled back against the car as Shay was dropped breathless to the ground. After a gasp or two, Shay realized his hand was still clutched around his blade. He took a bladed stance and sprang forward, staying low, and bowled over the silent menace onto the pavement next to the car. Shay knew his only chance to win and perhaps survive was to keep this column of a man off his feet.

Coming in low, he hamstrung the bastard. Pivoting and swinging wildly, Shay sent the steel blade to the hilt through the body of this beast another dozen times as the body writhed, seemingly stunned. He got on his knees, wheezing for his breath. As he ran out of steam and tumbled away to regroup, he saw the demon was possibly done for and lying very still now. Stumbling to his tired feet, Shay's watery eyes saw not a man there but something inexplicably worse. The thought struck him that no man, not any man who walks this earth, could take such punishment as this beast had.

Almost immediately, with gore still dripping from his blade, Shay realized that in the state of things now, it might appear more like a terrible crime, head injury notwithstanding. He decided it was not his place to dispose of the thing but to escape toward town without disturbing anything further. It would stand to reason that with no witnesses, he could walk away with his injuries and avoid being fingered. The thought of defending his own life by taking another and subsequently being locked up for murder in one terrible night did not sit particularly well with him. After a quick pat-down to ensure he hadn't left anything behind, he set off quickly as his wobbly legs would take him.

...

That string of events had played out in his mind as he let hot water run down his body, except for the knot on his head. Standing there, breathing the steam, Shay tried hard to make sense of what he had seen, but was further from answers than he had been the night before. His hands shook as he pleaded silently for the water to wash away the dread and guilt of what had happened. The hot water diminished to tepid, but the burden remained.

Billy, what sort of carnival sideshow have you gotten us into?

Reluctantly, he lurched out of the shower and ready himself to face the world once again.

With little desire at this moment to get back on the trail, no matter how hot, the gumshoe decided he'd take the train North to Seattle and have a sit-down with the boss. Billy would want updates a couple of times a week, but this was no discussion for the phone. So, after a tiny bit of food and several cups of tea, Shay calmed his nerves enough to collect his things and catch the overnight train to Seattle. It was cheap and easy if you found a well-maintained seat in which to sleep. He made preparations with a small suitcase and a selection of cigars. With his body aching from the brutal night's melee, Shay paused in his mirror to ensure he looked his best. His hat tilted at an awkward forward angle; he'd tried not to rest it on the lump adorning his head that marked his night's failures.

You look like you slept in a cement mixer, old boy.

The rest of the suit was the perfect traveling attire: ash-gray slacks and soft black shoes, a stiff white shirt, and his best tweed coat. He never could describe the color; it was such a mix of earth tones that he'd simply refer to it as his 'dirt coat.' His favorite part of the coat was its hidden zippered liner, which concealed a pistol pouch so he could carry a firearm without the ungainly under-arm shoulder holsters some men preferred. Right now, all that the pocket contained was a farmer's almanac, which Shay withdrew. Using the little attached (by an elastic band) pencil, he opened the calendar and crossed the day off. This day was Monday, November 20th, 1950, and the almanac called for snow. Thanksgiving was merely three days away.

Shay sarcastically joked to himself, "What a prediction, you loons. Snowfall on the cusp of December? Unheard of!" and he laughed to himself as he zipped the almanac back into the pocket.

Auld acquaintance

A train conductor in a spotless blue uniform woke Shay with a gentle jostle of the shoulder. "Time to get up, pal. We're at Union Station, last stop, don't ya know?" His tone was friendly but insistent. Shay raised his head off the lounge table, imprints of his sleeve creased red into his forehead. He picked up his hat, tucking it down over his eyes.

"What's the time, sir?" Shay was groggy and unenthused about his throbbing head.

The conductor checked his watch, apologizing, "We had some delays, there was a cattle truck on the tracks back a few towns. It's five o'clock sharp, sir. Don't forget your bags!" and he sauntered away.

Half-waving to the conductor as he stood up, Shay stretched his back. He felt well enough rested; the prior evening's tumbler of top-shelf whisky from the railcar bar put him right to sleep. He recalls leaving a dollar gratuity; perhaps that's why the barman didn't boot him for sleeping on the counter. With an exaggerated yawn, Shay made his way back to the coach car, where he retrieved his bag.

The blue dawn was crisp and clear over Seattle's ornate Union Station. In the morning chill, Shay knew there was time for a hot coffee and to sit for a spell before Billy would be in the office. His walk took him North, then Northwest. He recalled Billy speaking highly of a breakfast cafe on Cherry Street, which was just past Billy's office in Smith Tower. So, Shay made his way to 2nd and Cherry, strutting right past Smith Tower along the way.

Arriving at Cherry Street, Shay paused. To his right, Cherry went uphill. To his left, it was good and flat all the way toward the waterfront. Shay thought about his Billy, confined to a wheelchair after having lost both his legs in a mountaineering accident. He turned left and went toward the water. Six steps later, Shay paused. A sly grin crept across his face, and he spoke to himself there on the street corner.

"Shay, you daft fool. Billy may be the most stubborn man alive; you've known him to outright refuse to die at least twice. *When* does he take the easy way?" The answer was obvious, and Shay turned on his heel to head uphill.

A few short and keenly decorated blocks later, Shay had found the cafe. It was a delightful little place, very European in decor, and funny little handwritten signs hung on the walls with ramblings like 'every day is a new start', fancifully scrawled in chalk. The flowers outside were bright and probably fake, and the chairs were little wrought-iron things with soft striped cushions. In no time, Shay had settled in and was reading the day's papers. His eyes darted across headlines, and he flipped page after page, trying to avoid almost insultingly dull political exposés and opinion pieces on everything from curbing one's dog to Mccarthyism and the growing red threat. Shay missed the hopefulness and enthusiasm of the mid to late 1940s. He didn't miss the war that opened that decade.

Those Russians better watch their step, or they'll be the next Germany. Sure, it's a big place, but it's mostly fookin' tundra…

Finding a page dedicated to local pursuits was rather nice. An article written by a botanist described lovely rose gardens hidden throughout the city; it sounded serene. Shay thought back to a time in '26 or so when he visited France with ten dollars in his pocket and no hint of a plan. After a few days of bumming about, he'd gotten tired of showering at hostels but was in no rush to leave. He'd come across a kind restaurateur who needed someone to clean tables and scrub dishes in the mornings, which garnered Shay enough francs to enjoy for the summer he spent wandering the city looking for inspiration. He'd found little, but it was the hunt that he truly enjoyed. It was a wonderful summer, and he deeply missed Paris now.

Taking his time reading the paper, the travel-weary man had lost count of how many 'warm-up' mugs of coffee he'd drunk. It was a touch bitter but very earthy and plenty strong. When eight o'clock struck, he departed for Smith Tower. As he hit the sunshine in the street, he realized he'd worked up a bit of sweat just from the coffee and the morning sun beaming through the cafe window. A dab of his forehead with his handkerchief and a few choice words later, he donned his hat once again and took a walk back toward Billy's office.

In short order, he'd made his way up the stairs to see his friend; he was never fond of elevators, and he'd already begun sweating, so the decision was easy to possibly save a few riders from smelling him in the lift. The lifts in Smith Tower were famously original, mechanized elevators with polish everywhere.

As he reached the 9th floor, Shay realized his feet hurt, and he regretted taking such a hike; he'd take one of those beautiful lifts back down. Taking the handkerchief to his forehead once more, he breached into the 9th floor's narrow hallways and closed the heavy glass-paned door behind him. Pausing for a moment just as the door closed, he noticed the view over downtown Seattle was breathtaking this morning. The sun shone brightly, and despite winter, the golden light, refracting and piercing every little street in the city, almost felt like a late summer day.

With a few steps down the hall, he had arrived at the offices of William K. Bigsby, Private Investigator. It was heralded by a brass plaque on the wall, not painted onto the doors as with many of the businesses in Smith Tower. Preparing a smile, Shay twisted the knob and swept into the room to surprise the young woman, a Miss or Missus Reese (he could never recall which) at the desk, who diligently handled field calls, among other duties. As he stepped into the front office, he took off his hat with one hand and shook it in a vaudeville fashion as he started to sing, "Hello, my la-." He was met with a sharp glare and a finger pressed to the lips of the girl behind the desk as she 'shooshed' Shay before he could make a scene.

Shay tiptoed the rest of the way into the office, sheepishly hanging his coat and hat on the oak rack near the door. He could overhear the girl was likely talking to another investigator working remotely for Billy; from the sound of the voice, it might have been Michaelsson or the new guy, Leonard. Either way, Shay felt no need to fret. Her tone implied she'd be done with her call soon, and in fact, she was. Shay simply sat and smiled, waiting for her to address him. The chair embarrassingly squeaked a bit as he shifted on the cushion, but he stifled a chuckle.

"Mister Hayes, you're not expected today. Do you know that you were not expected?" She tapped her finger on a desk calendar.

"Sorry, Miss Reese, no, I wasn't expected. I prefer to sneak up on Billy like a proper old friend, thank you. Is he here?" His Irish lilt in no way charmed this stern woman.

"He will be in shortly, sir. You should know he never misses a day.

Still, he is quite busy, and his time is rather valuable, wouldn't you agree?"

She was trying to diminish Shay with her sarcasm, but he paid no mind.

"I'll wait as long as it takes; I'm sure I can bend his ear for just a bit, miss. You'll see."

With a smug smile, he leaned his head back on the wall and closed his eyes. Not two winks had passed, and there was a familiar sound in the hallway. It was the sound of hard rubber on tiled flooring, and it sounded rather hurried. Shay stood, donning his best grin, and folded his arms in defiance of the receptionist, who was sending daggers right through him for his insolence. In fact, he rather appreciated her stern manner for its potential aid to the office environment, as Billy was... well, Billy was sometimes less than professional.

With a clunk, the knob turned, and the door swung open; Billy had arrived. He came into the office in a bluster as though he'd been in a rush. With a vice-like grip on the rims, he brought his wheelchair to a halt in front of Shay and jutted his chin forward, squinting, eyeing his cheerfully grinning friend as though he were an obstacle.

"Hot damn, Shay, you sure pick the worst days! You know what sorta workload I got in front of me?" His one raised eyebrow was serious as all hell.

Shay stammered out the beginnings of an apology, and one word into it, Billy half-assedly slapped him in the stomach. "You horse's ass! I'm just fuckin' with ya! Good lord, Shay, you're one of my oldest friends. When did I ever not want to see you, pal?" He was roaring in laughter as Shay caught his breath.

"Get into my office, let's go. We've got catchin' up to do!" He was in high spirits, while Shay was amused but winded.

"Christ's sake, Billy, ye got t' not kill me every time I come through, yeh?" He was half-joking, half-serious. Billy had a hell of a strength that perhaps he wasn't fully aware of.

"Oh, sit down. You'll be fine. Oh, sit on the chair. There's... there's that mess we gotta clean up." He motioned toward the tufted couch, where a man was sleeping under a blanket.

Shay turned, seeing the man on the couch."Billy, you're still pickin' up strays?" And he poked the lump on the sofa, whom he very well knew was Johnathan Talbot, the man who climbed mountains with Billy for years until Billy's unfortunate stay on a cold mountain lost him both legs. John had hiked for a day and a half alone to find a sherpa who could help them save Billy, and Billy never forgot. Outside of being a hero, John had been a good friend and co-investigator to Shay, but it had been a couple of years since John had worked or even called; he'd been an on-and-off PI since he got booted off the police force in some little town in Minnesota. His home life hadn't been very enviable the last few years, but they all took strides, not to mention it.

Shay poked him once more. "John, wake up, pal. We've got loads to talk over. You might even want to hear a bit of it, yeh?"

With a groan, John turned over and slowly sat up. Billy and Shay patiently waited as John rubbed the sleep from his eyes and stretched like a cat before opening his eyes and seeing the two men there, observing him. John paid little mind; he simply grunted, "...coffee?".

Billy took his station behind his desk and buzzed the intercom. "Sarah, three black coffees, please? Get the darkest they've got, thank you."

His request was met with an icy voice from the next room: "I certainly will, sir. I can hear you just fine from here. You don't need the intercom. It's rather... *grating*."

A wicked grin crept across Billy's face as he pressed the button once more and spoke into the intercom, "Sure thing!"

With an audible sigh of frustration, she stood up and left the office. Billy leaned forward and gently shared, "I'm going to break her. She can't really be this stiff!" He leaned back in his chair as he withdrew a hand-rolled cigarette from the tin case in his breast pocket.

Shay looked to John, who looked like ten pounds of shit stuffed in a five-pound sack. He turned back to Billy and sat down on the couch next to John.

John grumbled toward Shay, "You stink, buddy."

Shay shot back, "So do you, Talbot. You smell like a boot full of bar rags. It's not even Thanksgiving yet, ye loon." His lilt hung thick on the word *loon*.

John Talbot sneered back, but only halfway. It was a half smile. "Maybe, Irish, but you shoulda seen her. She was a story on top of a story, honest. Worth every drop, but... maybe not this headache..."

Knowing well John's pain from many a night celebrating and socializing, Shay withdrew the small flask he carried. Nudging John, he handed it to him and offered, "Just a sip. Any more, and you'll be green, okay?" To which John leaned to make a snide comment, but decided against it as he was being offered a kindness. Sitting back, he took a short swig with a flick of his wrist.

"You'll feel better soon, lad. Honest."

Across the room, Billy knew precisely what Shay was up to. He well knew that Shay's flask was often filled with the family brew, something Shay shared with very few people. It was a rarity of a drink, with both a draw like a well-aged whiskey and a uniquely invigorating herbal effect that would help keelhaul John out of the mire.

"Boys, I'm glad we're all here right now. Shay, tell us what you've been up to while we wait for coffee?"

"Well, we can start by saying that my head is killing me, perhaps worse than Talbot, here.' He stuck a thumb towards John, who was a bit slumped over but steadily improving. 'I spent last night on the train, but the night before? I had to fight my way out of a car that was being driven by some massive, mute, fookin' lunatic. Honest, I'm not sure what to think at this point, boys. It's an odd one."

Talbot looked confused and clearly hadn't heard the news. He handed back the flask, asking, "What makes your case so odd, Irish?" Shay took a small swig from the flask and tucked it away before continuing.

"Johnny boy, you'd be hard-pressed to believe it, but I'm half sure I was assaulted by a dead man last night. Truth be told." John started to chuckle, but saw the deadly serious look on Shay's face and stopped cold.

"You mean like a *zombie*? Like in the cinema?"

He was incredulous and quite clearly now paying attention.

"No, John, not quite. Let me tell you what took me there, and I'll explain." Just then, the receptionist stepped into the room with a silver tray and three good coffees. She hadn't been gone long, so the brew was hot. She dutifully placed three white ceramic mugs of coffee, each replete with a small saucer underneath. Billy leaned back in his chair, looking out the window as he continued chuffing on his cigarette. Now and then, he would tap the ashes into a small tin jar with his initials monogrammed on it. Shay crossed his right leg over his left and turned to John, who was holding his coffee under his nose like a miracle cure.

All three men thanked her for the mugs, and she closed the door behind herself as they settled in for a tale. Billy offered, "Go take a paid break, Reese. Lock the door behind?" And so she did. After a few swigs of his cup of Joe, Shay laid out the story of what had brought him this far.

"So John, Billy here called me up a handful of months back, wondering if I was looking for any work. Of course, I told him I was certainly not because I really can't stand the sight of the man, but that's beside the point." He winked at Billy, who was smirking with a cigarette dangling from the corner of his mouth. "Now, Billy here doesn't take *no* lightly. He rang me up a few times and poked and prodded, even promising me a good steak dinner. Of course, I folded like a handkerchief. Once he spilled a few of the details, I was hooked. He told me a few pitiful towns outside Portland, mostly along the coast, had been suffering a spate of crimes of a very peculiar nature. Cars were stolen, windows broken out of buildings for no cause, barrels of chemicals and gasoline were stolen from various locations. All very much out of character for folks who live in a place so small… y'know, the way everybody knows everyone. Nobody thought much of it until somebody came forward claiming they saw a man looking much like a recently deceased schoolteacher committing one of these rather bland acts of vandalism. Suppose that is what put all this on Billy's radar?"

Billy piped up, "I got a call from one of the local bureau boys, a G-man I met in my travels. He didn't think it was worth his time, but he has a subcontracting budget to spend, and it's the third quarter. So I got the case, silly as it was. And that was about it, but now Shay is sitting here telling me it's not so silly." He shrugged, and Shay continued.

"I'd have called, but this feels bigger than that. My eyewitnesses were just a couple of old kooks and one half-blind fishmonger, who said they'd seen something odd, but nothing I could use. I was ready to give up!"

John chortled. "You never give up, slim. My favorite thing about ya."

Shay grinned through a few more sips of coffee. He could tell by John's face that the old remedy in the flask was taking hold. "As it goes, Billy dared to send me a cheque for incidentals! I never pocketed a dollar I didn't earn, so I kept at it. Took a little trip out to visit the county mortuary with two local uniformed boys in tow."

"How much did *they* cost?" Billy dryly inquired.

Shay rapped his knuckles on the desk, "You'd be surprised what you can accomplish if you knock on the right doors, Billy. Oh, and bought 'em each a steak dinner. So… eight dollars, gratuity included. Less if you consider they drove!"

"Cheapskate!" John chided him.

"*ANY*-way, with these boys behind me, this old funeral director had no choice but to confess. He'd lost the body! Even worse, after a little digging in his records, it seems it wasn't the first. Isn't that damn strange?"

John smirked and, in his dry tone, remarked, "Shay, literally everything you've ever said to me is strange."

Billy wheezed out a puff of smoke, trying to stifle his laughter. He ended up spilling a bit of his coffee across his desk. Shay paid no mind.

With a shrug, Shay continued the tale. "So I take my findings to three other towns. Same issue… nobody figured it was more than incompetence or, at worst, shady dealings. Suppose it's simpler to sell someone a trophy box full of gravel and tell them it's their loved ones' remains than to own up to such a foible. Now, here I was, palming a list of names of dead men to these local uniforms, and one of the boys came up with a theory that we should check local universities and such for these bodies. Nothing there; we looked. Not a shred of evidence; it's like these dead men just up and walked away. Silly idea, until a recent friend I made got me considerin' we may be dealing with more than just grave robbers here."

John looked to Billy with a quizzically furrowed brow as if to say, 'Sounds like a load of bull. ' With a wave of his hand, Billy set him straight.

"John, you know I'm not much for all that fiction stuff. I don't believe in folks rising from the dead, and I certainly don't believe in any of this Vincent Price hoopla that Shay is keen on… but there's *something* here. So, up to this point, what we know is that some bodies are missing, and we now have at least two *credible* witnesses who say these dead men perhaps aren't dead. Last week, I ran it up the pole to my buddies at the Bureau, and they cast a net. Turns out, this isn't the first wave of missing bodies in our area lately. This past March in Snoqualmie, they lost a freezer's worth of men who had passed in a car accident. It was a real mess, a hunting trip. Beer cans all over. One thousand pounds worth of bodies gone from cold storage overnight, and nobody is saying a word. So… combining that with the ordeal Shay has been through, I'm sending you boys over to Snoqualmie to keep this momentum up."

Shay raised a hand like a student. "Snow-what-me?"

Billy rested his cigarette and his coffee and closed his eyes, pinching the bridge of his nose. "Seems you two should get out more. Hell, it's not even an hour from here, and you both are practically locals."

Now, John raised his hand like an equally confused student. "We gotta go together?"

With a sigh, Billy lifted his cigarette and took a powerful drag. "They have this beautiful waterfall; it's a nice little place. Honest, it's a slice of heaven—a hell of an experience. I've hiked there a few times… well, it's been a while. You mugs could use nature; Shay, you're looking as pale as ever. It'll be a good trip! Two days tops."

Shay and John leaned forward in their seats simultaneously, with Shay extending an open hand as if to plead his case. "Billy, I didn't pack for travel. And Talbot? When's the last time he worked a case outside of a stakeout or a benefits scam?" John looked as though he had just been punched in the gut.

"Not to offend, Johnny-boy, I just don't wish to drag you along if you're not… ah… *ready.*"

Billy leaned forward with a steely gaze and growled, "He's ready, Irish. Because I say so, listen up. While you're pretty good out there, I can tell from your head that you could probably use somebody watching your back. I know John's had a bit of a rough patch, but he's as much one of the team as you or Cameron, anybody. I don't want to hear any hemming and hawing, especially not from you, who almost refused to take a damn job! Don't make me remind you what you promised me when you got back. Now, you and Talbot are going to head out there and figure out what the devil is going on. If you don't like it, you can feel free to hand me that check back, and don't forget your hat on the way out."

"I could use a pair of eyes in the back of my head, fine, Billy, fine. It's all fine. You are as wise as ever. Suppose if John were on my arm, I might not have this thump!" he tapped the bump on his noggin and winced.

John poked him, offering, "Who says I'd have stopped him?" and they all chuckled a bit, tension dissipating, and John made his case.

"Listen, Hayes, I know I'm not part of the little inner circle. I never asked to be. I'm only here 'cause Billy knows me from way back, not because I was much of a policeman. Hell, I know I spent too many days at the bottom of a bottle. I can't really change that, but what I can do is show you that I'm still worth my salt. Show you that I'm still good with a little responsibility. Just watch my back, I'll watch yours, and we can cover more ground this way."

There was nothing in his eyes but honesty and hope. Shay felt guilty already for what he had said, knowing that, regardless of work performance, John was a good man and would do his best in any situation. He knew, as well, that John was probably doing his best to keep things together with his family in shambles. Of course, Shay knew about the *incident*… everybody on the team knew because it happened on the job—nearly shuttered Bigsby's agency, shy of a few favors owed to Billy within City Hall. Without wanting to delve into messy details, Shay changed the subject.

"Talbot, you damn sod. You know we appreciate you; last time we worked together, you saved my arse… or at least saved me from acting a fool. Christ, if it weren't for you, Billy wouldn't be here to pay us! I'd be blessed to have you on the job with me, a partner. Not a subordinate. All I ask is that you give me a sign if anything starts to slip. Is that fair?"

With a grin, John reached over and took Shay's coffee, downing the last bit. He nodded his head and handed the mug back to Shay. "I know you're right… about some of it anyway. I appreciate another chance. I don't care much about pay, but I would love to earn some respect. Anywhere you go, anything you need, I will back you up. Besides, I can't sleep another damn night on Billy's couch. Do you know there's nowhere to *go* in here? It's a damn office… Where am I supposed to take a piss?"

In an instant, Billy's face turned beet red. "Jesus Christ, Talbot, is that why the plants are all dying? You've been here for a week. You could've said *something*. Look at the front door! There on the nail, see that key to the toilets in the hallway?" he slammed his clenched fist on the desk in futility. Shay took a gander around the office and noticed that all of the plans were, in fact, faded and looking somewhat troubled. He reached over and almost grabbed one of the wilting leaves, but thought better of it. He burst out in laughter, which only made Billy's face redder.

Through clenched teeth, a wincing Shay managed to seethe out, "Fook's sake, John. You killed the man's plants? After he gave you a roof and a bed?" he pointed at the couch in a teasing manner, and Talbot lost his composure as well, joining Shay in a fit of laughter. Soon, Billy drifted from mad to laughing with the three of them.

Wiping tears from his eyes, Billy pressed the intercom button. "Hey, we need some new plants in here!" he wheezed. From the other room, his blunt and clearly perturbed assistant shouted back, "I can hear you all in there. I know *Mister* Talbot has been using those plants as a lavatory. I'm not touching any of them, not one single plant! Or, you can speak to my attorney." She sounded absolutely livid.

That sent the men into an uproar. John tried to apologize through tears, and Billy just covered his face with his palms. It took a bit to regain their composure, chuckling like lunatics in a padded room. It was cathartic and very much a relief to see John, who was known for his serious tone, let loose a little and have a laugh.

After the din subsided, Billy wheeled from behind the desk and stopped just in front of the two men on the couch. In the suitcoat, you could see that his shoulders and arms were powerfully built. He was clutching the armrests of his chair tightly and leaning forward, eyes wide. His tone had gone from joking to business—he was known to do that.

"Now, boys, I'm going to pay you well. Don't I always? I'm in touch with the attorneys of two of the families out there, one more down outside Portland. They are paying a pretty penny, so we had better get some results. At its core, this is about seeking trials for official negligence, but if we do some good along the way, that's always the right thing. You guys get out there to Snoqualmie and do some fact-finding. You've got two days and two nights, then I want you back here with some answers. Thursday, that's it. I'm out of town Saturday for ice fishing, so just get back here before then. It's Thanksgiving, and of course, I'll be paying you boys double on the holiday."

John gave a double thumbs-up, and Shay nodded along.

"I got you boys a couple of decent rooms out there at the hotel over the waterfall. I think you'll enjoy it. I need your best work; I want this story in the Gazette and Herald and the Daily fucking Planet, just like last time. Remember that cockamamie with the elections? I made a pretty penny off the interviews and editorial exclusives. Not to mention juicing up my standing with the Bureau; it's probably the reason they keep knocking on our door. I expect your best, so if you need anything, I'll expect a call. On the way out, have the little lady give you some petty cash to pack for the trip; she's got the dossier as well. The usual cover, use those IDs I gave you if you get hemmed up, and please make me look good."

Shay shrugged, "You always look good, old boy, but we'll have the media knockin' at your door again, sure as can be."

In the lobby, as they departed, John Talbot leaned forward onto the very organized desk of Miss Reese. His hands were on the corner of the desk, and his right leg was crossed in front of his left; he looked like a lawyer at the banister in some serial crime drama. "My apologies, miss. I know we can be boorish. You seem like a smart sort, and Billy probably doesn't deserve your help. I hope he pays you all right."

Miss Reese was visibly surprised. Clearly did not expect such polite candor from some down-on-his-luck alky. Her cheeks turned a bit pink under her effervescent makeup, and for the first time that anyone in this room had seen, the corners of her mouth upturned a bit, and she softly replied, "I do all right, sure."

John nodded slowly, affirming her positive demeanor.

"Well, he's finally going to pay me something, but I'd better earn it. I hear you have a file well and some petty cash for us. That would sure help us get on the road and out of your hair, miss."

He was not being charming; in fact, he was simply being nice. This was a side of John that Shay hadn't seen often, if at all. Demurely reaching into her drawer, she withdrew two envelopes and set them on the desk. With fingers splayed out and her pinky in the air, she slid the envelopes across the desk to John and nearly off the edge of the desk. She wasn't paying attention; she was looking directly into his eyes the entire time. John stood up straight, his stature now notably more respectable than when he was slumped over the couch. He smiled and gave a cheeky salute to her, tucking the envelopes into his breast pocket. She sat back and waved to him in a coy fashion while Shay followed John out, absolutely befuddled.

Swaggerin' hungover sod, and ye've still got moxy... Johnny fookin' Talbot. Pish!

Roadies

Shay and John strode down the narrow hallway toward the elevator. John paused for a moment and placed his hand out, catching Shay dead-stop in the hallway. With a curious look on his face, John asked Shay, "Say, what was in that flask? I'm no stranger to a little bite in the morning, but I feel great. Don't tell me it was that little lady's coffee that got me feeling so light?"

Shay patted him on the back and replied with a bit of cynicism in his voice, "John, you don't often drink the good stuff. That was just a bit of what I bring from back home. There's a reason the Irish are always so chipper!" and he continued down the hallway, John now in tow shrugging his shoulders like a child who's given up searching for answers. Their strides were equally long; in fact, Shay took note of how John seemed to be in excellent physical shape despite what a shabby state he had been in that morning. John was also wearing a nicer suit than Shay, but again, Shay hadn't really packed for work.

"Listen, John, I'm a bit tired, and I sure could use a rest. What do you say we roll that sedan out there and find us those rooms where I can kick back for a bit? I took the redeye up here."

"Well, I could use some breakfast and another cup, but I wouldn't mind getting out of the city before we find shade. Let's get to the garage and see what that cheapskate has in store for us!" Shay laughed; he knew John was half-joking, but Billy was not known for being extravagant in his expenses. That he'd put them in a car, Shay figured it would be some scrappy little prewar Ford coupe with five working cylinders… just like last time.

As they entered the small parking garage beneath the building, they spotted the attendant booth, where a kindly young man in a white hat sat at a podium, rocking idly on a very creaky stool. At the same time, the baseball scores came over a smallish box radio on the floor. Shay extended a hand and greeted the young man. "How d'you do, lad? William Bigsby sent us down to retrieve the car. I hope you've got one in here with his name on it, which has all its doors and windows?"

The young man had a laugh and waved his hand, putting Shay's mind at ease by pointing toward a sedan in the corner. "Gentlemen, I believe that's your chariot there. Mr. Bigsby gave me the keys yesterday and even had me shine her up for your trip!"

As he spoke, he withdrew a set of keys from his podium and held them out. John swiftly reached out and snatched them before Shay had the chance. Shay said goodbye to the attendant, and John was almost on top of the car before Shay skipped to catch up. They each reached their doors and stopped, looking across the roof at each other. "Talbot, are you sure you want to drive?" Shay was hoping to get a crack at the brand-new and quite comely 1950 Dodge 4-door sedan.

John shook his head, "I get bored in the shotgun seat. You enjoy your rest, Irish. If it takes to rain later, you're going to want me behind the wheel on that highway out there. In fact, this is a '50 Dodge, and I've been looking at these in the latest issue of Popular Mechanics. Smooth Chrysler power... bet she has overdrive! You can take the wheel this evening once we get out to Snoqualmie. How's that sound, partner?"

Shay felt he had to concede. In truth, he wasn't an excellent driver; he simply enjoyed driving. With defeat in his voice, he shrugged his shoulders. "I suppose, but I may not even want to drive later. In fact, I might insist you be my chauffeur for the rest of the trip! Give me a chance to write my memoirs..." He joked; John chortled through a straight face as he slid into the bench seat. Shay slid into the bench seat and buckled up. John fired up the six-cylinder engine, and it absolutely purred.

"You know, this is a 235 cubic-inch engine. It's got 10 more horsepower than just a few years ago! I read an article about how these are sleeved and have some new bearing technology. Supposedly, they can go further on less fuel, too. Quite a fine machine." Shay was only half listening and didn't understand much about the technology, but he nodded along. "Sure, sounds like a fine engine!"

He ran his hand along the wood grain of the dashboard and quipped, "Really, really nice. All this chrome? It feels like a much nicer car than Billy deserves!" John laughed as he nudged the car into gear, and they departed.

"Irish, that's why *we* are taking it."

...

The damp, wintry roads were clear and easy this day, and they rode along in comfortable quiet, listening to the single-speaker radio humming big band tunes in the dash as Shay dozed for much of the trip. Not long before they reached their destination, John found a nice overlook just off the road and pulled the car into a dirt lot overlooking a lush valley. The cold air in the trees had a mist clinging to the air despite the sunshine above.

"Shay, I need a minute. I need to ask you some questions, and I need you to be real honest with me." He was sitting there with his hands on the steering wheel, staring off into the distance.

Shay didn't know where the conversation was going but simply replied, "Anything."

John shuffled in his seat a bit; clearly, something had been bothering him. "I know you and Billy go back; I know he has put you onto some of the tougher work. That's not me. See, for the most part, Billy had me working on insurance fraud these last couple of years. You know, hiding out and catching people trying to fool the system. Fake crutches and all the sad sack shit they try. Easy work, yeah?"

Shay patted the seat, "Easy, if you've got a nice place to sit and wait, sure."

"Well, you two are on another level. I promised Billy I would take on some work, but I've never done anything around dead bodies… or ghosts and ghouls. You guys are in there talking about a walking dead man. Is it some sort of… *normal* thing? I know you've seen a lot of dark stuff, but I wasn't in the war, and I never saw anything too shocking in the line of duty. There were a few big brawls, sure, but I trained for all that. I can handle normal. I'm a family man, well… I *was* a family man. Anyway, I can't be sure anymore whether this is the right line of work for me, whatever the job. You get what I'm saying?"

Shay took a minute to think of a good answer that might not spook the man. John was quiet and patient, as he always had been. After a time, Shay figured he would do his best, just to be honest. He couldn't see how telling John it would be an easy assignment would help if it turned out to be risky or violent.

"Talbot, listen. Right now, we're just on fact-finding. If it comes to a bad sort of work, you can bow out or just man the fort. That's fine.

Here, all I need is for you to watch my back and ask sharp questions. Think of it like a fraud case; this is no different. We have some people doing things they shouldn't, and likely somebody covering it up. You've done that a hundred times; you've solved a dozen cases like that; easy, pal. Easy work. If you can promise me that you won't spook if we come across something a little strange, I promise to have your back and get you through this so we can get you paid. Is that fair?"

Shay's answer seemed to be the perfect answer of any answer there could have been. John pursed his lips satisfactorily, nodded, and put the car back into gear. He mounted the road back to the highway toward their mission. Shay hoped that would be the last he would see of 'worried' John, as years prior, he had worked with 'brave' John, and that was very much his favorite version of John.

In short order, they arrived in Snoqualmie. Driving through town, they noted a sizeable and well-maintained Railway depot on the main street. Apparently, this was quite the burgeoning logging community some years prior, and there was still a lot of money and business in the area. Snoqualmie was a charming little town, but, indeed, not a big town. Shay was pleased with the idea of not needing to dig too hard or ask too many questions in these parts; he hoped that in the small towns, people would probably be itching for a little bit of excitement and an opportunity to tell any story they knew. Generally, that's the way small towns were.

Shay had John stop the car when they saw a men's clothier —a sweet little bay-window shop with a few manikins in the front displaying dashing suits and some very warm, comfortable-looking winter wear. As they walked the half block from the car to the shop, the chill really hit Shay through his outerwear. He knew that the 'dirt coat' was great for day-to-day, but would not play the part if he wanted to come across like a big-city PI. He told John he could use a long overcoat, and John simply pulled the petty cash envelope and handed it to Shay. "I'll follow your lead, pal!"

Thumbing through the bills inside, Shay saw that Billy had been generous in his petty cash for the boys. It would handle outfitting them a bit and covering their stay. Now, Shay almost felt guilty as this was practically a vacation. After trying a few things on and bothering the sweet shopkeeper a bit about the town's history, the duo each had a bag with a new suit and changes of shirts and undergarments. They knew they could get the bath and sundry items at the hotel for the traveling man.

"I hope they have little knick-knacks here, John. If you see anything with the name of the place, let me know!"

"I'll look out for snowglobes, Irish!" John offered as he swiped a few snowflakes off the roof of the car with his finger.

They idled their way out of downtown and the short distance to the Snoqualmie Falls Lodge, a beautiful resort perched on the cliff where the local river became a massive waterfall tumbling down into a crag. They parked under the awning, and a valet traded the keys for a ticket, remarking how sharp the new Dodge looked; that gleaming lacquer paint really stood out in a lot with square-roofed cars that were as old as perhaps the 1930s and typical to Washington state, a bit rusty. There were a couple of nicer vehicles in the front of the lot, and the valet puttered off parking the Dodge right next to a gaudy new Cadillac with its sweeping long fenders and plump button-leather seats.

At the lobby, a broad split-log welcome desk was almost diminutive in the grand lobby space. High arched ceilings, wood beam construction, and everything shellacked in a golden glossy finish; this place was certainly outstanding compared to many of the seedy motels where Billy had directed Shay to shack up on a job. "I'd rather sleep in this Dodge than another ramshackle motel, John," he'd commented earlier during the drive up.

As they were assigned their rooms and each received a key, John extended a hand to Shay and gave him a firm handshake. "Get some rest, pal; chow in the morning? Let's say seven sharp downstairs in the restaurant. I want to clean up and make some calls, plan our day." Shay was beaming at the idea of John taking charge.

"Absolutely, Talbot. Rest well!" And with that, he headed toward the gift shop.

...

The morning brought the sound of the massive waterfall churning. Shay hadn't noticed it in the evening, but he'd been damned tired. He cracked his window; the air carried a crisp, distinct smell of moist pine needles. After a few minutes, with teeth chattering, he realized it was a mistake to leave the window open in the mountains of Washington during the dead of winter. He saw that a light rain had begun falling, and from his room, he could see across the waterfall. On the other side of the banks of the river, railroad tracks were rounding the bend and leading off. He took a few last deep breaths of the perfect air and shut the pane.

After dressing and cleaning up, he made his way to the lobby. It was five minutes til seven, and John was there, leaning back with both elbows behind him on the counter of a banister. He was sharply dressed and clean-shaven, looking like something from a Hollywood detective movie. The idea was almost silly, but Shay was glad to be working with someone who really played the part. They said their brief hellos and decided to get breakfast at the hotel so they could set a plan. John had brought down the dossier; it was a bit short but had plenty of contact information and footnotes on what Billy had found, which the boys needed to follow up on. While Billy had made enough calls to gather some perfunctory leads, he knew and had ingrained in his subordinates that it was always more effective to investigate in person to capture the little details people forget when they talk on a handset.

Shay had wanted to eat on the run, but the lobby host insisted the men take their time and enjoy the restaurant. He even handed them a menu —a nice little bifold with an embossed logo stamped in the corner. Shay saw they were harping on what was known as 'The Farmer's Breakfast.' Under his breath, Shay mumbled the included items in this morning's feast.

"Oatmeal, brown sugar, that sounds nice… three eggs, bacon, ham as well? Oh my."

"That's a big plate, Irish."

"Sausages, cornmeal, potatoes, biscuits! John, you've got to look at this. Something called honeydew and buttermilk pancakes to boot. On me ma, I don't think I've eaten this much in a week, much less in any morning. John, we've got to go. I won't even bother you about lunch!"

John smiled and nodded, and they made their way to the dining room, where they were seated at a small table near the windows. From there, they peered into the valley which the waterfalls had carved, so many thousands of years in the making. It was a postcard-worthy scene.

John poked Shay in the chest and said, "I know this is romantic, but don't go getting any ideas."

Shay was bemused by his friend's sense of humor. They laughed and got into the coffee that had been left at the edge of their table. There wasn't much bustle this early in the morning, but a few folks were enjoying their meals. Each table's spread was different, but the boys saw one table where it seemed the man was enjoying the farmer's breakfast, and Shay pointed it out. "You see that? That's what I want. That right there."

John looked up from the menu, for some reason still debating his options, and under his breath, grunted, "We're gonna need a snooze afterward…"

John had decided to take the leap and order the farm breakfast with Shay; there was hardly a square inch left on the table that wasn't covered with a dish. The two sat there in silence, only the sound of forks scraping platters and the slurping of coffee. There wasn't much to say about it, and the dossier John had been cradling was under a plate piled high with hash brown potatoes. It was an absolute delight, and neither man had finished the meal when they relented and agreed that they were full. Shay had said 'full to the brim,' while John had grumbled he was 'stuffed.' Those idioms amused Shay, and in the few languages that he spoke with any usefulness, he found that America was the best place for folksy novel little sayings.

As they sent the plates away, John leaned forward and very subtly unbuckled his belt to make a bit more room for his stomach. "All right, pal, we are losing daylight, and we have a lot to do. See, Billy wants us to get in touch with three different folks. I've got a list here. We have the coroner first and foremost. He seems uninterested. At least, that was Billy's estimation. You have a way with folks, so I'd like you to go and make contact. Maybe don't push too hard. We can always go back later. I'm going to head down to the King County Sheriff's Office and speak with this detective, some D. Parks. He came across as levelheaded, according to the boss; he was the point man during the investigation when all that weird business happened. Not much paperwork, but he sounded like the only one who paid attention."

Shay nodded and took a gentle sip of hot coffee. "Sounds like a plan, Talbot; who is the third?"

John looked down his nose at the papers and almost rolled his eyes as he looked up. "Local yokel, some old timer who lives out in the sticks. He was the only witness, but he didn't seem too credible, according to the sheriff, whom Billy prodded. He sounds like he might be fit for a padded cell, but Billy wants us to follow up. Parks recommended that Billy avoid the man unless he 'wants to waste time.' Suppose we'll find out?"

"Ye never know what you'll find, John. Leads are leads."

"Agreed. His notes here say that the old codger Sterland is a veteran of the First War. We can visit him together. Seems he told Billy that he had something he wouldn't share over the phone. Hell, that might be the only *real* reason we got sent out here. Let's work on that tomorrow. Today, I figure you'll have enough fun with the coroner and maybe dig into some records down at City Hall. We can meet back here this evening and go over everything again. How's that sound, Shay?"

It was a good plan. John seemed eager to get to work.

"I tell ya, Talbot, I don't mind you running the ship at all. Let me focus on digesting!" and he went for another sip of coffee. Not long after, the two had finished up and parted in the lobby.

Just as he was walking away, John turned back. "Hey, noon sharp. I'll check in with the desk at noon sharp; you call a quarter after. I want to call back myself at 1230 and know where you're at. Can I hold you to that?"

"Yes, sir. I'll stay on track!" and he donned his hat, heading out with his copy of the notes. Outside, Shay was damn glad he had brought a coat. The rain had let up a bit, but it was damn cold, perhaps just above freezing. He stepped back inside and scanned the felled lumber walls of the lobby. Seeing the valet, Shay waved him over.

"Boy-o, I wonder if you can call me a cab?"

The young man tipped his hat and joked, "You're a cab!" and his grin was almost too much; Shay had a good chuckle over the silly snark. The valet quickly continued, "No worries at all. I will have you a set of wheels here in just a few minutes. Have you seen our gift shop?" He waved his hand toward that beautiful little boutique of gifts.

"Already bought something nice there, but here's for your troubles!" and he palmed two quarters to the valet. He took to a front window where he watched the rain pattering down. In minutes, the valet returned and put Shay in a taxi headed for the county hospital.

Panning for Gold

Climbing into the back of the yellow cab, Shay was already missing the Dodge. He was plenty comfortable, but that well-worn faux-leather upholstery was very cold on this cold morning. Fortunately, the driver was well aware of the best route to the county hospital that Shay had directed him to. King County was a strikingly pretty place and lacked much of the industrial mess that surrounds Seattle. From his rear seat, Shay was able to take in a fantastic view of the quiet highways and points of interest, the occasional business tucked away down some gravel road. He saw two taxidermist signs and wondered what sort of animals they might be stuffing on this chilly morning. He hoped it was something ridiculous, like a gazelle or perhaps a man-sized Seabass.

After perhaps half an hour, the driver had pulled up outside the double doors that led into King County's primary hospital. Shay leaned forward and handed the man a few dollars, joking, "…ye sure this is the place?" in a good-natured lilt. The driver, lacking coffee or perhaps personality, simply grunted and snatched the money from his passenger's hand. Not one to be bothered by other people's problems, Shay simply shrugged and tipped his hat on the way out of the cab. Standing there on the curb, he smoothed his suit with his palms and then took out the notes that John Talbot had assembled for him.

In the pattering drizzle and cold air, his thumb and forefinger pinching this note, he balled up his other fingers, trying to keep them warm. His opposite hand was shoved in the pocket of his new coat, a lovely grey all-weather men's coat that was just long enough to cover his also-new suit coat. Reading the notes, he murmured a few of the scribblings aloud.

"March 17th… three missing bod… doors forced, nothing else taken… blah blah… two identified… Doctor Mabry. Incomplete police report... of *course.*"

He prayed the doctor was in. Shoving the flittering paper into his breast pocket and leaving his hand in there as well, he shouldered through the front door and put on a good smile for whoever might be inside to greet him. Much to his delight, the front desk was absolutely barren and unoccupied.

Looks like I'll find it meself.

Making his way to the plastic-lettered sign adjacent to the elevators, just inside the lobby, he noted the Medical Examiner's Office was located in the basement along with the mortuary. Poking the button on the wall with a knuckle, he stood there waiting patiently for his lift. After a few moments, a graying man in a white lab coat walked up to the elevators and stood there next to Shay, facing the closed doors. Calming chimes from the elevator panel told the men it wouldn't be long before their moving rectangle arrived. The doors opened, and Shay took a sip of coffee as he motioned with his other hand for the man to step into the lift.

The old man in the lab coat pressed the B button, the only floor below. In a pleasant tone, Shay turned to the man and asked, "Headed to the examiner's office or...?" in a leading manner. The man looked up from the newspaper he was halfheartedly perusing and peered over the top of his glasses at Shay.

"Can I help you find something, young man?" Shay was always delighted to hear that term applied to himself, and he showed a genuine smile there in the elevator as it came to a rest in the basement. He had just taken a swig of coffee, so he nodded in agreement until he could finish swallowing.

"Possibly, sir. I'm seeking Dr. Mabry, your Medical Examiner. Any chance you know the fellow?"

"Dead."

"Excuse me?" Shay inquired.

The old man sized him up, giving him a swift look to the toes and back directly into his eyes. "Irish."

"Well, *sure,* but it's no secret once I've spoken a bit, wouldn't you say?"

"Hell. Sorry, just... I'm working a double shift. My mouth doesn't hold the words in after twenty hours. Kip Mabry... passed away; my apologies... I was *referring* to Dr. Mabry. I'm Dr. Lowell. You can call me Paul if you'd like; you're not a patient. Kip and I worked together most of the last twenty-three years, so... I suppose I could be as good help as any." He shrugged and adjusted his spectacles.

"No offense taken, old boy. I've had those long days. I'm sorry for your friend."

"Kip was good folk. You look like a reporter."

Shay chuckled and finished his coffee with a swig. "Not in the least, Doc. I'm just a curious fellow earning a paycheck. No reporter; those folk work far harder than I do. Séamus Hayes, Private Investigator. *Irish* if you wish,' he offered with a wink, 'just in from Seattle, hoping to ask a few bits about some troubles you had not too long ago."

"Interesting. Suppose I would have lost a bet there. Say, you're telling me your name is Shay, and you're a shamus?" he was referring to the way that 'shamus' was a term from some decades prior for any private detective or gumshoe. On several occasions, Shay had to point out that in his country, the name had an entirely other meaning. In Ireland, the name Séamus or Shay meant to 'replace' or 'supplant'—an odd meaning, to be sure, but a different meaning nonetheless.

"That old irony isn't lost on me, to be sure. I'm working under an Investigator up in Seattle named Bigsby. If I had my way, I'd be back on stage singing show tunes!" he rattled his hat at the old man, who let out an exasperated chuckle and shook his head, almost as if to shake off the silly notion of this lanky fool dancing about under spotlights.

"I've no time for reporters nor gumshoes. If you've got questions, you can ask them in the administrative wing. Look for anyone with a red name tag. Good day."

Shay started to protest, but the elevator doors opened, and the man stepped out, raising a flat hand to say, "Go back upstairs." Befuddled, Shay let the man walk away without a word.

The old sod needs to make time for me. He works for the County, and I work for the taxpaying survivors of the dead. Suppose we do this the hard way…

Ten minutes later, the gumshoe found himself seated on the curb outside the emergency ward. Their ambulance lane roof made for a nice shelter from the cold rain that was still spitting from silver clouds. He palmed a cigarette he'd bummed off a passing visitor, from which he took slow drags as he ruminated.

"On me duff again… what would Billy do? Scratch that… what would Cameron do?"

He thought back to a jam-up they had encountered in New York a couple of years prior. At the time, Billy had expressed his displeasure that Gabriel hadn't stuck around, or he would be to go-to for a job in old Gotham. But after what Gabe had gone through? No one to blame him for packing up and leaving West. He needed time to get his head right, time to settle down a bit with that doll who saved his life. The flipside is that now Billy had somebody to call if there was any trouble in the suburbs of Chicago. That wasn't much comfort, save for the fact that it brought the boys closer again. Gabe was gonna be 'right as rain, in time…' as Billy said. Shay hoped it was true.

Cameron had been up against the wall, dealing with a hotel fire that had claimed the lives of a couple of nobodies. Just some poor girls who thought they'd finally made it, living in the big city. After the rubble cooled and someone figured out the girls were gone, their families came calling and got nowhere; they had no recourse for the lost lives of those young women. The place had been nearly abandoned, and it took Cameron three days in city records and a dozen palmed bribes to suss out who, in fact, owned the damn place. It was a fire trap from the get-go.

"It's always about money, Irish." Cameron's words rang out in Shay's head. "The reason most people do nasty things is to get money or to keep it. Sometimes, the only leverage you've got against them is the threat of taking it away."

You wise bastard, he'd thought at the time. He remembered stealing a couple of waiter uniforms and sneaking up to a penthouse party with Cameron. He recalled how easy it was, how quickly everybody had assumed they were the help. "Show up with a ladder and a clipboard, and you could strut in just about anywhere, I bet!" Cam had mused in the elevator.

In just over an hour, they'd taken the keys to a very fancy car, loaded it with everything they could find of value in the rich bastard's home, and driven it out to a rented stall on Pier twenty-something. Shay chuckled at the memory of that phone call late the following night.

"Can you swim, you sonofabitch?" Cam had opened with. It took the voice on the other line a few moments to catch on, or perhaps just reel in the shock of standing in an emptied-out penthouse over Fifth Avenue; that robber baron must have felt like a pauper. Cam had even hauled away the entire sealed wall safe!

Heavy sonofagun, that.

"You'll never get away with this!" the man whined, his voice cracking.

"We already *did*. Now, I'm no Harvard graduate, but I can count, and from my count, it looks like I've taken enough from you to pay for a proper burial service and a little something for the families of those two girls, but maybe tenfold… maybe more. You didn't think this was random, did you?"

Lord, he kept his cool. Cameron is always so levelheaded. Shay truly admired the man.

"What do you want from me?" the villain had asked, as though the answer was unclear.

Cam sneered into the phone as he responded. "It ain't what I want; it's what I *need*. I need you to make things right. That building went down on those girls…the way they suffered. You didn't strike the match, but you owned the kindling. So I'm gonna send your shit to the bottom of the Atlantic if you don't cut a check to each of those families, and you have exactly one… goddamned… business…. day. Otherwise, I'll sink all your shit… and after you buy new shit, you rich cocksucker, I'll come back, and I will do it *again*. You know I can, and I will because I'm everywhere. I might be in your lobby right now. And I'll be *watching*. Tick-tock, fatty." Cam set the receiver down and returned to smoking his stogie with a grin like he was on a tiki cabana vacation.

11 hours. That's all it had taken. At 9:08 the following morning, the threadbare-coat attorney for those two unfortunate families received the call. A check was courier-delivered that day, so an anonymous letter with the waterfront address of a particular Rolls-Royce loaded full of upper-crust trinkets was dropped in the rich man's lobby postbox before dusk.

"Why didn't you just *sell* all that crap and give them a better payout, Cam?" He recalled asking of his friend, only half-serious. "What if that safe was loaded with cash and jewels?"

"Because, Shay, that's the difference between good guys and bad guys. The bad guys… they take the easy route. They take whatever they want. The good guys? They use their brains. They use leverage and tactics to force the bad guys to do the right thing. That's how we stay on the righteous side of it, no matter how messy it gets. That's how I sleep at night, Irish. Like a baby."

Shay would never forget those words in particular.

"That's how we stay on the righteous side of it."

Suppose there's some honor in being a vigilante, especially when everybody else is so damn crooked these days. Thank you, Cameron, old boy; suppose I will tear a page from your book on this one.

* * *

...

With a dour look on his face, a uniformed guard escorted the smiling Irishman into the furthest corner of the basement. Behind swinging doors, under blinding fluorescent lighting, Doctor Lowell stood holding a beaker of what looked to be isolated fluids, as one might withdraw from a centrifuge.

"You got the call?" the guard inquired of the Doctor.

"I certainly did. You're dismissed, thank you," he replied, and the guard left via the elevator.

"Didn't mean to twist arms there, Doc..."

"You're okay, young man. You're doing your job. And with the director's blessing, I can perhaps help you do it better informed."

"Sounds like you've got a story for me, yeh?"

"Well, let's get to my office where I can take a seat for my old back, and we can chat. Perhaps I won't send you away empty-handed." He smiled a bit, and his gray mustache upturned at the corners. He seemed like a genial man, and Shay was glad for that. Without saying anything and returning to scanning his newspaper, he led Shay back through the seating area of the Medical Examiner's Office. In no time, and without looking back up at his walking partner, the man shuffled into his own office and back behind his desk. Now settling into a tall leather wingback chair, he swiveled it toward Shay, who had taken a seat on the visitor side of the desk.

"Well, lay it out. Tell me what you have and what you need. I'm a busy man, and I'm not always a patient man. At least, that's what my wife says. I like to think of myself as blunt."

He made no eye contact. Instead, he withdrew a small comb from his desk drawer and began brushing his mustache, appearing to be deep in thought. It was a ridiculous mannerism, and Shay absolutely loved it.

Sounds like it's brass tacks for this one. Wonder if I can get a rise out of him.

"Sir, I can appreciate and respect that, so here's my conundrum, silly as it may sound. A while back, your offices found a handful of dead men who had, apparently, stood up and walked out of your freezer. At least... after witnesses placed one of those dead men upright, engaging in late-night petty larceny, that's a bit of a working theory. I won't insult your intelligence, so if you'd like to tell me what you think *really* happened, I would be much obliged."

For a while, Dr. Lowell sat there in his comfortable chair, gently combing his mustache. His left eyebrow arched, and he ran his fingertip back and forth along the edge of the leather pad on the desk. He never looked at Shay.

"And those families, you leveraged their pending lawsuits against this hospital to pry yourself into my office?"

"Sure did, Doc."

"Then you're willing to take a loss… er, financially, as it were, to find some closure?"

"Nothing less than the whole truth," Shay replied in earnest.

"Then you're more foolish than you look… but your heart is in the right place. Perhaps that matters more."

Shay shrugged and readied his notepad.

"That was some accident. I think it was April. No, it was March. Those men from North Bend went and met their maker out there on the highway in the middle of the night. Now, these were local folk, and they were all dearly missed. A funny thing happens when tragedies occur: people can't get it out of their minds. They can't stop thinking about those folks they lost."

"I'm following."

"Yes, well… unfortunately, it's much like after ending a relationship with someone you still care about. You end up seeing their face everywhere. Now, I'm not one to diminish the loss of these folks or what their loved ones did in the aftermath; what I know are the facts. We had four bodies in cold storage that went missing. That's a fact. Kip had found the door locks busted, so somebody had gained access. That's a fact. Later on? Some crimes were committed in the area, I believe a couple of burglaries, and somebody was assaulted. It happens. Those are facts, sure, but you'd be hard-pressed to convince me they were related. No facts for that, just… opinion."

Shay was enjoying the man's thoughtfulness. Perhaps those eyewitnesses were just heartbroken fools and hadn't seen a damn thing?

Shay piped up, "So, to be clear, there was never any connection afterward? Just a few eyewitness accounts and a bit of petty crime?" The doctor nodded and shrugged his shoulders with his palms toward the ceiling.

"That's all I would know; all we did was intake those poor men on the night they had their accident, finish a few forms covering the cause of death and state of remains, and pack them in the freezer. Sorry for the terminology, but that's essentially what it was. Very routine. We didn't have time to complete the autopsies. Perhaps we completed two the following day… hardly a need anyway. Drowning. They upturned into four feet of water off the embankment, and all drowned. It would have been survivable if it weren't for the standing water. I cleared their airways of fluid, and Kip tagged them; two of them were autopsied, and that's as far as we'd gotten. Then, a day later, they were simply *gone*."

Shay thought it might be a good time to tug at the man's very reassuring story. "You see, Doc, I want that to be the end of the story, just like you. My files state that only one of the bodies was recovered. What are your thoughts on that?"

"Ah… the crux of the matter." The doctor picked up his comb again and returned to brushing his mustache a bit more vigorously. His brow furrowed deeply; he was troubled by something he had not yet said. "You are correct, young man. That was an odd turn of events; yes, they found one of the bodies. It was one of the sons, I'm certain of it. I had seen him on my table just a few weeks prior. That body was nearly in the same condition as when it left, with no significant decomposition and about the same lividity as when the body was brought here originally. I matched it against Kip's and my notes. No mistake. The mother ID'd the body herself on that table outside my office."

"But it was no ordinary thing, was it?" Shay implored.

"They found that poor man a mile and a half up the highway, fully dressed and practically ready for a square dance. The body had attained some… recent damage. You see, it had been run over by a newspaper delivery driver just shortly before dawn. The man was terribly frightened, that's what they say… but I can't fault him."

Shay was intrigued now and hoping for just a bit more than that. "What had him so spooked?"

Still combing, the doctor stared off into the middle distance and replied, "he claims he hit a man who was *walking*. I spent eleven years studying psychiatry, and I don't believe that boy was lying; he seemed genuinely distraught." This fact clearly still bothered the doctor, and his brow remained furrowed.

"Well, what do you say to that?" Shay inquired, leaning back and clasping his hands on his lap. He tried his best not to sound excited.

"I say it's ridiculous. It's not possible. Dead men… dead men don't walk."

"Then why do you look so bothered?" Shay played his hand.

"Off the record?" The doctor inquired. Shay nodded.

"Off the record, all the new damage to the body since we had initially examined it was to the back of the legs and the spine. For instance, you can see where that truck's hood ornament took a piece out of the kidneys. There was directional impact damage consistent with a vehicular strike. Soft tissue, fluid displacement, and the like. If this body were struck lying down, that wouldn't be possible. There was no blood, just an excess amount of embalming fluid. There was no way, under the science, I understand, that man was walking... so the evidence just doesn't add up. I never really had an answer for it. Hell, neither did Kip."

Shay nodded and gave an affirmative 'mmm-hmm,' leaning forward and putting both of his hands palm-down on the desk. "Tell me, what happened when you brought this to the attention of the Sheriff's Department? Local police? Anybody?"

He was being assumptive that the Doctor had even done so.

"They brushed it off. Collegiate shenanigans, some kind of initiation ritual, perhaps. Or a thief with a morose sense of humor, a vendetta? Who's to say? There's value in bodies, which is why it's such a tightly regulated thing. Laws on the books in every state with regard to handling, disposal, and sale."

"Sale..." Shay repeated.

The doctor raised his eyebrows and sighed a long, almost disappointed sigh. "Never said a word outside of the Sheriff nor Kip himself. Kip had insisted. He believed it was probably a prank. He said he would speak to the sheriff further about my concerns, but I was never privy to any of that. Of course, I never had the chance to do any follow-up. Kip cremated the body at the insistence of the director... and after that? Well, neither Kip nor I wanted to seem like a raving lunatic, so we simply closed the book on it. There was nothing we could do."

Shay wondered how forthcoming the man was or perhaps how honest his associates had been with him. Still masking his excitement at the new information, the detective took a deep breath and leaned back. "May I ask, since we are being candid, as you disagreed with Dr. Mabry, is there anything else you might want to share?"

"Such as?"

"Well, Doc, I can't give too much in the way of details, but what I can tell ye... is that you are not the only little quaint hamlet dealing with this strange nonsense. Otherwise, I wouldn't be here."

The doctor raised his eyebrows and looked up at Shay. "You're not here for the families? Private investigator, I assumed…" and trailed off.

"No, sir, Paul, not for the families. At least not the families in this town. Perhaps I was a bit of a storyteller there, with your Director. Too late for us to turn back, anyway. I was hoping you could tell me a little more than you already have. So far, I don't really have much to go on, but I could sure use a little help. Somebody is desecrating bodies, and it's just not right. It's simply not right." Shay shook his head with a downturned maw. He supposed he might try for heartstrings since he had gotten this far.

The old man sat up in his chair and reached into one of the lower drawers of his desk. He pulled out a shallow file, just a few pages in an unmarked envelope. Rifling through the pages, he let out a small "ah…" and took one sheet out for Shay, placing it on the desk and sliding it across.

Shay picked up the document and looked it over. He scanned through a diagram of ratios, fractional numbers, and what was clearly the names of unusual chemical substances. It didn't make a lot of sense to him, but just enough to give him an idea of where this was going.

"Is this… a blood test? From the body that was recovered?"

Dr. Lowell nodded and pursed his lips. He raised a finger and waggled it emphatically as he spoke.

"When I autopsied the body, I found extremely high concentrations of what I thought was some modified embalming fluid. You can…" he waved his fingers around, clearing some invisible stench, "…you can smell it. It's acrid. We ran those tests, and I was nearly correct. The other half, well, that's what you see there. Some sick individual performed an autopsy and then pumped that husk full of all manner of substances; I don't know if they were attempting to embalm the body further…

Shay offered, "…or perhaps test chemical effects on fresh tissue."

"Ah. Not so foolish, it seems. Kip wouldn't look at it, but I ran those blood tests *twice*. They came back the same; that's a copy you can keep. It's all I have left of this damn thing. Samples went in the bin, or the burner… or god knows where."

"You're opening my eyes here, Doc. Much to take in, y'know."

"Well, now you know everything I do. I don't know if it will help you, but I've been in family medicine for over three decades, and I only took this role as Kip was getting ready to retire. It sickens me to see people out there outside the boundaries of medicine, and I haven't been able to get off my mind the idea that this person may still be doing it. It's… It's *draconian*. If you are sitting there telling me that this was not an isolated incident, then you need to stop this person. In my experience, it takes a man with a strong constitution and a bad intention to toy with the deceased. It's against our natural revulsion, that deep-seated primal urge to avoid death."

The geriatric doctor seemed indeed perturbed about it. His outstretched, wagging finger was stern, like that of a father or teacher. It wasn't directed at Shay but at the situation in general. Shay folded up the document he had been gifted and slid it into his breast pocket. He stood up and reached over to firmly shake the hand of the man who had been of so much help. Dr. Lowell didn't stand up, but he offered a solid handshake and one last word of advice.

"Young man, if you find any closure or even any more to this story, I'd love to hear it. I know the families of those men, and I'm sure it would put some minds at ease if they knew there was some justice. Their sons, fathers, and brothers may never be laid to rest, but any comfort is still comfort."

Shay nodded and stood, feeling a bit green, perhaps reeling from the revelations.

As he departed, he turned back. "Doc, the local boys never recovered anything else? No bodies, no sightings? Cold trail?"

Turning away in his chair, the old man muttered back, "Nope. How about you fix that, *Detective* Hayes?" And Shay grinned, rapping his knuckles on the doorframe as a way of saying goodbye.

Knowledge is Power

Walking out of that hospital into the dreary morning air, Shay looked up at the sky and to the west, where the sky was clear and vividly blue. He turned and looked to the west, where a broad and roiling stormfront was stretched across the horizon. He stopped in his tracks for a moment and patted the medical examiner's report that was nestled in his pocket. In the office, he'd seen plenty of words in that document he'd not encountered before. It occurred to him that he knew little about medicine or chemistry aside from what primary school or the Army had taught him, so his next move would need to be research.

Calling up a cab from the reception desk was swift; he was informed it might take a while for his ride to arrive. Just then, he wished this drab and looming building behind him were an airport; at least then, there'd be a taxi handy. In the meantime, he found a huddle of four lightly dressed medical professionals outside under an awning, seeking shelter from the drizzle that misted down, giving every surface a gloss and a permeating wet chill. The men were arguing over something that Shay tried to overhear, words drifting in the air about *too much damn noise in the cafeteria.*

"Can't you boys smoke in the cafeteria?" he inquired cheerfully.

One of them chortled and offered, "Only time we get outside when it's daylight. Don't you know we work twelve's?"

Shay countered, "Fair, fair. I'll trade you a fact you've never heard for a cigarette if you're game."

"You're on, slim! We're pretty smart guys," one of the men shot back.

"Queen Elizabeth, boys, is a trained vehicle mechanic." With a chuckle, one of the men handed over a stick.

"Roll a single die. The opposite faces, in fact, will *always* add up to seven." There was some deep thought, a slight murmuring, and one more smoke handed over.

"Lastly, boys, the most important fact of them all...' they waited with bated breath; a quarter of the human body's bones are in the feet!" And they all laughed, one of them punching another in the shoulder.

"Keller's a podiatrist! He must'a already knew that!" The shortest of the men exclaimed. Yet Keller himself handed over two smokes with a wry grin.

Nodding thanks, Shay inquired, "Say, boys, you wouldn't happen to know where I might do some... er... heavy reading on chemicals used in medicine? Like an index of sorts?" he inquired as he struck a slightly damp cigarette.

...

An hour later, the rain began to fall as Shay and his driver reached Issaquah. It took no time at all to find the Town Hall, which served as the new home for the quaint city's burgeoning library. A storm that gloomed their skies now was moving quickly toward the East, and they had hit an eerily perfect wall of rain as they came into town.

It was noteworthy enough for the driver to comment. "It's cold, too cold for much rain. It'll be snow by the time we hit dusk, I'd bet". He tapped the brim of his hat with his index finger, proud that he was prepared for the winter storm.

Shay shot back, "Better get to it! It's nearly Christmas, and my almanac calls for it. I'd rather be cold than wet any day, pal." He patted the man's shoulder and handed him a five-dollar bill. The driver made the change, and Shay handed back a generous tip.

"How much for you to stick around a bit, perhaps thirty minutes?"

The driver rubbed his chin a bit with his thumb and forefinger. Looking like a professor challenged with quite the equation, he took a moment before smiling and meeting eyes with Shay in the rearview mirror of the tired DeSoto. He took to resetting the meter bolted to its scuffed, oxidized wood-grained dashboard. He'd been driving this taxi for some time. Shay noted that the steering wheel's white paint had rubbed away in two spots on the wheel, at precisely ten o'clock and two o'clock, where the hands rested perfectly on the spokes of the steering wheel hub. It looked so very comfortable.

"Buy me a coffee, and it's a deal. I won't have a fare going back if I leave you behind. I have a sports section to read, anyway!"

The driver fluffed a neatly trifolded newspaper that had been resting on the front seat.

Shay patted him on the shoulder and handed him two quarters.

"Buy us two cups, and I've got a crisp five-dollar bill with your name on it for the ride back to Snoqualmie. Cheers!"

Shay had held up his hand and five fingers when he'd said five, but it sounded much like *foive*. With that, he darted out of the cab as he left the smiling driver, who was now scanning the adjacent street for a good place to snag a couple of hot cups of joe.

The Town Hall was a stout brick building, and Shay nearly darted into the front door before eyeing a nice little hand-painted sign hanging over a side door. The archway was inconspicuous, but as the helpful cigarette-vending epidemiologist doctor had explained earlier, it was a new and very temporary location for the library. In the mist and the slight breeze that carried it, the small sign swung lazily back and forth on its black wrought-iron arm. Its font was a delightful choice, nearly olde English or medieval in origin. Shay lightly jogged up the steps and to the door. Just as he was reaching for the handle, a face appeared behind the foggy window of the door. An older lady in a lovely floral dress was just then turning the woodcut sign hanging behind the glass from CLOSED to OPEN. She stepped back from the door and, with a kind hand, beckoned Shay to come inside.

Her face showed a bit of concern as she commented. "Dear man, you're lucky I arrived just five minutes ago! You'd be stuck in that awful rain. It's so cold, come in. You must *really* need a book!" She joked, and as she laughed, she crossed her arms on her belly. The flowers on her dress were a welcome flash of color in the otherwise very dark, conservative wood-and-brick walls of the library.

Shay smiled and nodded as he took off his wet hat. "True, miss, true. I'd be forced to grow gills out there if it weren't for luck! Thank you for obliging me with a swift entry." He bowed just a bit, tongue-in-cheek. The woman clicked her tongue and uncrossed her arms, outstretching one toward the wall and pointing.

"You'll be so kind as to hang your hat and let me know what you need. I knew every title here. I helped purchase them myself for this county and two more North of Seattle. We've got quite the resources lately!" And she beckoned toward the mahogany racks of reading material behind him. He dutifully hung his hat and walked to meet her at the counter.

After drying his hands a bit on his trousers, he clasped them as though he were asking for a favor from a deacon. "Miss, please simply direct me to where I might reference a few names of various chemicals, mostly medicinal terminology. I suppose there's a fancy way to say that, but I haven't a clue what it might be." He withdrew the paper from his pocket and opened it in preparation for his search for answers.

"We're not organized by cards yet, so you'll have to rely on me." She smiled back at him, and a pit sank into his stomach. Initially, he'd planned on finding the books he needed and tucking them under his coat, 'going for a cigarette' and absconding with the books so he could get back to Snoqualmie sooner. It was a cheap but very effective ploy, as most folks who step out for a cigarette tend to step back in. Guilt now overrode his sense of hurry, and he realized he had no desire to steal books from an old woman, no matter if the county owned them.

Her kindness continued, "Let's have a look. I am certain we have what you need. I outfitted three shelves with all the recent tomes on science and medicine. We've quite an array of aspiring doctors around here. I suppose it's our lovely school system. I was a teacher for elementary; I should know!" she said with a wink.

The pit in Shay's stomach became a ball of shame for his dastardly plan. She reached for his paper, and he gently recoiled. "Ah, this is ehm… It's not really for public consumption, miss."

She clucked her tongue at him. "You don't know many librarians, do you? I taught twenty-four classes of children about the human body. I've taught science and, to a small degree, biology. If it's science you're after, that's just facts. We love facts and books about them. So let's have a look; I'm difficult to offend."

With a defeated sigh, he handed her the paper. She took a moment, raising the glasses dangling at the collar of her dress. She didn't unfold them or put them on; she just raised them for a moment to take a gander at what Shay might be seeking.

In a monotone voice, as she read down the list, she commented with a huff.

"Young man, this is a dire report. These are some severe substances. Barbiturates, amphetamine, cyanide… I certainly have the books you need. This looks like a medical examiner's report, in fact. Are you a doctor yourself?"

Shay sheepishly responded, "No, no. I was given the list as a sort of… It's a sort of test. It's a theory on chemical interaction, and I need to study these drugs individually and cohesively… does that make sense?" His bullshitting was not half bad, and he constantly peppered it with truth. This time, she looked over the rim of those glasses, and it was clear she wasn't biting.

"This is an official form, young man. While I'm no doctor, I'm no fool. I'll give you the books you need if you're honest with me. I'd wager you haven't even got a library card, have you?" Her stern tone was pure and unwavering, such is the way with teachers and educators.

Facing few immediate options, Shay decided to play it her way. "You're a tough one. And you're right. I've got no library card, not even a Washington driving license. I'm a private detective, miss, and I'm looking into some bad stuff that's been creeping around these parts. That chart is, in fact, a set of blood tests from a body found not far from here. I don't have answers yet, but I suspect someone was trying their hand at science on the stolen body of a local man. That name in the upper corner? That poor fellow was stolen from a mortuary in Snoqualmie. Awful business, I'm sure you can understand why I was hesitant to share."

For a moment, he could see in her visage what might be described as *mortified*. Nevertheless, she cleared her throat and returned to reading the list.

"Will you help me all the same, miss?"

She gently tapped her glasses frame on the paper. Shay stood in silence, patiently awaiting a reply. With her sideways glance, he could see that the woman was scanning the shelves mentally. A time passed, and she looked over the paper once more. "I recognize the name, that family in the paper who had that awful accident a while back. They went into a gully, didn't they? Terrible way to go, drowning…." She trailed off, and for a moment, Shay was unsure where she was headed with her decision.

"A tragedy that ended in a mystery, a mystery I need to solve."

"Ah." She replied.

Turning away on her shoe heel, she swiftly strode down the closest aisle. Shay stood still for a moment until she called out, "Catch up, now. I'm not carrying all these books myself!" Growing a grin, Shay jogged to meet her down toward the end of the aisle.

Within ten minutes, Shay stood in front of a stack of books that had him regretting taking half of the day's duties from John. He imagined his partner sitting at some desk in the county sheriff's office, comfortable and easy… sipping cocoa. Still, he knew he'd have a better lead than Talbot by the end of the day. His competitive side shone through in his smirk.

"You should find most of what you need in the glossary here, and as you can see, the different drugs and chemicals are sorted in a way that you can index them together." She waved the paper in front of him, pointing at the little lines drawn around a few of the long and very dreadful-sounding words on the paper. "Won't be much help without knowing your elemental interactions *long* before you consider the chemical response in a given envir-" she cut herself off. She released an exasperated sigh, staring at the books and then at the thin man eagerly awaiting hauling off the volumes. "It's a start, detective. I hope you're smart."

With a grim expression, Shay turned to her. "I've got to tell you, miss, I have a bit of a schedule. I've got a cab outside and maybe five more minutes until he leaves me behind. I hate to ask, but…" and he handed her his business card, the one that boldly proclaims WILLIAM BIGSBY II - PRIVATE INVESTIGATOR across the top, well before Shay's humble and italicized name shone below.

She clicked her tongue at him and looked over the card. "You want to take my books?"

He nodded, standing up straight and trying his best to look like someone responsible enough to return them. Her glare was icy, making him squirm as they stood in silence. Then, she looked down at the ME report in her hand. As leaves fell from a tree in the cold winter air, the dour expression fell from her face and was overtaken by one of care and sorrow. "No person should be desecrated in such a way. It's not right." She handed the paper back to him, folding it up along its creases. "Take the books, but do send them back. I had to blow the dust off their spines, anyway.

Shay nodded and placed the ME report back into his breast pocket, feeling that one of the cigarettes had burst in his pocket and scruffy tobacco littered the pocket now. "I'll send them back from Snoqualmie. I'm staying at the Falls Lodge. I'll have the desk wrap and courier them posthaste. Thank you so much, miss!" And he assembled the stack of books under his arm, keeping a hand free.

She tapped her foot on the floor, arms folded across her middle again. "Don't make me regret this, Mister Hayes! You'd best not get those jackets wet!"

As he retrieved his hat, he turned back to her. "I promise to take the utmost care. Cheers!" And he bounded down the steps, twenty pounds of books in tow. Much to his pleasure, the cab was waiting just outside at the curb. He could see the driver balancing two cups of Joe on his dashboard and the paper on the steering wheel. The steam coming from the sipping holes was enticing, and Shay tossed the books into the back seat before climbing in.

"Say, how'd you borrow so many books? I thought two was the limit! What, did you steal 'em?" The driver deadpanned as he handed back one of the paper cups.

It was just after lunchtime as the two men sipped their coffee as the rain pattered on the rooftop and streaked across the windshield, the old sedan lumbering quietly out of town and heading east on the highway. The rain had moved fast enough to encompass probably the whole county. The roads were slow; Shay was now listening to his stomach rumble from the coffee and was considering going to the Lodge restaurant for another one of their ridiculous farm breakfasts. Of course, looking down at the stack of a half dozen volumes on the seat next to him, he thought better of it and supposed he might as well hunker down in his room and order a meal to be brought up. The driver made some small talk with him about the weather, local lore, and a few of the little byways they passed on the perhaps thirty-something-minute trek back to Snoqualmie. By the end of it, Shay felt almost rude as he was not particularly interested in small talk.

Earlier, while he and the librarian had been reading down the list of substances he needed to investigate, one of the terms had stuck out in his mind.

Is that… wait, I know this one.

He couldn't figure out how the primary reactant of a military-grade nerve gas might fit in, but he was determined to find that answer along with many others.

The driver eventually returned him safely to the front driveway of the Snoqualmie Falls Lodge. Before he could open his door, a valet met him at the car with an umbrella and opened it graciously. Shay took a moment to cobble together his books and pay the driver. That folded five-dollar bill was enough to put a very wholesome smile on the man's face. Shay was out of the cab in a tick after he paid his due.

Shay stopped by the front desk, still plenty wet from the rain and his knuckles white from holding the stack of books against his hip. After a bit of help from the clerk and a glance at the room service menu, he decided upon the roast beef sandwich, and that was enough. Well, with a side of chips. And a cola. It was lunchtime, after all.

In nearly no time, our man was back in his comfortable room, doffing his coat and his shirt, everything but his shorts and his undershirt. He set the pile of books on one side of the bed and made a wedge of pillows on the other, taking his place in the comfortable makeshift recliner and crossing his ankles. Comfy as a cat in a pile of laundry, he opened the first book. It was a 2-inch-thick, leather-bound volume that claimed to be a compendium of substances and medicinal applications. He had just settled into his comfortable position on the bed when a knock at the door reminded him he had ordered food. Almost synchronous with the knock, as he stood up, his stomach growled like a dog at a postman. He threw on the complementary robe from the closet, greeted the fresh-faced young man at the door of the room, and traded the tray for a twenty-five-cent tip, declining to have it wheeled in.

He rested the tray on the corner of the bed and devoured the sandwich; now he was sitting there, looking at an empty tray with a full stomach, feeling his second wind.

Okay, time to get to work. God, I hate readin'…

He dropped the robe next to the bed and got comfortable once again; he picked up the bloodwork report and took the pen from the nightstand's complementary notepad. Faced with a complicated and intimidating list of words, he decided to reference them by group, just as the librarian had suggested. There were perhaps a dozen different chemicals listed there that were found in the blood work that were annotated as being abnormal for the blood work of any person, much less a deceased person. The ME had even gone so far as to put a little star next to each compound that might have been foreign to standard embalming, anything out of place.

Of note, next were the barbiturates. Two barbiturate chemicals were in the sample; neither dose was enough to tranquilize. At least, that's what the volume he was holding had offered. In fact, one of them was known to have a delirious effect, but he didn't believe that was particularly related. He put a star next to it anyway, in blue ink on the black print of the paper.

The third compound was confusing. It was an oligomeric distillate, almost like a petroleum product. He couldn't find any reference to it in the medical volume, so he switched over to the very portly book on chemistry. After a bit of searching, it seemed to be a combination of two things. The high carbon index indicated that it was a product typically used in combustion or as a fuel. Very toxic yet rudimentary. That was a low quantity. Slightly higher was the nearly unpronounceable and very toxic ester, like a stripping chemical. It was as though somebody had gone to a factory or rail yard and cracked open a couple of barrels of whatever they could find, injecting that garbage into this mortal coil that was so plainly dissected in the text there in front of him.

If those don't drastically affect the tissues' function, what if they're part of the delivery...?

He noted oxygen levels were spectacularly high compared to a healthy blood sample, even moreso compared to a still bloodstream.

The one that concerned him, he had saved for last. In his time in the service, he and several men in his unit, including Gabriel, had been detailed several times to travel with or help transport some very nasty nerve agents that were being used in some very controversial and often very secret operations on a select few battle fronts. Tabun, that was the name of the compound. A nasty nerve agent that had been around since perhaps a few decades prior and even been used by the Germans in a few instances was the substance in question. According to his book, this was an organophosphate that had near-immediate, very unpleasant effects on anyone in its vicinity, much less in direct contact with it. The way it shut down systems in the body was drastic and irreversible.

I wonder what it does to dead tissue... a defunct nervous system...

According to this book, Tabun was developed when it was discovered as a byproduct of attempts to create a new insecticide. While a very potent insecticide, it was also a potent people-cide, and the book in front of him warned of dire consequences if one were exposed to it. Of course, it wasn't an exceptionally high concentration in the blood sample. Apparently, it was low enough that it could have been a survivable dose by a person who sought immediate treatment, but... that wasn't the concern at hand.

Christ's sake... we flattened a factory making this stuff in '43 or 44... they bombed that place, let the chemicals take out most of the scum inside. Wonder whatever happened to that railcar of the stuff we packed off and sent back to the front.

Lastly, there was the footnote of the medical examiner's report. It was a short handwritten paragraph stating simply;

Results inconclusive as to the effect of aforementioned upon preserved healthy tissue sample. Primary introduction method appears to be pressurized injection through two punctures directly into cadaver kidney, wounds indicate high volume hypodermic. Vacuum/hydraulic abrasion evident along with postmortem tissue layer separation. Burns in surrounding tissues, indicative of application high-voltage alternating current; method unknown. Physical sample incinerated to avoid dispersion of hazardous materials not yet extracted.

"Ah… shite."

Physical simple incinerated. Shay was disappointed but wondered whether there might be another reason for that cremation. He had known of many cases where the body would be stored for a long time and quarantined for further examination. Hell, even Army hospitals had airtight portable storage units for such things, bigger than a Jeep. Usually, a double-axle transport. He remembers having seen them when he was working way freight on base.

Having added his tick or a star near each term, he was no closer to an answer. He knew a little bit of what was in this horrible cocktail that they had found in the body, and he sat in silence, reflecting on whether or not he'd encountered someone or something similarly afflicted during his little scuffle just a few nights prior. He realized that his hand was pressed against the side of his head. The bump no longer ached, but it was certainly still present under his hair.

The now more confused man sat there in his shorts, contemplating what a strange situation he was now in. Either somebody was out there experimenting on corpses and drugging living men into violent puppets, or somebody had sussed out a way to make dead flesh move again. He was absently gnashing the pen between his teeth and scowling, a headache coming on.

Just then, the phone rang mercifully, drawing him out of a dark headspace and bringing his attention back to the cozy room in which he was seated so comfortably.

He answered with a short hello, and on the other end of the phone, he heard a long and exasperated sigh. He knew it was Talbot. "Jesus, Hayes. You had me worried. You didn't check in! It's nearly 2 PM, you never checked in, and I had to call back three times, and now some kid at the desk tells me you were upstairs enjoying a goddamn sandwich."

Shay, being cheeky, responded as Sheamus would. "Well, hello to you, too, mister. You're right; I forgot to check in just as much as you forgot your manners! And before you ask, the sandwich was *delicious.*" He had embellished that last word, and in all honesty, the sandwich wasn't particularly delicious, but any opportunity he had to tease John Talbot? He simply *had* to take it.

"God dammit, man. Listen, I've got something. You sit there, and I'll be back in a couple of hours. Can you stay out of trouble until I get back?"

"Fine, fine. I won't even put me pants on.' Shay chuckled into the handset but stifled it, realizing that John was well and truly pissed. 'Of course, Talbot. I'll be here. In fact, I've got something big as well. We should compare notes, that's for sure."

"I'll come get you when I get back, and you're buying dinner. I want… I need a salad." John hung up just as Shay heard him let out another exasperated sigh. He stretched out his hands and interlaced fingers, relieved at the bit of progress and perhaps a bit at being able to get under John's skin.

…

A very insistent knock at the door woke Shay from his nap. It was John, of course, and Shay took his time getting up and putting on his slacks. He figured he didn't need anything more than the ribbed shirt he was wearing, but men don't sit around without pants. It's simply not done.

Shay opened the door to his friend, looking doggedly tired, leaning on the doorframe like he'd had a few drinks.

"Where the hell have you been, Talbot? You look like a hobo!" He smiled, and John smiled back. John sauntered in and plopped into the chair adjacent to the bed, so Shay sat down on the end of the bed and folded his arms, waiting for John to fill him in.

"Irish, you'll never guess what happened. I went over and met that detective, Danny Parks, as I planned. You know what? Great guy. Real standup lawman. Apparently, he and one of his deputies were the first on the scene when those boys sent their truck into that gully and then the first on the scene when they found that damn body. He seemed invested."

Shay leaned toward him a little bit and sniffed. It was clear what the boys had been up to. "So you went and emptied the bar with the man?"

John chuckled and shook his head. "Not quite, but pretty close. He had just gotten off shift, and I can always use a sip. We ended up getting into stories, and wouldn't you know it, he went to the same school as I did. Two years ahead, but he knew my older brother. It was a great time. Good man."

His words were slightly slurred, but he was in a fine mood. Apparently, his earlier frustration with Shay on the phone had waned in the face of a friendly inebriation. Shay balled up a fist and tapped him on the shoulder. "Well, let me know when the wedding is announced!"

"Ha! Go to hell, you goofy cus..." Shay doubled over in laughter, and his friend joined him. John put up a hand, trying to catch his breath.

"Say, maybe I'll give it a go. I haven't had much luck with the ladies in a while anyway," he chortled, Shay still jiggling with laughter.

Wheezing, John finally spat out, "Goddammit, let's be serious. This is serious! I mean, if not all the drinks, so... nah, He's just not my type anyway."

Shay threw the pen at him, and John sighed, relenting. "Okay, fine, back to business..."

Shay was happy that John could joke about something like that. A lot of people were really uptight about it, but Shay had a cousin who was privately homosexual; cousin Kerry was a great man and a fantastic welder. He had been teaching structural fabrication and now had his own shop and apprentice. Shay had been intending lately to catch up with the lad and see how life had been treating him.

"I found out what killed our dead man in Snoqualmie. Both times. Maybe. It's... It's a mess." He handed the ME paper to John.

John scoured the medical examiner's report, mumbling. Eyeing the stack of books, he commented, "You've been busy yourself. Parks told me all about the local burglaries, and a couple of laboratories burgled in the last eighteen months were likely missing some of these simpler compounds. I don't know much science stuff, but... that looks like a hell of a lead... I think you might actually be onto something!"

He tossed the report back onto the bed and sat back in the chair. "Irish, listen. I know we talked about me simply helping gather some information here, but by Christ, I haven't felt like myself in a while... and now I'm actually excited about finding out what the hell happened here. Do you know that there have been more than a couple of sightings of dead men around these parts? Four I can list for you — who knows how many more? None of them were considered... credible, but Parks gave me one name that I think we really need to follow up on."

"Your policeman didn't follow up on it?"

"Parks was told to drop it by his C/O. So... he dropped it." He shrugged.

Shay nodded and interjected, "Well, whom and what for? I love a good lead."

John crossed his legs and put his hands up behind his head like he was in a lounge chair. "That old man is living out in the woods just past the falls; he's not far from here. It seems he called up the Sheriffs around the time this nonsense was happening, but Parks said the man could be a bit of a handful. He says he's missing a few screws. Still, he said that was the only lead he hadn't personally followed up on, and I figured since everybody else gave their statement and that all panned out to nothing, we'd better talk to this guy. Same one Billy got on the line, but he wouldn't say a peep over the wires. So, yeah. We've got that now, too."

"That's pretty fantastic, Talbot. Shall we visit him tomorrow? In the meantime, I've been here doing some research on all the nonsense they found in that body. The medical examiner was a straight shooter. Doc seemed to be boiling about the whole thing, but he played it cool for me. He gave me that list there and set me on a path. Do you know that they found nerve agents and amphetamines in that body? If that thing was a dead man walking, well, I don't see how. I've got more questions now than I did yesterday.

"Join the club, pal!" John retorted.

"Still, there's more work to be done, Johnny boy. Also, it seems that there haven't been any body thefts before or after, just a window of time. Perhaps they moved on and headed south, and I suppose that's how they wound up out there west of Portland. So, let's go see this woodsman tomorrow and get back to Billy with the details."

"You know, Shay, it's Thanksgiving tomorrow."

A somber look fell across John's face. Shay took a beat and locked in on John, who looked deflated now.

"See, the way things have been, I can't really be with my missus right now. I don't know where else I would be if I wasn't here, I guess I'm saying... I appreciate you and Billy keeping me busy. The holidays aren't easy alone."

Despite his liquor-loosened lips, he was right. The holidays were a time for family, and it could be even harder to get through them if you had a family you couldn't be with. Shay nodded, mirroring his friend's straight face. He recalled many a holiday when he was away, or alone, and he wouldn't wish that on anyone. Not even fussy John Talbot.

"Ye know I give you a hard time, John, but you're a good man. There's nobody else I would rather be stuck on a mission with, and to be honest, if I weren't here, I'd just be at home eating a takeaway meal for the holiday… so I suppose you could say the feeling is mutual. Listen, get some shut-eye. We've got a good shot at making even more headway tomorrow, and you're in no shape to work right now. I'll get some food sent to your room. How's that sound?"

John smiled, lolled his head a bit, and stood up. "That sounds mighty fine of you, Irish. You get some rest too, see?" And with that, he shuffled out of the room and down the hallway. Shay took a minute to call down to the desk, following through on his promise to get John some dinner before long.

Extraneous business out of the way, he sat back down on the bed and picked up the thickest volume of them all: the 'Journal of Chemical Application Data [JCAD].' It looked to be an anthology of white papers. Shay knew he'd be thoroughly lost in that book, but any lead is worth the time. It was hardly 7 PM, and that nap fixed him up for the time being.

Get to reading, ye fool.

The Woodsman

Thursday, November 23rd, 1950
Thanksgiving Day

Dawn came around, and with it, the brassy ringing of Shay's bedside alarm clock. He went to the windowsill, where he could hear the constant and calming rush of the waterfalls outside. Snow was falling, slowly drifting in the gentle lofting breeze over the falls. Swiftly swirling white lace troupes of snowflakes danced to the music of muted winter air until they found ground. They joined their brethren in softening the lush green forest tree with a fluffy layer that looked nearly unreal, like white cotton balls on a church nativity scene.

In no time, he was rapping on John's door. He wasn't sure the state his friend would be in; the man, perhaps, had imbibed a few whiskeys past his limit the day before. Much to his surprise, the door swung wide, and John was dressed and ready. After a clean shave and a hot shower, John looked better than presentable.

"Ready for action, I see?" Shay teased.

"Guess we'll find out, Irish. Breakfast is on me!"

It was 8 o'clock sharp when they departed, full of the farmer's special, gingerly making their way through the slush in the parking lot toward the frozen Dodge. With directions sketched on a piece of hotel stationery, John took the little back road that led to the stead of a Mr. Clyde Sterland. Along the way, John explained to Shay a bit more about what he had been told about this reclusive old coot. Parks had shared that this Sterland was a capable but eccentric lumberjack who retired from the dilapidated millworks that had been knocked to rubble in 1947. It seems he had been a town regular before finding a solitary life in the woods.

"Takes all kinds, I suppose. Irish, how about you? You ever feel the need to get away?"

Shay mulled over it before answering, "Yeh, sure, but last time I got the urge? I up and joined the Army. An' we all know how that went…"

"Say, you'd never have met Cam or Gabe, Billy, or even me if that weren't the case!" John joked.

"Lucky me then, s'pose! How about you, wishing for a cabin in the woods?"

Wistfully, John peered out the windshield through the light snowfall and sighed, "I *have* a home. I miss it… Say, I think we're just about here."

The crooked road that led off the highway seemed treacherous at best. Both John and Shay were dressed in their long coats, and the snow was just dry enough not to ice up much. John chose to take the road on foot after explaining his not wanting to drive down a "slushy damn mess, that's what it is. I can tell from here! No, I'm not getting us stuck."

So, with their dress shoes and their pressed slacks, the two boys parked the sedan roadside and took to hoofing it down this rough and steep terrain toward their mystery man's cabin. As they trudged through the soft snow and the rocky mud underneath, they heard the report of a gunshot in the distance. John commented, "Hunting season, s'pose?"

After the second shot rang out from the thick treeline, Shay stopped walking and put out his hand in front of John's chest to stop him. "Hear that again? Small charge. Birdshot, but it's too close. Someone is out hunting. We'd best announce ourselves, don't you think?" John nodded in worried agreement.

The two began whooping and hollering and alternating, shouting "Hello-o-o!" and "We're here to visit Mr. Sterland!" with the hopes of avoiding taking birdshot in the arse. There were no more shots; the air was silent. They assumed they had been heard, so they carefully resumed their hike down to the old man's cabin. They had walked perhaps thirty yards before Shay pointed out wisps of smoke rising from a point just downhill and to the east, farther back in the woods.

"Hope he's making us coffee?" Shay mused, and John chuckled with a grin and a nod.

Another twenty yards or so, and the edge of the property, neatly staked, could be seen. Shay took to shouting once again, just to be sure anybody in earshot knew they were friendly.

"Sterland, ye've got visitors!" he exclaimed cheerfully.

As they reached a clearing in front of the cabin, Shay walked up the steps and knocked on the door. They waited silently, patiently. After a minute, no response was heard. Shay strutted back down the steps and stood next to John. Hands on his hips and looking over the tree line, "D'you think that he heard us? He moost've…" his accent lay thick as he became a touch nervous.

As Shay and John peered into the window, they heard the all-too-familiar sound of a shotgun racking behind them. The duo turned around with palms up to face the most confusing sight. There in front of them stood a sizable man with a bushy white beard, holding a shotgun pointed lazily between the two of them, clad head-to-toe in soft white fur and red velvet. They were looking at an armed Santa Claus.

"State yer business, or git!" Santa barked at them. The ridiculousness of it had Shay stifling a chuckle. Santa Claus glared a piercing eye at him, then swiveled at the hips a bit so the shotgun was pointing dead-center at Shay's belly.

Oh, Christ, this is it, huh? Shay mused, about to speak.

John stepped forward half a step, his hands raised in the air to show he was unarmed. "Sir, are you Clyde Sterland? I'm so sorry we had to intrude, but we didn't have a working phone number for you, and it's a matter of urgency. We are both unarmed; *please* don't shoot!"

Shay whispered under his breath, "Yeah, please don't shoot us, Santa Claus! Oh, I promise I've been *such* a good boy!" And John snorted, now holding a laugh himself.

Santa stepped forward with a filthy black boot and shouted at them, "The hell is he mumbling? And why are you on my goddamned land? What the *hell* is so funny?" He sneered at both men, contorting their faces and jiggling with stifled laughter despite being held at gunpoint.

Nearly in tears, John reached his hands out toward the man, who was maybe 10 yards away, and pleaded through his chuckling, "Please, sir, Mr. Sterland, we're private investigators. You spoke with the sheriff's department sometime back about some fishy business, but I am aware they didn't take you seriously. Our boss had you on the phone for a spell. We came to hear your story, that's all!" Shay was in stitches behind him, tears in his eyes.

Santa Claus grabbed the barrel of his shotgun near the end and swung the butt stock down to meet the ground. He marched forward toward them and shook a fist at them. "I told that sheriff to come down here! Damn idjits! And just *what* are you two laughing at? Just what the *hell* are you laughing at?!?"

Shay, wiping tears from his eyes, reached out and gestured wildly at the man's suit. "I'm so, so sorry, sir... Santa, sir, it's just... I never pictured I'd be put in the ground by auld Saint Nick himself!" and with that, Sterland glanced down at himself and let out a bit of a sigh and a laugh.

"Ha! HaHA! Oh, hell." Sterland shrugged his shoulders and chuckled at the sheer stupidity. He raised his hand and offered, "Boys, I honestly forgot I was *wearing* this getup. I used to dress for Santa Claus at the holidays down in the town center, but now it's just the warmest thing I've got to hunt in that I don't mind messing up with a little red. Know what I mean?"

Sterland doffed the red hat and rumpled his kindly face apologetically as he deftly swung the gun up over his shoulder, barrel aimed behind him, and extended his hand to shake John's. John shook the old man's hand vigorously.

"Well, sir, it's a pleasure to meet you. I'm John Talbot; this is Shay Hayes. We work out of Seattle for the Bigsby Investigative Agency. We've been working on that case you called about a while back—those stolen bodies and the sightings." Shay took to shaking Sterland's hand as John withdrew a business card and handed it to Sterland.

"Boys, I'm glad you're here. Hell, I haven't caught a thing all morning. It's cold, and cold hands can't aim proper some days. Three birds already got away... looks like I'm having potatoes for Thanksgiving. Suppose that's enough. Why don't you come in? I'll put a kettle on."

With that, he led the two men into the cabin and invited them to take a seat at his small table. As they entered, Shay looked around and saw that their host had a meticulous, rather charming, tiny home. "Ohhh, he's got knick-knacks, John..."

It was nowhere near the decrepit trash pit that Parks had described to John; instead, it was the perfect place for retirement, at least, certainly fitting for a holiday retreat. Red gingham tablecloth, pictures on the walls of varying silver and bronze hues, many years of memories in those handcrafted wooden frames. There were no stairs; it was a simple open floor plan, and the only closed door was likely the toilet. A few trophies hung on the walls, various animals with and without antlers, but Shay paid that little mind. He was more interested in the stack of newspapers by the front door, each well-worn and poorly folded, destined for the trash.

"Coffee, boys?" Sterland inquired. John gave a hasty two-thumbs-up.

The coffee kettle was put on a burner, and Sterland took the chair closest to the stove at the head of the table, leaning forward on his elbows as he looked over the men seated before him. "So, you say someone else seen one of these things?"

Shay nodded uneasily and took off his hat. "Can't say for sure, but something large and unpleasant stuffed me into the boot of a car after giving me this lump. I took him on, but... he didn't go down easy. It was damned odd, but I can't say for certain what the thing was. Perhaps with my injury, I wasn't seeing straight, I don't rightly know." He turned his head and showed Sterland the bruised lump on the right side of his head, hardly visible now but still helping tell the story.

Sterland leaned back, gripping the sides of the low wooden chair, betraying unease. "You wouldn't be here if that was all you knew."

Reaching into his pocket, Shay pulled out the medical examiner's report. He tossed it across the table in front of Sterland. "One of those bodies, local man, they found it sometime later. Somebody had done a real number on this fellow. That's the screening of the blood sample. We don't know what to believe yet, but all of this points to somebody at very *least* desecrating the dead... and our job is to figure out the who and the why."

Sterland took a moment to look over the paper and was murmuring some of the words to himself. After he finished reading it, he folded it back in three and slid it back in front of Shay.

"Big words, but most of that sounds ungodly," Sterland offered as he stood up to prepare the coffee. He opened the cabinet nearby and retrieved three small copper mugs. Quietly and diligently, he poured each of them a coffee and returned to the table, all three mugs in one big hand. It was clear he was deep in thought.

Shay filled the air, "Anything you can tell us, we'll add to what we know. You're helping these families with closure more than anything, sir."

"Well, let me start by telling you what I told the sheriffs. It was a late afternoon just this past March... a nice day, humid and warm for the season, but that doesn't really matter. I walked down through the woods to the riverfront. You know, I can't quite see the waterfall from here, but I can hear it. I paid a good bit for this place just for that; I used to have a cabin out by Crater Lake. Sold it 'cause I never went anymore. So, anyway, I had my fishing gear, it had been a nice day, and y'know, sometimes in the evening you catch the biggest fish. I think it's because of the swarms of little flying jiggers over the water. Never really got taught how to fish… had to teach myself."

Shay cleared his throat as if to say *Get on with it, boyo.*

"Anyway, I was out there with all my gear and I was on the river for 'bout three hours. I was gettin' bored, collected a few smooth stones for my garden. It helps keep the soil warm after the sun goes down, you see. It was nearly dark when… when it happened."

Shay and John had taken to loving dark, strong coffee. A bit of coffee grounds swirled around in it, but neither of them took much notice.

Shay leaned in, "John says you spoke to Officer Parks about it. What did you see?"

Sterland was mid-sip and nearly spat it out, blurting, "Those damn badges don't listen. Told 'em to come down 'cause I saw something damn strange. They never came to take a report or nothin'! I told them it was in the river."

"You saw one of these things in the water? Was it floating?" John inquired.

"No, no. It didn't come from the river; it came *through* the goddamn river. Walked from the other bank right underwater, came out maybe 10 yards upriver from me. Hell, at first, I had thought it was some fool trying to drown himself, and I was already stripping off my boots and pants to go haul him out. Low water, maybe six or eight feet, that time of the year. When he came bubbling out of that water on *my* side, it scared me half to death! I had no pants, I had no shoes, and this son of a bitch walked out of the mud, trudging towards me, looking like death. Pale, puffy. Just an awful sight."

Sterland's grim countenance told that he was serious. Shay was wide-eyed and, in his lilt, exhaled 'Sheeeesus *chroist*…"

"My thoughts exactly. I shouted at him, and he was dead mute. He just kept on marching toward me. Seemed to me like he wanted a fight or worse. I warned him that I would stand my ground; he just came right for me with his fists balled up tight at his sides. He looked like he was takin' something, not liquor… eyes wide, he looked like he had been through a meat tenderizer. Honest, I was spooked, y'know. All I had at hand was a fishing rod and some fancy river rocks, so I did what I had to do."

Shay leaned forward, brushing aside his coffee cup. "You ran?"

Sterland looked down into his mug, clasping it with both of his sizable hands. His shoulders heaved up and down as he took a breath and let out a long and very strained exhale. "I picked up one of those damn twenty-pound river rocks, and I defended myself, that's all. I just defended myself." Sterland was nearly pleading.

John placed a hand on the table near Sterland. "Nobody's telling you that you've done anything wrong, sir. We just came here for facts. If that's what you say happened, that's the truth to us. Sounds like you had mixed feelings about it."

Sterland raised his chin and met eyes with Shay, and there was a sadness there that hadn't been present before. "Still do. I suppose I was just defending myself, but… it still feels wrong. I picked up that rock, and when the man got close enough, I did the deed."

"You killed the thing?" Shay asked, recalling his tussle with something that sounded eerily similar.

"Bashed his head in since he was grabbin' at me, but… now listen up, boys, I've been a hunter for about as long as I could walk. I've killed the game with every weapon you might think of: bow and arrow. Shotgun. Rifle. Even a goddamn axe when we took to killin' wild pigs out at my Uncle's ranch in the wetlands! But in all my life, I have never killed something that didn't *bleed*. Unnatural, that's what it is."

John was shifting in his seat, obviously a bit green over the thought of it. Shay took the lead. "Tell us everything, Clyde. We're on your side about all of this."

"I'm saying any living thing you kill makes a damned mess, and after a while, sure, you get used to it. When I took that thing down? It felt like butchering, like halving a lamb that's been strung up and drained. It was… *cold*. Had my nerves set off for a week, thinking about that feeling. That *give*, the… the way the bone and flesh was there, but there was no life in it."

Shay responded in a hushed tone, "I know what you're speaking of; as I said, I know it firsthand—nearly lost my head to one of these things. Took everything I had to get away. I… he paused, thinking of how to pose his response best. 'I believe that you made the right decision. I know it because the thing didn't bleed. It didn't make a sound. And y'know, it tried to *kill* me, no question. Were you injured?"

Sterland let out a long breath and pushed away from the table to stand up, pacing. His chest was heaving. John looked at Shay with his hands up as if to say, 'I'm not sure how to proceed.' But Shay just waved him to settle and wait. Sterland was clearly upset, but he returned to the table after a bit and refilled his guests' cups with more steaming dark brew from the percolator. Still in silence, he sat down and bellied up to the table.

"I'm sorry, boys, and I woulda made some food if I knew I had guests coming by... coulda run to the corner market. I like the Piggly Wiggly out in Portland, but I don't like those city drivers... I'm just..."

Shay patted Sterland's forearm, "Sir, you're too kind. We came here out of the blue and upturned your day. I'm sorry. You're a good man for thinking of it, but we're here to help. So... tell us how we can help."

"Well, yeah, so... I wasn't really hurt. That thing barely got a swing at me when I put it down. Just... I never took the life of any man. I never had the constitution for that."

"What did you do with the body?" John's tone was dry as ever, but the question was genuine curiosity.

Sterland looked to John, and a wry smile crept across his face. "Ah... that. So maybe... maybe I forgot to mention when I called the sheriff. I couldn't leave that thing layin' around for the wildlife, could I?"

Shay caught on first, but John was just behind him. "D'you mean to say ye *kept* it?"

Sterland grunted. "Hmmph. Do you boys want to see it?" He thumbed over his shoulder toward the back door.

John's jaw dropped, and he placed his hands on his thighs. Shay was standing up; Sterland reached over and grasped his shoulder. Shay sat back down like a child being scolded. This older man had a kind face and was wearing Santa Claus's uniform, but he had a grip like an iron vice, and his eyes were serious.

"Sit down, just for a moment. Let's all finish our coffee. I... I need a minute." And he returned to his mug, taking gentle sips as the boys sat there in stunned silence.

Shay's mind went racing with the trauma of what he'd experienced so recently. He felt flush and raised his hand as if he was in school, asking, "Sir, I can surely wait, but d'ye mind if I...?" and motioned toward the closed door in the corner that had a funny little hand-carved wood sign hanging off a nail next to the door; "loo." Sterland nodded and waved his hand as an open invitation. Shay took to his feet and headed for the restroom, stepping in and closing the door behind him. He ran the tap and splashed some cold water on his brow and cheeks, feeling the hot waves of adrenaline and the pulse pounding in his head.

You've stepped in it again, old boy. Keep it together. Can't have John seein' ye sweat bullets, as they say...

Catching his breath and running his hands under the frigid tap, he felt a bit of relief in that little toilet. It was small but serviceable. A clawfoot tub pushed into one corner, a fading, yellowing porcelain sink below an oxidized mirror. On a shelf just under the window, there was little decoration save a dish that held a bar of soap and a photograph of a lovely woman with her hair pinned back and waving in the silvery light, looking like a thinner Greta Garbo. He focused on the picture to cool his nerves. Drying his hands, he picked it up and leaned back on the sink.

On the left side of the frame, the paint was worn through in one spot. Shay reached for the frame and put his left hand around it, his thumb resting perfectly where the imprint was. It was clear that this was a cherished possession, that it had been picked up more times than its varnish could sustain. With a sullen feeling, Shay set it delicately back on the shelf. He wondered about the old man out in the room and what that lovely young lady might have meant to Sterland. It was a nice distraction from his excitement about seeing something impossible.

Returning to the room, Shay found John and Clyde chatting comfortably about the town. John had mentioned they were staying at the Snoqualmie Falls Lodge, and Sterland had some stories about its history in the community. He told John that the place had burned down many years ago and had been rebuilt at its current location. He proclaimed, "I cut half the wood that built that place, I bet!"

When Shay arrived at the table, Sterland stood up. His shoulders were thrown back, and he looked almost happy for the first time since the boys arrived.

"Son, you've got an interesting friend here. Do you know he collects trains, too? And he pointed into the far corner of the cabin, where there was a table draped in a green cloth. Shay had only half-noticed it before, but on top of the green tablecloth was a ring of black and silver track, and in the center, a little mountain that appeared to be made of glue and cardboard. Underneath the table were a few boxes with the brands of a few toymakers, and lazily lying on its side was a toy steam locomotive that was perhaps a foot long and looked heavy.

Shay nodded at the scene and turned back to Sterland. "Lovely trains. Do you collect them, Talbot?" He hadn't known John to be a fan, either, but he supposed it might have been something John did with his family for Christmas. John shrugged and nodded.

Sterland spoke, a bit exasperated. "My brother's trains. He passed a few years back; he was a real fan. Before he came to work with me at the mill, he was a ticket agent down at the station in Snoqualmie. It was a beautiful place… he used to gripe about how cold they kept the ticket rooms, but otherwise, he was absolutely in love. You could see it in his eyes any time he saw a loco or heard a train whistle, that little sparkle of excitement. I keep that stuff around, and I play with it when the mood strikes me. That locomotive is quite a puller. Hell, it even makes steam out of its stack with these little chalk pills! Maybe I'll show you boys later when we get through with the nasty business."

John patted Sterland on the shoulder and said, "I'd love that. Haven't played with my trains in too long."   Shay knew the reason, and it made him sad.

Sterland turned towards the back door, waving his hand to 'come along' and heading out. The boys grabbed their coats, with John slipping his on and Shay simply carrying his under one arm. Sterland was wearing just his shirt, but a man his size didn't get cold so quickly.

Outside, they could see there was a beautiful forest beyond the cabin. It was quiet and a bit remote, but the ground had been cleared and stumps removed, which curtailed the forest back about 20 yards from the cabin. It was a nice little plot, though if it were grass or rock, nobody could tell under the 2 inches of snow that covered it. The garden was covered as well. Across a clearing was a small but very sturdy-looking brick shed. It had a redwood door, much like the cabin's front. Sterland moved directly toward the shed, and Shay had to stretch his stride to follow in Sterland's footsteps. John was just behind them, fumbling in his pocket for a cigarette. By the time the three men reached the door of the shed, John had already struck a match and lit a smoke. It waggled from his lips as he tucked away the matchbook. Sterland slowly leaned forward and turned the knob of the shed, pushing the door open and inward. He stood about 3 feet back from the doorway and did not step in.

"You go ahead, Shay. I… I need a smoke real quick, yeah?"

Shay stood there for a moment and then perched his hands on his hips, looking up at Clyde. "You've got the body in there? What sort of state is it in?"

Sterland shrugged a bit and, with a bit of defeat in his voice, said, "Honestly, I don't know. I installed this Sears electric cooling system last year for my fresh game; it worked pretty well… uh, up until I turned this shed into a damned morgue. The light switch is on the right when you step in."

He was clearly not interested in going first. It was cold outside, and the air in the freezing shed was even colder. With the door open, Shay could hear the hum of the refrigeration unit running.

Reaching into the pocket of his coat, Shay removed a small flashlight that he kept with him most days; this day, it was in the same pocket as his almanac. Aiming it into the shed like a pistol, he flicked the switch. He saw nothing at first, his eyes adjusting there at the doorway. He stepped one foot inside, the slight creak of the floorboards echoing in that open yard. He took the flashlight in his left hand and reached for the light switch with his right. With a flick, the single bulb hanging from the ceiling began casting its warm glow onto the center of the room, but objects along both sidewalls remained in darkness.

Shay had a strong stomach; that was generally true. He'd been around plenty of death and bodily destruction, both in the wars and in his various careers before and after. He'd seen a hunting shed before; that was nothing special. Shay had himself hunted as a youth. He knew John had a strong constitution as well, so he wasn't too concerned about what they might find. He swept his flashlight beam across the somewhat dim sides of the shed. Just then, John stepped in behind him and placed his hand on Shay's shoulder. Without a word, the two men stood there for a moment as their eyes adjusted to the light; it took them several moments to distinguish what they were looking at.

As with some nicely equipped hunting sheds and anywhere fresh meat is left to drain or cure, one can find metal rails spanning walls or hanging from ceilings. On these steel rails are cast iron hooks that can be moved along the rail, depending on the size of what is to be hung. On one side of the shed, the beam of the flashlight moved across the bellies of deer of various sizes. They had been tied up at the ankles and hung upside down with their throats slit over basins. Nothing out of the ordinary, to be sure. Shay swept his light beam across the opposite side of the shed. Two turkeys, one rabbit, and in the corner, a strange shape that appeared almost like a massive butterfly cocoon. Unsure of how to proceed, Shay turned back toward the door but saw that Sterland was not near the doorway. Perhaps he had stepped away or gone back to the main house for more coffee. John smacked Shay in the arm and barked, "Flashlight!" and with that, Shay handed the flashlight over to John.

Stepping closer, the men realized what it was they were looking at. At the top of this confusing shape, large leather boots were clearly visible. They had been hogtied with heavy rope and hung from one of the massive hooks. A tattered navy-colored drop cloth had been wrapped around this object, gathering frost and hiding whatever it was from prying eyes. Shay reached for John, and before he could say, "Wait-" John had grabbed the corner of the drop cloth, yanking it away. He aimed the beam toward the boots again, slowly moving it downward to get a look at the corpuscle hanging there, now swinging slightly after its jarring uncovering.

"Shay, this is a…"

"Yes, John."

Talbot took a deep drag on the cigarette, tossed it on the floor, and tamped it out with his toe.

"Okay, Shay, let's take a look."

The denim jeans were stained and dark, mud and other debris still clinging to them. Hanging upside down, the shirt had been untucked, and the stomach of the body was hanging out. This man had some weight on him. The arms had not been bound; they hung toward the floor, and one of the knuckles dragged along the planks. A gray jacket and the shirt hung down, obscuring the head. John reached out and placed his hand on the body's hip to stop it from swaying so unsettlingly. He stepped back a foot and handed Shay the flashlight.

"Give me some light. I want to see if the face could be used for identification." John's monotone statement spoke to his ability to remain calm under duress. Shay was no scaredy-cat, but most other men in a similar situation might be hesitant to put their hands on such a mess. Not John; he was all about the work, even if he'd been doubting himself as of late.

Shay aimed the light toward the bottom of the hanging form, and John reached down and slowly lifted the shirt hanging between the limp arms. When the shirt was lifted enough, it became clear.

"Fookin' hell…"

The head of the body had been completely removed, and only a stump of the neck remained. The gore at the cut glistened in the light like cranberry pudding.

"I miss that cigarette," whispered John.

There was a creak behind them at the doorway. Both men turned back to see Sterland standing there with his hands in his pockets. The light barely cast on him; his silhouette and the fog of his breath in the cold, refrigerated air were the only things they could see from inside.

"I didn't want this thing moving on me again, sorry boys. I took off the head. It's in a box over there on the shelf". He motioned toward a corner shelf adjacent to the light switch. He then stepped back out and started pacing around in the yard outside the shed. Sterland was clearly uncomfortable, though that was perfectly natural after having strung up and beheaded a walking dead man in your shed.

Shay went to the corner shelving, flashlight in hand. John was just behind him, hand on his shoulder, also submitting to morbid curiosity as they went to open the only box on the shelf. Ironically, it was a waxed cardboard box with a beautiful color paper print glued to the side—an advertisement.

CALIFORNIA WHOLE HEAD LETTUCE

"Ye've got t'be shitting me."

Shay handed the flashlight to John, holding it up over his shoulder and wiggling it to indicate that he wanted it held high. John reached out and obliged, so Shay had both hands free. He grabbed the box flaps of the cardboard and, in one jerking motion, split both sides of the box apart and downward. As the front flap of the box fell open, they could see, through a cellophane wrap, a well-preserved, though admittedly rather bashed-in, head of a dark-haired and rutty-faced man. The strike from Sterland's garden rocks was readily apparent by the way the head bowed inward on one side.

Shay stood up straight, patting John on the shoulder. "I think we have a fair bit of evidence here, wouldn't you say?" John nodded with a low whistle that indicated his overall surprise at the scene. Still, he held that beam of light at the head and just... stared at it. The eyes were sallow but open, with an eerie presence. Fine crystals of ice glistened over everything.

Shay stepped back out into the much warmer air and made his way toward Sterland, who was pacing a lovely oblong pattern into the snow.

"Sterland, that's quite a find you have. It seems like you might not want the thing here. I'm wondering if you might be obliged to let me and Talbot take this mess off your hands. In fact, I think it's *my* luck that you've got it, and I am sure it's *your* luck that I'm here to take it."

Sterland stopped in his tracks, his hands still stuffed deep into the pockets of his Santa Claus costume pants. "Is it that obvious that I'm uncomfortable around that thing? I still have nightmares. I don't know.

Maybe having that out of here will help me sleep a little better. I suppose I don't have a use for it; when I put that thing in the freezer, I figured the cops would be around to pick it up any day. I haven't walked in that damn shed since. Beautiful kills in there, but I'm going to burn that thing to the ground. Can't stand the *smell*."

Shay put his own hands in his pockets, still feeling the cold. "I wouldn't presume to tell you what to do with your property, but like I said before, you've done nothing wrong, and in fact, what you did might end up saving lives. If you'd like, I'll come back and let ye know how it all lands."

Sterland looked up with a raised eyebrow. "You think so? This could help folks?"

Shay nodded, "In fact, I'm *sure* of it. We've still got our part to do, of course. Thank you, Sterland. By the by, I'm happy to forget where I found it… lest anyone come looking for answers."

Santa Claus smiled, offering, "I'll make you boys a coffee for the road."

Mortis

"Just drive like a grandmother, and it'll all be fine, John."

"I'm fine. This is fine. What makes you think I'm not fine?" John shot back, clutching the wheel of the Dodge. The creaking crunch of snow under the tires could be heard as they puttered down the highway.

"It's no worries, lad. Your nerves will give you fits after something like that once the shock wears off, don't you know?"

"Yeah, I know…" John relented.

"So, don't worry one bit! We're on our way to the hospital, and that chap Lowell will surely help us. He said as much to me directly!"

John peered over his shoulder at the tarp on the rear floor of the car.

"I just… I think it's illegal, Shay."

"What's illegal?"

John struck another cigarette off the ember of his last. He rarely smoked, but today? He was chaining them.

"Driving around with a headless popsicle fat bastard shit-ass corpse in the back of your Dodge Sedan, that's what."

Shay burst out laughing at John's blue words.

"John Talbot, don't ye worry… It's not headless. We have the head in the trunk!"

"I mean, it's not *connected*!"

"Pish, that's a technicality. We'd have put the whole thing in the trunk, but ye can't easily fold a popsicle, it seems. We're taking it to the authorities, anyway."

"…fuck. I need a drink, Shay."

"You and me both, Talbot. You and me *both*."

…

* * *

The Dodge idled in the far corner of the hospital parking lot. Shay came trotting out, announcing, "Got 'im! He's coming out!" and climbed back into the warm sedan.

Before long, Doctor Lowell pulled up in his Buick, right next to the Dodge in the parking lot. Rolling down his window and leaning out halfway, he suggested to John that it might be difficult just to waltz their grotesque new evidence into the hospital unnoticed on such a quiet day. To avoid raising any suspicion, he suggested that the boys meet him somewhere a bit less populated than the parking lot so they could hand the body off to the back of the staff hearse.

Sometime later, in an abandoned parking lot behind a shuttered grain and feed with a burned-down freight dock, they parked the vehicles end to end. The exchange went off without a hitch, though Dr. Lowell spent a few minutes admonishing them for how they might have damaged the body during its transport.

John stopped the doctor mid-sentence, "Yeah, sure, we could have sat him up in the backseat if, you know, his HEAD was attached."

His sarcasm was not lost on the doctor, who realized his demeanor was lacking; he bit his tongue and begrudgingly shook both their hands before climbing into the hearse. "If you boys have the time, we could start finding some answers right now. I cleared my schedule for this."

"We're on your clock now, Doc. Lead the way!" Shay cheerfully replied.

"I'll handle the gurney for our new friend. You boys get a bland meal, then meet me in my office. It's going to be a long night!" And with that, he drove off.

After a brief bite in the hospital's coldly lit cafeteria, a meal that John could hardly stomach, the boys made their way down to the ME hall. The Doctor was already set up at a steel table, poking and prodding the thawing subject. Excitedly, he insisted on hearing the story of how they came across the body. Shay declined, offering, "Our benefactor will remain unnamed, Doc. You just look at those wounds and tell us whether this thing was moving when it received all this damage, okay?" The old man grumbled at him and turned back to the body.

"Oh, it's going to be some time before we can do that. It needs to thaw to a temperature at whereupon I can inspect soft tissue, so nothing today. I can start with the surface. I just want as much information as I can get! I am, after all, going to need to explain this to the proper authorities when the time comes."

"Let's cross that bridge when we get to it, yeh?" Shay gave him a knowing look.

John leaned in and put his hand on the edge of the cold slab, locking eyes with the doctor. "What we need is for you not to say a word until we got something concrete; if you can't do that, I'll pack this freak show back up and find another Medical Examiner. How's that?" He was smoking another cigarette, and his tone was half joking, but he was serious. Doc withdrew his glasses and rested them on the bridge of his nose, not making eye contact with John as he responded.

"I'm the only man outside Seattle qualified to do this. Don't worry; I won't say a word until it's all ironed out. Besides, I want some closure myself." He sank a brass-handled scalpel deep into the temple of the thawing, decaying head. With a spin of the knife, he sliced a core of meat and shattered bone, then yanked it free with forceps and placed it with a *plunk* into a glass dish. After that, he beckoned the boys over to help him undress the patient. As they lifted the limbs, he cut away the pants and the sleeves from the body. Now, he reached forward and slit the shirt from belt to throat directly up the center. He paused, and a quizzical look came across his face.

Shay looked to John, shrugging, and John spoke up. "What's the matter, see something odd?"

Lowell had set aside his tools and removed his gloves and spectacles, pinching the bridge of his nose for a few moments before lifting his glasses back up to his face. He leaned in, looking closely at what was clearly an opening in the chest of the man that had been from a prior autopsy. In a quiet and dry tone, he commented, "I autopsied this man myself with Kip."

Shay leaned in close. "Say you did… which opens another enormous can of worms… what's with the scowl?"

The doctor looked up over the rims of his spectacles and said to Shay, "Because that's not my stitch. Somebody seems to have opened this body *again*."

Shay and John moved to the edge of the table, where the doctor was pointing very closely at some punctures that surrounded the large slit down the man's sternum. "In an autopsy, the sternum is opened and all of the organs removed, but for respect of the dead and ease of transport, the wound is sewn shut with heavy-gauge thread." The doctor instructed. His tone was that of an educator; he wanted the men to understand where his line of thought was headed. "You see, I sew in a particular pattern. It's no signature. It's just a habit."

Furrowing his brow, John asked, "So some amateur was digging around in there?"

The doctor raised a finger for emphasis. "Not at all, young man. These are proper stitches and are the sort of work you would see at any qualified mortuary or Medical Examiner's Office. Competent hands worked here; no thread pulled too tight. My concern, young man, is that this is *not my pattern*. I begin with a double backstitch, and I tie at the end with a single-loop knot; this is a simple double knot, and the thread is a heavier gauge. Somebody has opened this incision up after I completed my examination, but what concerns me more is that this body was closed back up with the suturing skill of a doctor." He used a ballpoint pen to point out where the stitches had been run through the flesh, mere millimeters from the original punctures that Dr. Lowell had placed during his initial autopsy.

Shay poked the ribs of the cold body. "Why does it all look so clean? Like it's healed a bit?"

"Don't be silly, Mister Hayes. That would be *impossible*. It appears some sort of adhesive must have been used. Very curious indeed. Well, we need to wait a while before we can get in there and see what other secrets our friend here is hiding."

After retrieving a rubber sheet and a heat blanket from a cabinet, the doctor draped the rubber sheet over the patient's body and slid the electric blanket over it. Clearly, he was aiming to quickly soften the stiff, cold tissue.

"How soon, Doc?" Irish inquired.

"Five to six hours, I'd say."

"What about the head, then?" John asked, leaning over the body's stump of a neck.

"Right, if you've got the stomach, let's get into it then. This sample seems thawed enough for some cursory probing, I'd say."

The men each found a metal folding chair in the corner and placed it near the wall. They sat back and watched as the doctor worked with small saws and other gleaming instruments around the concave head, removing flaps of skin and retrieving tissue samples. The doctor deftly used forceps and a scalpel to remove the eyelids, placing them into another glass tray next to the core of the skull and flesh.

John lit a cigarette, sparking it without moving his gaze from the process.

With a fine-toothed razor saw, a cut was made longitudinally from the brow over the scalp, then another following the arc from end to end beside it. With a twist of the saw, that portion popped out of the skull like a slice of cherry pie. Made a similar sound, as well.

John handed Shay a cigarette and lit the end while Shay just stared in horror and awe at what he was witnessing.

The Doctor had moved that long, narrow slice of skull over to an exam table equipped with bright lighting and several microscopes.

"Boys, would you like to see something spectacular?" he inquired.

John looked to Shay, grimacing and pale as a ghost.

"Okay, doc, John will sit this one out, but I'm curious as can be." He went to the table just as the old man removed a paper-thin slice of brain matter. Shay could see light casting through it.

It looks like an Italian delicatessen… God, that's morbid.

The Doctor spoke as he worked, preparing the sample for the microscope.

"You see, when I conducted the autopsy, we removed organs and weighed and inspected each of them. Everything was placed back where it should be to prepare the body for cremation. I remember this case; I had spoken to this man's wife personally. As it goes, this body was generally complete and intact when I was finished. The organs were bagged and replaced in the cavity, as is standard procedure. The head remains untouched during our procedures and is less vascular than much of the body. Much can be learned from the sedentary tissues of the brain, you see…"

"So what's with that brackish hue, Doc? We're all red and pink inside, so far as I've seen. Is that from the embalming?" Shay asked, seeing some discoloration.

"No, the color is wrong for any embalming procedure I've ever seen, and the smell is… off… but most importantly, this man was not embalmed… whatever gave this tint of black-green and the associated smell seems to be just what we found when that first body was returned to us in such poor condition. The lab report I gave you."

"All that toxic stuff, yeh. I did a little reading. We should be very concerned about a couple of those ingredients, Doc."

The Doctor turned back and placed his hands on his knees, frustrated.

"We'll need to get into that body before I can speak on anything, gentlemen. Please… take some time to rest and recuperate, and see me after eight o'clock this evening. We should have it warmed enough for incision by then."

And so, they did.

...

Hours earlier, when dusk fell, the detecting duo rested in their rented rooms, although neither had slept. They now found themselves silently riding the elevator back down to the ME's section of the basement.

They found the heavy double doors locked upon their arrival.

"Old boy said after eight, didn't he, John? This place looks shuttered."

"Sure, he did, and it's ten after. Wonder what gives?"

To their surprise, the sound of a deadbolt latch clacked from inside the door. They were both grabbed by their lapels and yanked into the darkened laboratory!

"What giv-!" Shay blurted out while John reached for the billy club he'd been hiding in his back pocket.

Before they could get their bearings in the dark, the latch behind them slapped shut, and the Doctor himself switched on the light in the now-sealed examination lab.

"You men, *keep your voices down* now. It's Thanksgiving, and the only people in the building are security guards and critical staff. We must be *cautious*!" He hissed, nearly in a panic.

Shay put his hands on the man's shoulders and locked eyes with him. "Old boy, you're scaring us. Are you in a bad way? Did we get you in hot water?"

The Doc shook off his grip and pivoted toward the dimly lit table in the center of the room. He was visibly sweating. John stoked up a smoke, and Irish joined him.

"Sit, both of you." The man implored. So, they did. "I need a few moments to collect my... I need to show you. Just... ah, just sit." He fumbled with some sample trays and a beaker as he gathered his thoughts. In short order, he had come back to the autopsy table to the now splayed-open body and beckoned the men to join him. He gloved his hands and moved back into the corpse cavity, fumbling around for something in the pelvis.

Shay leaned on the table over the open torso cavity, the flesh inside looking gravely gray and sticky. "Eh... so, how does everything look inside?" somewhat tongue-in-cheek.

The doctor paused his work for a moment and raised his now-slightly-wet gloved hands. He was scowling, voice taut with excitement. "I'm both curious and distressed, to be sure. These organs have been *reattached*. Do you see the scar tissue? Exactly! There is little to none!" He exclaimed and leaned in elbows-deep once again.

As in, all the plumbing was stitched back together? Or, like you said, *adhesives*?" John questioned as he tapped cigarette ash onto the floor.

"I wouldn't know how to explain this any better than to say that this man's organs look as though… It's as if we had never autopsied them. It's as though they've never been taken out of place. Aside from the entry cut on the chest, it's as though this man could have been walking around again. Except…"

"Except?" another nervous tap of John's ash on the floor. Shay stood quietly, stomach turning at the *glush-shlorp* sounds of the doctor moving innards to and fro.

"*Except*, young man, I can't find blood. There's no measurable blood in his body, only this blasted makeshift embalming fluid, just as we had found in the other body that was retrieved. That report which I gave your friend,' he motioned toward Shay, 'this viscous formula looks to be just what we found in the other body. It's pervasive, as though a hydraulic procedure was used to… I'm not sure how it connects to all of this, but I'm hesitant to speculate right now. I have more tests to conduct! I've already arranged for access to the most powerful microscope in the building!"

Shay stepped back from the table and gathered his coat. "John, I think we can get back to Seattle. I believe the doctor here needs his space. Doc, can we count on you to follow up with whatever you find?"

John relented. "How about, Doc, can you give me a sample? Something to show the boss?"

He was met with a fiery gaze and the rumbling voice of an awoken titan.

"You… will do… NO such thing, young man. This vessel has suffered more desecration than I can accept. I will not be handing out *souvenirs*!"

"Okay, okay, Doc! I'm sorry!" John offered as Lowell hurried them out of the ward. As he shut the door, he said, "Monday. You may return on Monday, and we can discuss this further. For now, I must work."

John followed Shay down the hallway, where he grabbed his Irish friend by the arm and stopped him. "Just hold up, now. Are you sure we can leave this behind?"

Shay smiled and patted his friend on the shoulder, reassuringly telling him, "One body is evidence, Talbot, but two could be proof. Let's get back to Billy soon as we can. Maybe catch a hot meal…"

"I'm not eating for a goddamned *week*, Irish."

…

The little sedan took a while to warm up, but outside the windows, it was a cold, unforgiving night. The stormfront, overtaking the state and heading briskly east, brought with it a ceiling of moonless clouds and a metallic cold. John commented that the cold felt so piercing through the long coat he was wearing as the duo made their way to the car. Having made some miles west and the car having adequately warmed up, the old bench seat squeaked happily while John rustled about and removed his coat as Shay worked the steering wheel.

"Crazy day, Irish, one for the books."

"Yeh… looney."

Fogging had covered the side windows, and the car's defroster was working full-time to keep the windshield clear. The wipers were moving like the tail of a happy Labrador.

"Snow's falling a good bit, probably going to get worse, pal," John remarked through teeth that clenched gently onto his next smoke. His hands trembled a bit, likely from being exhausted and starved.

"Ay, it's a chill, but I don't mind much. It's the heat I can't bear, that sun they love so much down in California."

John nodded, finally releasing his sleeve from his arm and taking the wheel back from Shay.

"It's nice there; you should visit. Just…" he surveyed his friend's white hand that was releasing the wheel. "Just take a hat and a long shirt, I suppose?"

Shay snickered and sat back into the corner of the seat, half lying back on the door. The little round Dodge had plenty of room for reasonably-sized folk, and Shay now sat facing John as he drove, but wasn't really looking at him. It was simply comfortable.

"Talbot, if Billy likes the progress, you s'pose we should head back to Portland? I mean to say, that's where the action is… out past town…"

"Oooooooh buddy, I got roped in this far, and you bet your skinny ass I'm going with you to Portland. I can't let you go headlong into a case without backup now, can I?"

Shay looked thoughtful but concerned as he was half-frowned at the thought of having a once-reluctant partner in the matter. "It's just…. It's what ye said only days ago, ye had no mind or heart for such a mission. I'm sayin' like, the superstitious sort of work?" He awaited an answer as his gaze lolled along the snow falling outside.

John was clenching the wheel as he scrolled it back and forth to follow the winding mountain roads headed back to Snoqualmie. He glanced once again at Shay and set his jaw a bit. It was clear he was deliberating on how best to answer the contention Shay had raised.

"I know you're not calling me chicken. You're absolutely right. I was apprehensive about all this. I'm just getting my legs back under me, and this is a long way out of my comfort zone, yeah. At least, if it is what you think it might be… but, well, what the hell do you think it might be?"

"Reanimated bloody corpses walking 'round at night?" Shay teased him as he waggled his eyebrows saucily and poked John in the ribs.

"Goddammit, man, be serious here. I'm trying to have a conversation, you horse's ass!" He was laughing but still chastising his friend.

"Sorry, old boy, I'll be serious for a time. I have some conflicting ideas about what this could be, sure… I know medical science and the Hollywood sort of science fiction have been bedfellows for a while. For all I know, the other night I was thumped by some twit loaded up with those pills they gave the Nazi goose-steppers in the trenches when things got dire back in forty-four… but at the same time, part of me feels like it might just be bigger than what we understand. Something we simply haven't seen before."

John nodded and replied, "So you don't think it's some supernatural, satanic mumbo jumbo?"

"Scientists today are planning to put men in rockets to the moon, while me grandpa was certain a woman's baby-making parts would just *fly out* if a train moved too fast. We're a stone's throw from the Stone Age, old boy. Science is moving faster than any one man's understanding of the world, and I'm just tryin' to keep up. We gave the husk to a scientist for a half-dozen hours and already got *some* answers."

"Those were answers? I'll give you, they were *clues*, Shay. Suppose that's fair. Still… you think the two of us are up to working this case?"

"Talbot, you worry too much. Of course, I'm gonna work this case, and if you're with me, then sure… we work the case. Close it. An' if it gets bigger than us, we take it to Billy's friends in the suits. I don't think you're risking life and limb just yet."

"I agree. Let's head to see the boss first thing tomorrow. We're only a short way from the hotel. I need that drink, Shay."

"Top shelf an' the tab's on me, Talbot."

Check-in

Friday, November 24^{th,} 1950

Coming to a stop, the little sedan parked idling in front of the garage of Smith Tower. An attendant met the boys at the driver's door, so Shay grabbed the men's bags while John handed over the keys. The attendant, a scrawny boy perhaps 20 years old, had just about put the car into gear when Shay put up his hand and implored him to "Wait, stop!"

The attendant put the car back into park and leaned out the window. "Forget something, sir?"

Shay put his palm on his forehead as if to say *I'm such a fool*. "I believe, in fact, we'll be returning shortly. If you don't mind, we can just leave our baggage here. How's that sound to you, John?"

John tapped the brim of his hat, nodding, and turned back toward the street to watch a gleaming silver Lincoln roll by. The attendant hopped out of the car, retrieved the keys, and collected the bags from Shay. "They'll be in the trunk. See you shortly!" With that, Shay grabbed John by the sleeve, and they headed upstairs to debrief Billy.

...

Arriving at Billy's office, the boss was sitting behind the main reception desk next to a new girl. This girl was dressed in all black, a wool suit that looked like it belonged in church.

Billy backed up his chair and came around the front of the desk. "Boys, this is Kate Crane. She's going to be taking over phones and some paperwork up here, and I know her father from the piano store up the street."

John scratched his head under the brim of his hat and inquired, "Where's the last one, missus Reese?"

Billy lifted his chin and peered incredulously at John. "You didn't think she would last, did you? She quit right after you boys left. I don't think she could handle my..." he peered back over his shoulder at Kate and decided he would be polite rather than honest. He'd always sensed the previous girl didn't much respect him, which was why he was always joking with her and trying to get a rise from her.

"She had some family obligations. Miss Crane here —she's going to be a star anyway. I just bought her a new typewriter, in fact."

Kate settled into her chair and was eager to share some of the information Billy had clearly been imparting to her. "Did you know that the man who built Smith Tower made his fortune on guns? Oh, and typewriters. I'm told this is the best typewriter; it's a Smith Corona!" She beamed with pride as she held out one hand toward her beautiful new machine, its case a shiny, medium-green gloss that matched the cover resting nearby.

Shay loved the girl's enthusiasm. "That's quite nice, quite nice indeed. Did Billy say he was going to purchase you one of those guns as well?"

Deadpan, Kate replied in the most innocent tone. "Oh, I don't think I'll be needing one of those. This seems like a rather safe place, what with all you men doing the work you do." She smiled sweetly and looked back at Billy.

"Yeah, unless Billy puts you on a case!" Shay teased. The three men burst out laughing, and the girl's cheeks turned red. Billy reached out and placed his palm on the desk in front of her. "Kate, don't listen to them. These boys they're always joking. You never really know when Shay is being straight with you. I'm sorry. We're not laughing at you. This is a fine place to work, and you're never going out in the field with these clowns. I'm glad you feel safe here; let's do our best to make sure you feel comfortable, too. How's that?"

Kate nodded a bit sheepishly and placed her hands in her lap. She had begun to smile and realize the silliness of the situation. "Certainly, Mr. Bigsby. I certainly do like my typewriter. Shall I finish organizing my desk and cleaning up that cabinet?"

Billy nodded and patted the desktop. "Sounds like a dandy idea. Your antagonist here, Shay Hayes, and my longtime friend and associate, John Talbot, are the boys working my current local case. Please feel free to get familiar with everything here in the front room.

We can meet up later to finish discussing my expectations and iron out your salary. I can promise it's better than your old man was paying you."

She smiled shyly and nodded to the men as she returned to her desk, closing the door hbehind.

The men shuffled into Billy's office behind him, and John shut the door. Kate turned back toward her typewriter and finished removing the protective bakelite plastic guard over the ink band. Dutiful and demure, she paid little attention to the raucous laughter that was emanating from the office just behind her.

"Boys will be boys," she commented to the empty reception room.

As the men in suits took to getting comfortable on the couch behind the closed office door, Billy made his way back behind his desk with a sigh. He leaned forward, clasping his fists in front of him, and his shoulders hunched. "You two jamokes look damn sharp. I'm glad I was so generous in that envelope. I can assume, from your lack of communication until now, that you've been busy. So tell me, for all my dollars, what have you come up with as of now?"

John leaned back into the couch and patted Shay on the shoulder, "You're the storyteller here, pal."\

Shay was flattered, but he knew that John was nowhere near as excited about the case as he was, so he leaned forward and rested his forearms on his knees. Locking eyes with Billy, he offered up, "D'you believe in the dead rising, Billy?"

Billy was lighting up a smoke. He had a stare that could call out bullshit from just about anyone, and he could tell his day was about to get more interesting. "I might."

"He's being dramatic, Billy. It's queer as can be, but we don't know anything like that yet."

"That's true, but I'm just measuring the room. Honestly, Billy, we don't have solid answers yet. We do have some mutilated bodies and some compelling witness statements."

Billy leaned back, puffing. "I like witnesses. And bodies. Hollywoodland fantasy bullshit aside, what did you boys *find*?"

Shay grinned, and his toes tapped a bit. "We found one. A body, that is. It seems the boys in blue are so poor at their trade out there that we hauled a carcass out of that old codger's meat locker. Looked a might similar to the demented bastard I handled meself!"

Billy stopped puffing mid-draw. He got excited. "Well, where is it? Did you bring it?"

Shay waved his hand, "No, sir, we weren't prepared to be playing at illegally transporting cadavers… more than we had to. It wouldn't suit your reputation! We found a professional out that way, Dr. Paul Lowell, one of the original medical examiners of the bodies that went missing. He's on our side. In fact, he's probably elbow-deep in that corpuscle as we speak!"

Cynically, John chided, "You and your five-dollar words…" but Shay and Billy paid him no mind.

Turning to Shay, Billy laid in with more questions. "How did you boys acquire this body? Did you see it move? Did anyone see it move?"

"In fact, yes. Well, two out of three, Billy. As I said, we pulled this old boy off a meat hook in the back of Sterland's refrigerated shed. He claims this man, whom the doc insists had been dead weeks ago and already well autopsied, had stood up out of the river and came after him. He says he had to make a bloody mess to stop this thing, and I don't doubt it. He seemed genuine."

Billy peered at him and squinted his eyes a bit. "You might be biased, considering you met one of these characters yourself, and I wonder if your detecting might be a bit tainted by your excitement to prove yourself *not* crazy."

His blunt words might have offended anybody else, but Shay was unfazed. He put up a thumb toward John. "He was at my side. We found all this together. No room here for stories."

John nodded and simply shrugged, grunting, "Ayuh." Billy's squinting became a relaxed, 'well-if-you-say-so' smirk.

"So you boys believe in the mission, and you've got evidence in the field. A body and a witness tell a great tale, but that's not going to be enough to close this case. You boys up to the job of seeing this through?"

John piped up, wanting to show his confidence. "I've thrown my hat in the ring, and Irish needs a ride home to Portland anyway. If you're covering expenses, I'm in." He gave a big, cheesy grin to Billy, knowing his friend was always covering expenses, so there was no being 'out'.

With a clap of excitement, Shay stood up. "Billy, old boy, you've got a fishing trip to take. We've got some bodies to dig up, er… bury, and the only thing on my calendar is Christmas alone. I say we find a little help and get back to it?"

Billy raised a hand, palm toward the boys, in an almost benevolent fashion. He took a final drag of his cigarette and tamped it out in the ashtray near his phone. He had two ashtrays on his desk, and both were littered with various brands of butts. It was clear he had been lax in cleaning up during the two days he didn't have a receptionist. He opened his top left desk drawer, drawing out two brown envelopes. Billy looked down at each envelope in turn and tossed them across his desk to the boys. John caught his in mid-air with his left hand. Shay had not been quick enough, and it bounced off his lapel onto the floor. He bent over to pick it up and saw a smiley face drawn on his envelope. He turned to John, who was already stuffing his envelope in his breast pocket.

"Hours tallied, those bills are flat. Extra holiday pay is in there, folded long-ways. Happy Thanksgiving. The rest of it is folded half-ways, and that's for incidentals. I need you both to understand something. From here on out, things could get a bit messy. I'm keeping Kate here; she'll be working every 9-to-5, even some weekends, for a while. I'll give her time off when shit un-hits the fan. I need somebody around to answer the phone while I'm out. Now, I'm not going to be too far from town; we're headed out to this beautiful spot on the Snake River that has some heavy catch this time of year. I'll be checking in with Kate myself each day. If anything gets too big and you boys need backup, you can call me through her. Of course, if it gets… messy? You boys both know that the local bureau is up to speed on this, as much as they need to be anyway. I made sure that they know who you are in case you sound the alarm."

"Sure, sounds like a plan; thank you, Billy." John stood up and rubbed his hands together. "Shay, let's get back in that warm little car. Maybe you've got a couple more cigars on you; I figure it's a five-hour drive back."

"Talbot, it's been rather a day. You sure you don't want to stick around here until morning?"

"We'll get coffee on the way." John spun his hat around on his finger before placing it on his head. He shook Billy's hand and waved for Shay to follow him out as he went to say goodbye to Kate. Shay turned back to their boss, who was wearing a satisfied look on his face.

"You see our old John shining through? I think I see it." Billy inquired of Shay; John was well out of earshot.

"I see him warming up, yeh. It's good to have the backup, Billy. I'll keep an eye on the lad!" Shay offered as he snatched two cigarillos from the humidor on the shelf just next to the door.

With a wink, Billy shooed him out to follow John. The boys made their way down the hall and caught an elevator just in time.

"Talbot, I've got a big fainting couch for ye. Best not snore tonight, or you'll sleep in the Dodge. I'm *beat*. Oh, but I've got a pair of short stogies for the way." John patted him on the shoulder as they stepped on the elevator and toward the garage.

Portland, ho!

The snow fell lighter on their drive south to Portland. They stopped at a small delicatessen on the edge of town and devoured a couple of decent hoagies, two cold bottles of pop, and chips to boot. It was a feast for two weary men on a dreary, chilly day. John's hands were now rock steady as he motored them through light flurries. His rosy cheeks had returned.

While John navigated, Shay reached behind the seat for his bags. His hand returned to view, holding two cigars, their gold bands setting brightly against the grey tweed-like upholstery and Shay's simple grey suit. It was the only color in sight, as the coming stormy skies sapped so much color and life out of the daylight.

"What are those… good ones? Cubans?" John questioned, not really caring, as his mouth was already watering from the thought of good tobacco.

Shay withdrew a lighter from his pocket, equipped with a flip-out cigar hole punch in the foot. He pierced the cigar's caps as he spoke. "I don't often smoke the cheap ones, 'less rent is due, or my taste is shot from spicy food. I won these in a coin toss with a Honduran newspaper chap in the cafe last month, and they've been in his humidor a year… or so he *said*. Think they're the good ones, smells as such anyway."

"Really?" John asked in surprise at the tale.

"Pish. I stole 'em from Billy an hour ago, you sod."

John snorted and shrugged. "You're an unserious man. Irish."

With a flick of the thumb on the side wheel of his lighter, Shay handed John a stick and offered the flame to him. John gripped the steering wheel with his right and sparked the cigar with his left. After he toasted the foot and took a few puffs, he handed the lighter back.

Shay lit his cigar in the same manner, toasting the foot of the cigar to a nice, even glow before drawing gently. He held the first few puffs of smoke for moments in his mouth, mulling over the dark and silky smoke on his palate. John was relatively quiet. Rich blue-grey smoke filled the cabin, swirling around the knuckles of the men gently holding their respective cigars.

"John, I'd forgotten, or perhaps I never knew… you're a lefty? That's fine luck!"

Without looking, with a smile on his face, John chided back, "I don't count much on luck, but I suppose you're the expert if I ever knew one…"

"Because I'm Irish?"

"No, because you're *alive,* you stooge! I know what you boys got up to back in Germany."

"The fightin' or the chicanery?" Shay asked, letting out a wisp of cold blue smoke from the stogie.

"Suppose both, but I'm leaning on the chicanery. I heard they called you the Brasswatch boys because you were always goofin' off when the COs weren't around. Took turns on the lookout like schoolboys playing with firecrackers behind the auditorium. Someone always watching out for the brass."

"That's half-true, Johnny Talbot—half at *best.* Cam was the worst of us. Once beat a man with a fish."

John chuckled, "Heard that was just a *toss.*"

"Not the way the CO told it. I swear, I never scrubbed so many dishes. I think it's why I don't cook!" Shay mused.

John teased him, "Maybe that's why you're so slim!"

Snorting, Shay tapped his ash into John's empty coffee cup.

"Nah, boyo, it's from the effort of carryin' around a pair of brass balls all day!"

John mocked a shocked face and shot back, "Is that what that sound was? I thought you had some loose change in your pocket!"

They erupted in laughter that lasted so long it became a coughing fit. John swigged the last of Shay's coffee and poked his friend in the ribs.

"You're a strange one, Shay. I'm glad you bastards pulled me back in." Shay smiled warmly.

Outside, the snow flurries became a snowfall, not enough to white out the road but plenty to decorate the boughs of the lush evergreen trees that lined the road. John had reached down to turn on the AM radio in the dash. The chrome surround of the stereo and speaker was glinting as the radio's tuning dial clicked, casting a glow upon the occupants of this fine sedan. With a slow and sure turn of the dial, John found a quiet jazz station. The music waned before a monotone gentleman's advertisement for shaving products came through, but just afterward resumed its repertoire of music worthy of a cozy drive. Ella Fitzgerald was up next, with some lovely, smooth vocals about a friend — or, more likely, a lover… it was a very 'holiday' mood, and nary a month until Christmas.

The two men sat back and savored their stout cigars as the Dodge puttered down the snow-laden, narrow roadways for a while.

It was nearly ten o'clock at night, the radio buzzing with poor reception but still ringing forth just enough classical piano to justify keeping it turned on. Shay had just woken up and was rubbing the sleep out of his eyes as Talbot handed him a cup. Some streetlights passed overhead on the passenger side, and the far side of the road was black as night. Shay finished clearing the sleep from his eyes and took the paper cup from John. It was hot, steam escaping the small hole in the lid.

"You stopped? How long was I asleep?"

John patted the dash. "Three and a half winks. And you farted somethin' awful in your sleep. Storm had us crawling a bit; we still have maybe thirty miles to go."

"Fair enough. Bet it was that Farmer's Breakfast haunting me." Shay breathed the steam escaping from his cup. "Chamomile?"

"Dunno. Whatever she had that was herbal. Seemed like your thing; I needed a coffee."

"Safer for me! We'll rest up tonight and get on the road tomorrow."

John cocked his head a bit. "Plan?"

Typical chatterbox John Talbot.

"It's simple. First, we go to the warehouse row where I was plucked. Nothing to worry about in the daylight, I hope. If that brings no leads, we head west."

"West?"

"It was in the file, Talbot. Those coast towns that were affected, or should I say afflicted, by some dark business like your lovely Snoqualmie. Should be able to dig up some dirt there if we're wise."

"Good." John nodded affirmingly, hands draped on the wheel as the hardly visible road unfurled in front of them. Snowflakes were caked on the cowl of the car. The hood and windshields were clear, thanks to the engine's warmth and the humming defrosters.

Shay looked to the seat between them; John had retrieved the file on their case from the trunk and placed it there. It had a coffee stain on the cover. Not wanting to waste the next hour or so before returning to town, Shay opened the glove box and raised the file to read by the dim courtesy lamp glowing within it.

He re-read the files, including several brief police reports that Billy had retrieved from the towns of Tillamook and Hemlock. Checking the map Billy had included, both towns were some eighty to one hundred miles west of Portland. The reports read much the same and were even similar to the findings in Snoqualmie. The reports detailed break-ins at both towns' small hospitals. In each case, two or three bodies went missing in the last few months. They were written off as pranks or general incompetence.

Hmpph. If they hired wise cops, I think I'd be out of a job…

Tillamook had a second report —an addendum. It seems that someone had also broken into that same hospital yet again, a month later, and 'relieved' the ME's office of nine recently deceased persons who suffocated in their sleep at a motel after a gas line break. The addendum report stated the basics but also referenced other police reports by number, which were not included in the file. The report also mentioned this tragedy, and the following theft of bodies matched a sad event up in Wheeler, an hour north, not long ago.

"John, here it is. All of this nonsense seems to be out past Tillamook State Forest. It's just forest until you reach the coast. Traveling might be hard. We should bring supplies in case it's a hostile trip."

"Good idea." John was squinting to see past oncoming headlights, snow still falling and obstructing the road. His breath fogged the windshield a bit.

Shay continued reading, reveling in the footnotes Billy had added. There were three reported complaints, which may have been related. It was no shock to Shay that two of them were folks claiming to have had terrifying run-ins with brutish men. The reports did not identify with certainty the assailants as resembling recent missing deceased, though it seemed much in line with the other towns' experiences. One of the reports duffed the whole thing as "drunken hallucinations." The third, which Shay was most engaged in, was the Portland Police report on the burglary and theft from a local pharmaceutical supply company, G.H. Welles Inc. The report was three pages, but two of them were a poorly handwritten eyewitness account from a night watchman who claims some slow, menacing form had accosted him and run him off.

The watchman, whose name was printed and signed Lester Callum on the witness statement form, filled the body of the report rather casually. Under the map light, Shay read the statement aloud verbatim.

"On June the second, I was posted in the North facility because Jay Drummond needed a week of vacation with his family. I knew his patrol because I worked this shift for couple years when I first started. I was outside the North facility near the main entry door, I had just checked the production building's doors and I was listening to my radio. It helps me work at night, and Mr. Grisholm said I can listen to it. I was patrolling outside and getting some air when I saw that one of our gates was swung open down by the road. I went to the gate and I could see that the lock had been busted, it looked like somebody went at it with bolt cutters or something like that. I didn't see that and I didn't hear nothin funny. So, I went to walk a full perimeter search again and I didn't find anything except for some footprints near the walkway that goes up to the visitor entry door. I know because they keep that garden real nice, and there were no footprints when I did my patrol that afternoon at maybe 4 o'clock when my shift started. I notice cause it's a great spot for a smoke break. I always work second shift, or at least evenings and nights. So I checked all the doors again, and I got back maybe 10 minutes later to the employee door of the North facility where Mr. Grisholm said I should stay because that's where all the expensive supplies is kept, not in the research building. He bragged how none of that equipment could be stolen unless you had a Mack truck. When I got back to the front door, I could see that somebody had jimmied the door because the lock was all split out at the frame but the knob was still there. I went inside the facility then I went in the main hallway and checked every door. The offices were tight, even Mr. G's office, which was good because I know he keeps payroll in there. Betty Lou locks it up nice every night, she's last out and I usually walk her to her car cause we like the same shows."

John scrolled the glossy black-and-chrome steering wheel back and forth down the highway as his friend continued. The ornament in the horn button glinted now and then as other cars passed.

"So I walked the facility, I got Clint on the radio but he was busy on a break so I told him I would check doors until he got there. Anyway, I came to the main storage room that's just on the left side of the testing facility doors. You go in there, there's a second door inside as well, anyway I went in and the handle fell loose in my hand. I used my flashlight, I could see there was a big dent in the door right in the middle. Looked like somebody took a battering ram to it. I went in, in that little hallway, and I saw the second door was partly open. So I went back out to the hallway, I got Clint on the radio again and I was looking for him he said he was coming in the hallway just about then. I felt some kind of, maybe like a person behind me and I was scared but I turned around like my training and I raised up my flashlight. They don't let us carry no guns there. All I have is my big flashlight. So I put it up, way over my head and shined it but there was this big guy there dressed in, I don't know exactly, but they look like maybe mechanics' coveralls. I barely caught a look at the guy, but he spooked me so bad I swung my flashlight down. I didn't hit him, I wanted to but this big guy who had broken into the place… at least, that's what I figured had happened, he caught my hand with a flashlight in it and he just squeezed. He squeezed so damn hard he broke three of my fingers. Then, he grabbed me by the shirt and tie and honestly he lifted me straight up, right off the floor. Something was wrong with him, like in the head. I have a cousin just like that, he got hit in the head with a baseball bat when he was a kid and he was just never all there again. This guy had those eyes, he wasn't mad or making any noise, he was just looking at me. It was like he wasn't hardly there, you know, mentally."

Tapping John on the arm, he motioned for his friend to listen carefully to the next paragraph.

"Then this big guy just tossed me to the ground like I was nothing. Like a rag doll, like my little daughter and her toy Susie dolls. I was scared, sure, but I got up and by the time I was up he was out of there. When I got to the hallway, I could see Clint was layin' on the ground and he was out. Not dead, I mean you guys know that, but he was lights out. I went looking for that big guy but I couldn't see him, I knew he had left because I could see the employee entrance door at the end of the hallway was wide open now. I remember I had closed it behind me, because that's what Mr. Grisholm had always told us to do was to close doors behind us. So then, I called the police they sent someone over but I don't even know what they found. Mr. G told me to go and get my hand looked at. I only called him because I was having trouble helping Clint, but Clint was okay. So they found my flashlight, and they found my radio because I dropped it on the ground when I was getting attacked, but the radio was okay. That was good because I know those are worth maybe a couple bucks. But the flashlight, Mr. G said I don't have to pay for it. But, it was all crushed. It was so crushed that they couldn't take the batteries out. So Mr. G showed me where they keep more flashlights, and I tried to squeeze one of those but it was real solid like. I was lucky this big guy didn't use that damn grip on me, on my neck, just my hand. So we went out and they found some more of those footprints near the footpath where they keep those flowers all nice, they were big but just regular big maybe size 12's. I don't know if they found anything after that."

Shay cleared his throat after he finished and set the paper down with a sigh. The report was an interrogation transcript, and surprisingly, the leading page of the police report said that evidence of the break-in corroborated the night watchman's story. One photo was attached to the report. It was a bit blurry, but you could see it was a standard Coleman flashlight that had been pinched in the middle like somebody had run it over. Shay studied the picture; this late at night, the image was surreal. He thought about his encounter; in his mind, he could still see the big hulking sonofabitch who had abducted him. He could see the face of that man, also eerily calm and expressionless. Even when Shay had been dodging around, sinking his blade into the chest of this guy, there was a calmness in those eyes that sent a chill up his spine.

John cocked his head and asked, "Evidence?"

Shay nodded his head and replied, "Maybe. I want to say probably; either way, we'll find out. I think a good place to start in the morning could be our Western precinct; they've been *much* help on certain occasions." His concerns about the type of foe they might soon face wouldn't do John any good tonight, so Shay kept them to himself.

Indicating toward the folder in Shay's hand, "I'll give that stack another look in the morning. We're here! I think…" As he pointed out through the windshield. Shay lifted his head and realized he had been so engrossed in reading that case file that John had driven his oblivious friend safely home; outside the window was Shay's little brick building with the cafe downstairs.

"I'm flattered you remembered where I live!" Shay exclaimed, with a hint of curiosity in his voice.

"Good coffee at that little spot last time we were here. That was the shotgun case. Say, whatever happened there? I got put on the bowling alley thing before you sussed it out."

Shay recalled that day some three years prior. John had been working with Shay on a theft case, an odd one. An old man had been killed by a shotgun blast in his own home, but he'd been a beloved and generally respected local bookseller with no family or enemies to speak of. John had left town for some personal business just before Shay got to the bottom of it.

"Ah! That loony case! Remember, they couldn't figure out the entry point?"

John nodded, shutting off the engine. "Place was tight as a drum! Doors and windows, anyway…"

"Not the doggy door."

John turned to him, eyebrows raised. "The DOG shot him?"

Shay guffawed at the idea. "No, you twit. Someone used the doggy door to reach up and lock the door as they left. It was the man's old business partner. He just had really, really long arms!" He outstretched his arms in front of him, over the steering wheel, into John's face, waggling them like a puppet.

John pinched the bridge of his nose and chortled into his cuff. "Fucking dog shot him. I know it! It was a frame job!" The two boys sat in the car and laughed together at the stupidity of the idea.

After a while, the two had unpacked the necessities and gotten settled in Shay's place, lighting up the fireplace and taking turns with their nightly routines. They made their beds; John insisted he'd sleep just fine in the plush armchair near the fire.

"Better than Billy's stiff couch!" He'd insisted to his host. John was wise; he'd fallen asleep before Shay had even a chance to turn out the lights and stoke a log for the night. It was a soft end to a wild day, and Shay was looking forward to sleeping in his own perfectly sallow bed for the first night in a while.

As Shay tucked himself in, he couldn't help but feel sadness for his friend. A pang of sorrow resonated in his chest at how unfortunate it might be to end up snoring on someone's armchair after life's inherent carelessness had its way with your kin and your marriage.

The thought subsided as Shay joined his friend in dreamland.

Pit stop

Shay woke with a start. Blinking tightly, he cleared his eyes enough to look around the room. He realized he was holding his breath, and he exhaled the old air filling his lungs on fire. His knuckles were white, clutched tightly on the blanket he was sleeping under. He had half tossed the bed, one leg out in the air, and pillows strewn about the floor. He could hear the shower running on the other side of the wall.

Taking a slow and measured breath of cool air from the room, he closed his eyes tightly yet again and tried his best to recall whatever horrid dream had him so worked up. Tears welled in the corners of his eyes; he knew it must have been something rough. He was lucky, some days, not to be able to remember the nightmares. Not that it was a pressing concern, but he had seen his share of ugliness in the world, and on many an occasion, he fought those demons from his past yet again while he slept.

Determined to make the best of the day ahead, he lurched out of bed and stretched his weary bones while he took a few good deep breaths. He figured that the fire had gone out in the night, as he could practically see his breath in the bedroom. It was a deep chill, and looking outside, he understood why. From the second-story window, his view was of a beautiful neighborhood almost entirely covered in serene white snow. Slipping on his robe, Shay made his way to the living room, where the fireplace crackled. It seemed an industrious John Talbot had already replaced the logs and stoked a new fire, and the heat emanating was recharging to this slender man who could feel a chill in his bones. He stood there, warming his hands and toes, for long enough that John finished washing up and came back out to the living room.

"It's nice, isn't it? The fire. I haven't used the fireplace in my home in years. Electric heaters, they say it's good and safe, but they don't warn you that they absolutely lack any measure of charm."

Warming his hands and nodding with a shiver, Shay agreed. It would be a few minutes before he was ready to converse. Eyes closed, he could hear John in the kitchen clanging about with some pots and pans. He listened as the icebox door opened and silverware and other dishes clinked. He didn't pay much mind; he sat there enjoying being a marshmallow on this campfire. After not too long, he smelled toast and could hear the sizzle of frying bacon. He could finally stretch his warmed-up fingers and spread his toes. In a beat, he could smell the bacon in the pan. John was making a hearty breakfast, and Shay felt very guilty about having his guest do the cooking.

"You didn't have to—"

John spoke over him with a grin, "I haven't cooked breakfast in *ages*, Shay. Happy to!"

Darting into the room, Shay grabbed a change of clothes and jumped into a piping-hot shower, changing from pajamas to dressed in nearly no time. There wasn't much time to stand around without clothes; the rest of the house had not yet warmed.

It had been perhaps fifteen minutes since he had awoken, and Shay came out dressed to find that John had already set the table and was placing plates eight with eggs, bacon, and perfectly golden toast at two of the seats.

"Much appreciated, but by social norms, I believe it was me who was supposed to cook for you?"

John smirked and set the last of the silverware down, motioning for Shay to take a seat. "Honestly, I haven't hardly used a kitchen for too long, been eating like a bachelor. It's really my pleasure. Besides, this place was cheaper than a hotel, and I slept like the dead."

Shay looked up from his breakfast, "The dead?" Phrasing, my man!"

John chortled and grabbed his utensils. Without blessing the meal, he dug into the impressive pile of food in front of him. Mouth full of eggs, he remarked, "Farmer's breakfast!" and smiled to Shay.

"Absolutely, John, as close as we can get!" He set about tackling the plate of food while reminiscing about the breakfasts at the Snoqualmie Falls Lodge.

Breakfast took little time to devour, and on their way out, the boys stopped at the café. There were a dozen customers, but all were seated and enjoying their food and drink: coffee, tea, cocoa, croissants, bagels, toast, and jam. The café was *just* worldly enough to keep folks trying new things and just local enough to take care of the regulars and their plain-Jane orders.

John took a table near the window and glanced over the front page of the paper that was left there by the previous patron. After Shay had ordered, and just as he was walking toward the little table where John was seated, he paused at the door where his delightful tenant and neighbor, Ms. Ginger Fisher, was just entering. Holding two coffees and a wide grin, Shay bowed a bit in a gregarious, show-business fashion with his arms wide, ankles crossed. The look on the fancifully dressed woman's face was priceless.

"Why, Mr. Hayes, you look thoroughly *dashing* in your coat today. Two coffees? I don't recall their brew being *quite* that good here!" she joked. Shay had opted to wear his airman's coat, the brown leather matching his tan slacks and crisp white shirt very nicely. Just before they had left the house, John had questioned his decision not to wear a suit. "Only one of us really needs to look professional. I work better when I'm comfortable, Talbot! Besides, this is my lucky coat. Nearly saved my life last time I ran into one of these nutters."

John relented. "Who could argue with that?"

Ginger was bundled in a plush and flowing blue sweater, furls of wool to stave off the morning chill. It wasn't enough to hide her lithe frame, and the turtleneck bunched nearly to her ears under her short and very stylish haircut. She looked like she'd just stepped off a Broadway stage, all style though with little flash. She was *quite* a sight.

Shay stood tall again and waved a coffee toward John, who was sitting nearby but not paying attention. "I've got a friend. A coworker, in fact, we're on a hot lead, don't ye know?" he said, with a sardonic tone.

Ginger had known of his work as a private eye, and she raised her eyebrows in mock amazement. "Sounds like you're a busy man! I wouldn't want to be in the way of your saving the world!" She clutched his arm and shook him a bit in mock excitement, the two of them chuckling.

"Ginger, come say hello. This is my old friend John Talbot!" John overheard his name and turned to the woman, and his eyes lit up. He moved to stand, and she waved him back into his seat.

"Don't get up, John. You're comfortable, and I wouldn't miss my coffee for anything. A pleasure to meet you all the same." Her voice was smoke and honey, and she put a hand on his shoulder as she stood next to him.

John stammered out, "I… we have… It's nothing serious. Just another case. But, certainly, you're… ah… *coffee!*" She giggled at this flush-faced younger man finding his tongue.

"It's going to be cold. You boys bundle up! Shay, would you like me to keep your fire going?" She was a spare keyholder for his second-floor abode, and he appreciated the offer.

"Ah! I'd fully appreciate that, if you're going to be around. We may return tonight, and we may not. Would ye mind keeping it up through tomorrow?" He had sat down adjacent to John.

She leaned in and kissed Shay sweetly on the cheek. "I'll tend the fires for the price of a dram from that bottle you keep behind the wicker basket, and you boys just get home safe. Okay?" She turned to John and took his hand in a demure grip.

Shay nodded and clasped her other hand on his shoulder. "Thank you, Ginger. Drink all ye wish. I'll owe you a dance!" With that, Ms. Fisher sauntered away toward the counter with a wry smile.

Shay patted John on the arm. "Say, let's get on the way, Talbot. I've got plans for us!" He stood up with a stretch of his arms. John stood up as well, though, with his eyes still on Ginger. She was oblivious, lost in the menu board, crookedly hung over the register.

"Sure, Irish. Let's… uh… yeah, let's get to it." Ginger had clearly made an impression on the man.

The pair made their way to the black sedan, where John warmed it up while Shay dusted off snow with the little plastic ice scraper they'd found stowed in the trunk.

They huddled in the car, engine idling, and both men waited for the heat to find their feet. Shay reached into his pocket and produced a small letter, handing it to John. Diligently, John opened the letter and read it. This was the anonymous letter imploring Shay to meet regarding the case, the one that had him walking into a trap and nearly meeting his fate.

"This reads like a trap. Is this the one you were talking about? This is what got your narrow ass stuffed into a trunk?" Shay nodded sheepishly. "Well, there's no return address or name. What should we do with it?"

"Not sure yet, but it's handwritten. Wrong nouns, see? Perhaps we should keep a keen eye out for that same handwriting. Whoever penned this, I don't suppose English is their native tongue."

Glaring back down at the letter, John nodded. "Postmark is from

Tillamook; can't be a coincidence… just hope the road's clear."

With his head nodding in agreement and his lips pursed in consideration, Shay simply replied, "Mmmm *hmmmm*".

After the windshield and side windows were clear, Shay scooted into the chilly seat. He could tell John had something on his mind as his friend was half-looking toward Shay and chewing on the corner of his lip. "Well, spit it out, ye twit!"

John counted his words, then spoke his piece. "That Miss Ginger… she's quite a lady. You're not…?"

Shay wiggled his eyebrows. "Not *what*?"

John turned back to the car and put it in gear. "Never you mind. It's just… no, you can't be that simple."

"She's a good woman, John. Ye'd be good to respect that. And sure, I noticed. It's simply not a good time for that trouble, that's all." He sat back, folding his arms. John had inadvertently reminded Shay of his lonesome ways. He'd not pursued Miss Ginger, as he'd outlived two extraordinary women and refused to put himself through that again. With all his might, Shay Hayes pushed those painful memories out of his mind and focused on the snowy sidewalks outside.

Seeing his friend scowl, John said nothing. Instead, he kept driving and aimed the car toward the West precinct, where Shay insisted they should start their day. Shay offered a few directions, but his subtle grimace spoke volumes about his mood.

Not 10 minutes later, the little black Dodge arrived in front of the police precinct near the industrial district. It was the closest precinct to Shay, and John had remembered seeing it on their way into town the night prior. The traditional white globes were lit outside. Under the snow caps, which resembled arctic circles, they looked like abstract world globes. Before stepping out of the car, John put his hand on Shay's knee.

"Sorry if I overstepped back there, pal. I don't know your life, and I wouldn't assume it's bad enough that I didn't fare so well in my own… romantic ventures. At least, not since… Listen, don't let me get to you. Let's stay cool and just focus on the job, all right?"

Shay looked outside, into the drifts of snow forming as the snow gently but continuously fell.

"I'll do anything but stay cool. How about you leave her running and keep the engine warm? Don't worry; ye haven't put me off or anything. I just need another cup of joe to find my charm." He lifted his empty paper coffee cup and rattled it around a little bit. John smiled, and they stepped out of the car.

"My treat, Shay."

"Talbot, as I said, I know a few of the boys in the precinct here. Would you mind if I took the lead?" John shrugged. They headed up the steps and stomped the snow from their boots.

Upon stepping inside, they were greeted with the most bullfrog-faced cus that ever manned a desk. He was tapping a pen on the massive wooden countertop, scowling. It was unclear whether he was scowling *before* they entered or *because* of their entry. His hair was cropped close, blond going silver, with a bushy mustache. He had little neck to speak of, but his uniform was crisp and tidy.

"PETER!" Shay shouted. "You look great! Hard to stay out of the snow, yeh?"

The scowling man slapped the pen down and let out a long sigh. "Whaddya want today, you skinny mick?"

John was taken aback and looked to Shay.

"Pete, I'm fookin' with ye. Get off your big red ape arse and come say hello!" Shay walked around behind the desk.

Surprisingly, the scowling man's eyebrows reversed their arch, and his jaw relaxed, turning one of the most grumpy-looking faces into a kind and rather younger-looking and fatherly face. The large man grunted as he sat up from the chair, which let out a relieved squeak. He turned to Shay and snatched him up in a bear hug that took Shay off his toes.

Relieved, John stood back and watched these men embrace as brothers. Once Pete had dropped Shay back to the floor and Shay had caught his breath, Shay shook the large man's hand unusually. He shook fists, then clasped Shay's hand above and Pete's below. It was an odd thing, and John was fascinated by it.

"John, you twit. Say hello! This is Pete O'Malley, my best mate from darts at the Irish League. He's been here longer than most. They built the building around him!"

"Hey, John."

Pete turned and reached his massive hand across the desk to shake John's. As Pete leaned forward, John could see that this man was far less fat than muscle. His shoulders were boulders set atop tree trunks for arms, and his grip told that he could likely take down a gang or perhaps a black bear. John smiled somewhat nervously and shook the hand of this man in a usual way.

"Boys, what are you doin' in my domain? You back to work, Shay?"

He hooked his thumbs in his belt loops and leaned back on the pillar behind the desk.

"Petey, I must say, it's been a while since I've seen you in uniform. So, it must have been a while since I came here begging for handouts... yeh, I'm workin' again."

"Don't tell me you're working insurance fraud again. That muck gets *tiresome*. I always say, if someone had *nothin'* and after a tragedy they got *somethin'*? Well, that's probably a con."

"No, no, Pete. It's far more dire than that."

"Cheating spouse?" Pete had a hopeful look as he offered his second-best gamble.

"Not even close. Go darker, boy!" Shay ribbed him.

"Uh... murder plot?" He had almost whispered the words, looking over his shoulder as he said them.

"Getting warmer!" Shay grinned ridiculously.

"Christ, I don't know... I don't wanna guess it's more nasty stuff. Just spit it out, already!" He patted Shay in the gut, which was almost a dead blow for a lesser man.

With a wheeze, Shay clutched Pete's shoulder and leaned forward. "Ye bastard! Watch the belly! No, it's even crazier than anything. Would you believe... *the dead rising*?"

Pete looked at his friend in disbelief. He turned to John, who shrugged and nodded. "He's not bullshitting you, Pete. I mean to say, it's lookin' that way."

"Petey, this is John *Talbot*. He's a long-time associate of mine, ye may recall we took a load of cases some years back. That doggy door murder? That was *mostly* him!"

"Oh! I remember that! The mess made the paper —front page, even! What a story. Damn that old man's long arms... he coulda probably reached the keys on the wall from his cell!" Pete waved his arms around, making them look as long as they could. Shay did, too, for a bit, and they waved their arms together, making groaning noises like crochety old men.

"Baaah!"

"Guuuhhh!"

John was nearly red-faced, embarrassed at the ridiculousness of it all.

After the chuckles subsided and the men came back around the desk, John could see the actual size of the man. He was nary five and a half feet tall, but nearly as wide. He looked like he'd stepped out of the

Viking art of old, with expansive shoulders and stout legs.

Thinking about the size of this man, John had an idea. "Can't help but notice, Pete, you're a big guy. Let me ask you… If you needed to, could you crush a flashlight enough to flatten it against its batteries?"

Pete looked at John, then back at Shay. "I uh… I don't really know the answer to that, Mister Talbot. Why do you ask?"

John had been holding Billy's case file; he opened it to the photograph from the G.H. Welles break-in. Producing it for Pete, he hoped for a more straightforward answer. "You're about the biggest lunk I've seen lately, and I figure I should ask a strong man if it's possible to do so, that's all."

Pete looked hard at the photograph. He looked down at his hand, trying to match the image with what marks his massive hand might leave. After a minute, he handed the photo back. "Sure looks like it was crushed by a hand, but I don't know if I could do the same. Guess I'd need a flashlight to try…" he rubbed his chin like Sherlock Holmes, staring off toward the equipment locker.

Shay butted in. "No worries, old boy, let's stay focused. How about John and I go relieve ourselves while you read over the file?"

Pete nodded, opening the file John handed him. "Go see the little. She's in the office. Give me twenty, yeah? I gotta tidy up the desk for the day watch."

"Sure thing, Petey!" Shay responded. With that, he let himself and John behind the banisters that separated the police from the public. John in tow, Shay made his way swiftly past rows of empty desks and dark offices. It was not a large station, but it was built at a time when offices were small and desks were close. Being a Saturday and hardly past waking hours, most of the precinct was empty.

Reaching the only lit office at the end of the large hall on the right, Shay waved John to 'hold back' while he went and knocked. With two fists, Shay let out a barrage of half a dozen bangs on the door of the office. From inside, John could hear paperwork being dropped on the floor and a faint voice grumbling, "Oh, for fucks' sake…" moments before the door opened. In the dim light, a small woman opened the door and stood hands-on-hips in the doorway facing Shay, whose obtuse grin meant he *knew* he was disturbing her.

"Hey! Who said you could… Oh, Christ. *Peter*. What do you need, Shay?" Shay slipped past her into the office, tugging at her sleeve. She turned and followed inside the office, leaving John in the hall.

One of the benefits of well-constructed buildings —perhaps also a curse —was that hardwood and marble echoed like a sonofabitch. John could hear half the words in the room, some of them blue as all-get-out, and others sounded like friendly banter. He overheard Shay ask to "borrow" something, and her tone was unkind in response. She grumbled about "last time" and "another car," but Shay was all charm, and within a minute or two, all that could be heard in the hall was laughter and hushed, friendly tones. The sharp words gave way to what, John surmised, was Shay getting his way.

After perhaps five minutes, Shay came out of the office and closed the door. He strode back toward John with hands clasped in excitement. "You'll never guess. It's a lucky thing we came when we did, John. I must say we are in for a treat." He was still walking hurriedly.

John glowered at him and stepped into Shay's walking path. "You can tell me in a second, Shay, but I actually need to piss."

"There's a potted Christmas tree just over yonder…"

"God*dammit*, Irish."

"Okay, OKAY! Jeezus, follow me." Shay led the way toward the washroom, where the boys each took a urinal.

"What did we get? I heard you ask to borrow something?" John mumbled head-down into the urinal. His words echoed.

Shay leaned back and let out a long sigh. "Not a some*thing*, John. A some*one!*"

John realized precisely what the inference was. Shay had asked the woman in the office if he could bring that hulking mass of man, Pete, along for the job. Closing his eyes, he pictured the little sedan. He imagined Pete climbing into the back seat, and the Dodge promptly rolling over onto that side from the weight of the man. He snorted, trying to stifle a chuckle, and it echoed in the restroom. Shay was already washing his hands when John finished, and John couldn't help but smile at the thought of having a gorilla on their team for this mission.

"You like it? The plan, I mean. Smart thinking, right?" John simply shook his head.

"Irish, you're gonna have to convince the man to come along. No sane person is going to volunteer to get mixed up in our case."

Shay shrugged and tossed the hand towels into the bin. From the hall, while John was just washing his hands, Shay commented, "Yeh, we'll see…"

A moment later, John was hustling past a number of empty desks down the side hall back toward the central clerk's desk. He caught up with Shay just before he reached Pete. As they came up to the banisters behind Pete, the man spun around in his chair with a slow and almost deliberate *creak*.

"When do we leave?" Pete asked, through a grin like the Cheshire cat. He was shrugging his eyebrows up and down like a drunk man taking a salacious pass at a cigarette girl. In a dark alley, it would have been terrifying. Here, this mountain of a man in a crisp blue uniform and his odd intonations put John's mind to rest, pleased at his fortune to have some stout and well-humored backup.

Within minutes, the broad and neatly organized precinct desk sat empty and gathering dust. As the three men bounded out the door, more uniformed officers were on their way in—three officers, in fact, two of whom gave Shay a very disapproving look.

The moments now seemed to rush by; there was an excitement about it all. Shay took the keys from John and tossed them over the roof to Pete, much to John's surprise.

"Talbot, we get the royal treatment. I'll take a backseat. I could use the legroom. Get in; we've got somewhere to *be!*"

"The place you got snagged?" John inquired.

Shay patted his shoulder, "Later. You'll see!' He slapped Pete on the back, shouting, "Giddyup, big boy!" whereupon Pete wedged himself behind the wheel with a beaming grin.

Good Company

In no time, the sedan had ambled out of Portland and onto the highway headed west. From the backseat, Shay couldn't help but chuckle at how John was shielding his eyes from the snow blindness. His hat brim was not doing the trick today, but he had brought along some very stylish black sunglasses. Under his coat, Pete was wearing his police uniform, and while it may have been inappropriate, nobody told Pete what to do. Since Pete had the good grace of being born nephew to the chief of police, so long as he generally did the right thing, he was relatively immune to criticism from colleagues. What Shay had not explained to John was that the lady in the office was Pete's sister Amelia, who, despite her lack of a badge, essentially supervised that particular precinct under the humble title of an administrator. Notably, she had been the first female hire in that precinct. Not all of the men had adjusted to it, but she kept Pete in line, and that was appreciated.

As he'd intimated to Shay over a pint not long back, Pete had employed kind words and firm handshakes to make sure everyone knew who the boss was, and nobody questioned that big, cheerful bastard lest they see a different side of the man. He knew what he was and used it to his advantage.

"John, we can check out that setup spot where they nabbed me, perhaps tomorrow morning. Today, with Pete here tagging along, I believe we should get closer to the action."

Shay was right. John hated sudden changes in plans, but they were part of the job.

"Sounds like a good notion. I'm in. How about you, Pete, you game?"

"I'm always up for a mystery. Are you boys gonna fill me in?

112

Anything I should know before we get out there to Tillamook?" Pete asked, eyes on the road.

With a shake of his head, Pete looked in the rearview, and Shay laid out the plan.

"Of course, and today's a simple one. We're going to visit those local coppers and see if they have any information we don't. Billy was only able to get so many reports before they started asking questions, as is often the case with small-town blues."

"I resemble that implication!" Pete chided him, teasing.

"Say now, without you and the boys from the league, I'm not sure I would've solved half of my cases!" He patted his big friend on the back. John was back in the file again and narrowly avoided motion sickness as he churned through those reports once again. While the state forest was undoubtedly pretty, one could only see so many snow-covered pines before boredom set in.

He read some bits of the reports aloud, pointing out their significance along the way. Pete listened and nodded along, the occasional affirming grunt, as Shay took over telling the juicier bits of the story, and John kept reading.

Sometime later, while Pete and Shay were busy chatting away about exploits on old cases, John looked up and took a glance at the dashboard. "Fuel gauge, Pete." Squinting through his sunglasses, Pete leaned forward a bit and rapped the fuel gauge with his knuckle, finding it not budging from its current location directly above the letter E.

"There's a Texaco five miles up, boys. Get the gas, and I'll buy us lunch. Hell, we're almost to Tillamook anyway." It was a generous offer, but Shay refused.

"Not a rat's chance in a cathouse, Petey. You're on our dime today! Don't be daft. I'll split my day's pay with you as it is."

Pete grinned and knocked the dash with his knuckles. "Good. I owe Ames a fiver for a lost bet."

"Sports trivia again?" Shay inquired.

"Babe Ruth. It's like Amelia has a dictionary for a brain."

"Encyclopedia." John piped up, not looking up.

Shrugging, Pete grunted, "Huh. Yeah, that one."

Within just a few minutes, the little black Dodge found its way to the pumps at a corner gas station. Its whitewall tires and piecrust edge scrolled their way through the snow on the ground, leaving beautiful tracks comprised of five grooves in the snow and four neatly arranged rows of snowflakes left unscathed by the straddling treads.

John had stepped out to stretch his legs; the attendant was working quickly between a small Packard coupe and a Chevrolet panel wagon at the far pumps. It was a clear morning, the sounds of chirping birds and the ring of those shiny red gas pumps doing their work. The chill in the air was certainly enough to keep the boys in their coats, and as always, Shay was in the mood for something hot. He called over to the attendant, as he thumbed towards the small shop at the corner of the building, "Any Joe in there, boyo?"

Through a shiver, the neatly uniformed college-age man nodded and waved him in. "Pots are full, and it's on the house if I fill your tank at least half?" Shay nodded and gave him an awkward thumbs-up. That was one of those American things that Shay had never really picked up, but it was popular, so sometimes he gave it his best try. In reality, as limber as he was, his thumbs tended to bend too far back and just look damned silly.

Ducking into the shop through the six-pane red corner door, Shay was distracted by the jingle of the bells mounted above the door, and he bumped directly into a dour-looking man who was just inside the door, waiting patiently for Shay to get out of his way so he could be on with his day. The look on his face said it all. Shay felt the need to apologize.

"Sorry, sorry! It's… there was a jing—" he trailed off, pointing up at the bell. He realized that his apology was further inconveniencing this man, who simply scowled at him through tired eyes.

As Shay stepped aside and let the man pass, this man, who was nearly a head taller than him but generally as lean, he noticed that this sour customer had a significant gait. In fact, it wasn't so much the curious walk but the fact that his spine seemed to curve in a way that offset his shoulders, making him look much like a broken coat rack from behind. His head was clean-shaven and pink from the cold.

"Twit," Shay murmured.

Grabbing a pack of cigarillos, mint chewing gum, and three paper cups of piping hot coffee, Shay left two dollars and a quarter on the counter to include a gratuity for the poor, freezing boy outside. Managing his three cups and pocketing the incidentals, Shay used his toe to open that bright red door, and he made his way back toward the car.

Thumbing back toward the shop once more, "I paid for my things, and I've got your money for the gas here. Looks like *you* could use a cup of this coffee!"

The attendant pointed to the price on the rolling numbers in the pump once it clicked off, and Shay thumbed through a few bills to cover the total. The young man shrugged and dusted the snow off his shoulders before responding, "I've had three cups already, sir. If I go back to that shop for long, it might be four, and then I won't sleep until Christmas!"

Pete had taken to rearranging the trunk, and this time, he had also taken off his uniform shirt. He clipped his gun holster back to his hip, where it sagged without the rigid leather duty belt to support it. All he was wearing now was a white T-shirt and his blue pants as he was putting his lightweight gray jacket back on. Some years prior, when Shay had met the man, he had admired Pete's fading Navy tattoos. Of course, Shay himself would never get a tattoo, as he could never be sure what might be out of style in a number of years. Also, he never really could decide on the art of it.

"Saddle up, ye twits!" Shay announced.

All three boys were now in the Dodge; Pete had taken to the passenger seat and was holding two coffee cups. John took the driving duties, with Shay in the rear seat next to that damn thick file.

Unprompted, Pete relinquished his sunglasses to John, who had been squinting over the steering wheel at the sheer whiteness of the snow. "Thanks, Pete. That helps." The big man simply smiled and nodded, sipping his coffee while he handed John the other cup.

Now clutching the folder but without opening it, Shay offered up an idea.

"Say, I've been thinking about something, you two. I've been mulling about those bodies, how they were snatched."

Pete nodded and replied, "Those files say they broke the doors open with a pry bar. Easy enough. I've seen it probably a hundred times back in town. It's simple; all you have to do is just grab the long end of the—"

Shay cut him off mid-sentence.

"No, you daft gorilla, no. I mean, as in the way the bodies were taken *away*. I've been in the trunk of a car recently; not a pleasant place. They took these bodies away whole and complete, didn't they? It must've been quite a sizable vehicle to move them. Say, a milk truck or a moving truck, perhaps… I can't imagine them stacking those bodies up in a pickup bed and strolling down the road like a grocery errand."

Somewhat embarrassed, Pete thought he'd better add something valuable to the equation with his experience in police work. His methods were often a bit more hands-on than cerebral. "I tell you, boys, we have a paddy wagon that can move a half dozen people with room to spare."

"That's a sore thumb of a vehicle, though…" Shay offered.

Pete continued his train of thought. "Anyway, a medium-sized box truck or maybe one of those Suburbans would surely be useful to haul all of those bodies. Heck, even a panel van, if you're not moving more than, say, three or four laid out. But… that's maybe one in ten cars on the road, so not much use trying to suss them out that way."

Shay swigged his coffee, offering, "Agreed. Too many variables."

At the steering wheel, John looked like Cary Grant in those sunglasses, and he was simply nodding his head at the logic of it. Pete had dutifully unfurled the map in the glove box to ensure they found their way. John had thanked him for that, but snickered to himself at the futility, as there was only one road into town, so navigation shouldn't be too difficult.

The boys spent a while offering musings on what to look for and what might be suspicious around these parts. They all agreed with a laugh that a black Dodge full of caffeinated shit-talkers was the *most* suspicious car in town.

A large, crudely carved wooden roadside sign indicated they were approaching state forest land, but this meant little. The woods had already surrounded their drive, sprawling and vast. The scars of past forest fires were obscured by the snow on the ground; above, seemingly endless boughs of green hung heavy with it.

Their windshield's center divide bar was a perfect split of Shay's rear-seat view, with light snow starting up again and collecting in the corners of the front glass panes. The wipers droned rhythmically as they drove slowly through Tillamook Forest. Each of the passengers minded the scenery, scrolling by like the canvas mechanical backdrop of a stage play. Nobody in the car was sure whether they might strike gold today, but the road was calling, and the three men were all itching for the following hunch or clue to come to light—a jittery excitement of the known unknown. There was blue sky to the South, though they were traveling under dark silvery clouds. The sun shone behind them, making the white snow even more blinding. They rumbled West for Tillamook, the highway twisting and rolling through those forests.

"Pete?" Shay piped up, not breaking his gaze from the passing woods.

"Yeah, Shay?"

"You think we're crazy?"

"Sure," he smirked.

"I mean, come *on*, lad—this case. What we saw... think there's a chance we're loons? What if it's all a goose chase? Worse, just a silly fiction... a prank or the like?"

"Shay, when a friend asks for help, ya help him. But no, you're probably not mad."

John was quiet as they spoke. Something somber in Shay's voice held him pensive.

"It's all so damn strange. Feels like we're characters in a book written by a madman. It's… It's like walking in a fog these past few days. I need to get above it, outta the haze... I need answers. I just don't want ye to think we've lost our senses and play along for the sake of drinking buddies."

John chewed his lip but nodded in agreement.

Pete let out a chest of air and shrugged as he replied.

"The Wright brothers flew in my papa's lifetime. Nineteen ought two... no, *three*. Shit. Now folks are globetrotting in planes, smoking cigars, and chewing roast duck, readin' magazines. Imagine what we'll see in another few years. Hell, they want to put men on the *moon*. Think of what they'll have to do to those men to make 'em suitable for living on a rock in space—the far-fetched nature of putting a body out where it wasn't meant to function. I can't say you're crazy. Maybe I think you're just ahead of the times. I don't believe in magic, but science musta looked a lot like magic to folks too simple to grasp it."

"So we're looking for a scientist, then..." Shay grumbled, simultaneously unsettled yet feeling satisfied with Pete's answer.

Soon, the quaint and very sparsely populated little town of Tillamook appeared as they rolled out of a deep valley. Three empty coffee cups lay about on the floor, and a colossal man complained that he needed to use the latrine. After a few minutes of circling blocks, John found a parking spot on the side of the local precinct. The white snow on the ground seemed to have no edge where it met the white plaster walls of the building, and the little black sedan cut quite a profile on that parchment-white background.

Shay patted John on the shoulder, offering him to take point.

"You're the most professional lookin' of the lot of us. I say ye take the reins after Petey-boy makes introductions."

A crow swooped down and perched on the hood ornament just as the three men made their way into the station.

Movement

It was a bit after eleven in the morning as Pete bellied up to the lobby desk of the patrolman on duty. Shay leaned back against the corner window and folded his arms. John stood nearby with his hands clasped behind him. Shay thought it best to observe and give the boys space to work. He noted that the patrolman was dressed for the weather, uniform taut with layers of thermal cotton underneath, his winter riding boots nearly reaching his knees. It was a small station with only five desks and an office in the back, a marked hallway leading off to the holding cell and the toilets. Nobody else seemed to be in the building; aside from the conversation between John and the patrolman, the station was as quiet as the snow-muted street outside.

With a flash of a badge, Pete's status as a Portland Police officer ingratiated them. John managed to smile and get friendly with this officer, bantering about the snow and all the hooligans they must be ready to round up on the looming Saturday night. They chatted about busting a few heads, and Shay enjoyed watching the officer's demeanor loosen up a little. Pete leaned into one of his tales about the pretty girls working the rough side of Portland.

"You'd have died, sonny. She was all gussied up and at her height. I swear, I was worried I was gonna need backup. I couldn't end my shift 'til the corners were clear, and I was so damn tired. Name was... Gerta. German gal, real *farm girl* type. Christ, she coulda been a linebacker before she started hookin'... anyway cost me a cigarette and two dollars to get her off that corner. I think it was the only two bucks she was gonna make that night, seein' as she picked a corner with a working lamp over it! I got home in time for hot food and a backrub, so I say it was a good shift."

They guffawed and patted shoulders; Pete had this guy properly

loosened up. The cop took his glasses off to wipe them, offering, "…
Shucks. Maybe I shoulda been a city cop… all we get here are drunks
and domestics. Petty farmer bickering over horseshit. Lieu works
maybe ten hours a week if you subtract the coffee breaks and the hours
he spends in the can with a magazine. Well, it has its perks, I suppose.
What can I help you boys with?" He was still smiling as he asked.

After a few fishing questions about unusual sightings and utilitarian
vehicles, it became clear that the policeman was friendly but not too
invested in the conversation. Still, Pete was fishing without using good
bait. John leaned in and turned the questions toward the files on hand,
asking about some facts and recent occurrences rather than the
opinions of this bored copper.

The men discussed those absconded corpses. They spoke about
other local witness reports. Tillamook was the place where the
strangest sighting had occurred; an old lady, a widowed woman who
volunteered at the town hall meetings and bingo night, had seen a man
closely resembling one of her bingo participants dragging what looked
to be electrical utility equipment from the bus maintenance yard. She'd
spotted him across from the school on a late Wednesday night after
bingo had wrapped up at the Elks' Lodge. She hadn't thought much of
it at the time, calling out the man's name and receiving no answer. So,
imagine her surprise when she happened to chat with the police
captain about it after church services and was informed that the man
she'd thought she had seen… had suffered a fatal 'widowmaker' heart
attack some three weeks prior. The officer told John Talbot, "Cap said
her expression was *priceless*. Dunno what he meant exactly. I figure she
just needs spectacles worse than I do."

John mused about it, "Old ladies aren't known for their eyesight…
but my mother? Rest her soul. She could spot our neighbor smoking
down the block on a moonless night to remind him to put out his trash
for the bin men, so there may be something there."

After a few minutes of passing gossip and stories back and forth,
the patrolman shuffled off to one of those back offices and returned
holding three brown hanging folders, passing them to John. Claiming a
seat, and with Pete barely squeezing in between the arms of his chair,
the three each took a folder and got to reading.

A few minutes passed as the boys studied their files. John was quiet,
and Pete let out several small but acknowledging grunts; Shay had
already finished his file and was now reading over Pete's shoulder.
Then the men rotated files, and each read a new one. They repeated

this process for the third file each, now all fully up-to-date on what the patrolman promised was the entirety of the information that this small station had about those missing bodies and their subsequent alleged encounters. It was sparse, primarily consisting of statements from mediocre witnesses who offered more speculation than observation.

"Boys, seems to be all rather boilerplate. There's not much of any use in here aside from the trail heading out of town. Did you see where that hiking couple came across that old boy in the red coat? How damned odd. Luckily, they were able to leg it to their pickup; it seems they thought he was going to take that hatchet right down on their *heads*!"

The cop chimed in from across the room, "See? Bickering farmer *horse-shit.*"

Pete was excited about the file he had read. He had this habit of bouncing his heel with his toe planted, which sent his knee moving up and down like the head of an oil derrick. It shook the row of seats noisily against the wall.\

Shay and John nodded at each other, and both stood up together. In the past, they had made a point of discussing cases out of earshot of the cops who, more often than not, either mishandled things or overlooked clues entirely. For the sake of staying on good terms, they didn't want to offend the officers they might call later for backup or a collar. Taking the hint, Pete stood up with them, and Shay returned the patrolman's folders, thanking him profusely.

Outside again, the trio had collected in a circle behind the Dodge. John cranked the motor to get her warmed up. Shay flipped up the collar of his coat while the other two men looked to be suffering in the just-below-freezing breeze. With snowflakes collecting on the wool of his collar, Shay took charge of the debrief.

"O-kay, ears open and brains working. Let's get something accomplished today, shall we?" He received affirming nods. "Great. Firstly, I saw three good, consistent facts across all those reports that fit with everything we have read so far. These suspects don't talk, that's-"

Pete cut him off. "Not even the one *you* ran into?"

"Not a word, Petey, not even when I put him down."

"Okay, strong silent types." Pete joked.

"Strong as hell, big guy. It sounds mad. That's to be sure. When I took my blade to this mad bastard, he went down only after I practically butchered him. Didn't say a word. Damn funny business, but I've seen injections and pills change every bit of a man into something you wouldn't recognize. So maybe it was a drug or a mental thing, y'know. It could be some drugged-up cult… but last I checked, fanatics don't tend to volunteer for autopsies and then hop back in the car for an adventure, yeh? "

John had a chuckle at the sarcasm there. With a significant shrug and a sigh from Pete, Shay continued his point.

"Nobody's seen a thing outside dusk to dawn, so we've got to expect they like to stay under the cover of night. Or, that's their order. Assuming there's some hierarchy or someone is in charge of all these shenanigans. That's gonna help us, certainly. Gives us the days to work this thing."

"Sounds like you're saving the heavy hitter for last?" John asked.

"Old boy, some days you know me too well. We all saw the third file, the skinny one from the night things went missing?"

A round of nodding heads. He was referring to the report, which was written in haste and relatively thin on details. It was accompanied by a note from the DA investigator who had handled the case. In this particular case, seven bodies had been pilfered from the cold storage at the County Morgue. What caused the state to step in was not the theft of the bodies. That would likely have been handled on a local level. In this instance, it was the desecration of a corpse that brought the state in. In every other case, corpses had gone missing wholesale and in their entirety. Apparently, that's common enough from either incompetence or malfeasance not to warrant a close look.

"Seven bodies gone, right? That's a lot of beef!" John offered.

Shay, quick to correct, raised a finger.

"Johnny boy, in this instance, they were looking for exactly six and one-half bodies. The morning after the break-in and disappearance of the bodies, one of the cleaning staff had stepped out for a fag while the police chatted up the coroner. Lo and behold, in a ditch out back, this poor lass, trying to enjoy her cigarette, tripped across two recently and very crudely-severed legs that could be identified easily, seeing as one of the toe tags was still attached."

Pete shoved his hands deep in his pockets, "Fuck… that's gruesome."

"Oh, it must've been. Seems the legs were a matching set, so the state investigator concluded that whoever was making off with all of these carcasses likely only had room in their vehicle for *just* more than six bodies, which would include three overweight men, two average men, and a young lass who had met her fate behind the wheel after a rainstorm. The math was around one thousand, three hundred and twenty gross, assuming the coroners' postmortem recorded weights were accurate."

John shouldered Shay and joked, "With or without the legs?"

"Don't be crude. Apparently, the legs belonged to a portly fellow, George Emerson, who had met his end after an electrocution. Reported as an accident, as nobody was willing to accept that this well-liked dairy plant middle manager might be a bit unwell."

Pete smirked and commented, "Sure… *plenty* of folks enjoy bathing with their prize toaster."

"Boys, they came upon two big pieces of evidence then, which we haven't seen in any other case. Know what those might be?" After a side glance and a shared smile, both John and Pete held up their hands to 'go first' as though this frosty curbside were a classroom.

"Pete, you first." John fake-scowled at being chosen second. He was in rare form today.

The big guy spoke up. "The mud! They said it contained traces of bunker oil and metal filings, and pine needles."

Shay gave his awkward thumbs-up. "John?"

"Well, I had two… but yeah, the muck on the floor. Lucky it was rainy, s'pose. Also, we got those legs! The report stated that the blade used to remove them was rough, something toothy. Gnawed those bones up something foul. Amateur hour, with no precision. Not like the tools a medical professional might use. Like we saw in Lowell's office."

"John, you're spot on with that. Not that I wish to think about him takin' a wedge of that head."

Shay made a sawing motion with his hand, and Pete squirmed a bit. The idea was dark, to be sure. Shay stepped closer and clasped his hands on the shoulders of the other men.

"So what we know is, we're out here in the woods looking for somebody who's also in the woods. But, they've got only a medium-sized truck or wagon and a stomach for hacking up bodies in the rain, using a toothy saw, likely the kind you'd use for hacking tree limbs. Sounds like some proper clues, lads! Say, how much d'ye think a severed leg could weigh? It can't be more than twenty or thirty pounds, I'd say. One of ye lads wants to lie down, and we'll give it a lift?"

His enthusiasm was shared but shrouded in general disgust from his mates. John scowled at the open sky behind Shay, unsettled. Pete crossed his burly arms in front of his chest and shrugged his shoulders once more, offering no advice but a solid 'okay' nod. Shay took the lead and presented his plan.

"Ask yourself, boys. Where might one find the combination of toothy saws, metal shavings, and pine tree detritus?"

In a moment of realization, a devilish grin crept across John's face. He knew precisely where Shay was headed with this. Pete was looking at John's face, waiting for a cue but not doing the math himself. Shay grasped Pete on the shoulder.

"For Christ's sake, Pete. You grew up in Portland! What's the biggest industry west of Portland? Hell, west of Seattle?"

Pete scratched his chin, and in an instant, his eyes lit up.

"Logging?"

"Absolutely right, you big genius. That's where most of this money to build this scrappy town came from, I would hazard a guess. Seems to me we should head South toward Hemlock and Blaine, as we saw in those case files. Doesn't seem like much happening North of here, at least that we've got a lead on."

Pete piped up, "Not much out there but logging and farming."

Shay was jazzed. "Yes! If we can make a few contacts and dig around a bit, it might not be a waste! We could be back here by nightfall and catch a hotel room."

He patted his friends' shoulders, playfully pushing each one toward the car. Pete went for the passenger seat, rubbing his mitts together and warming them with a hot breath.

"John, you're driving. Shay, can we get more coffee? Maybe a refreshment? I'm peckish."

"Right on time!' Shay shot back, 'My treat, Petey-boy. John can have milk."

John flashed him a middle finger and a smile, then hopped in behind the wheel, Shay settling into the rear seat with their files strewn across the woven upholstery. John mapped the route South on a winding county road. In the middle of the backseat, Shay was worked up. His mind was spinning with the possibilities of how they might suss out their culprit. He knew that there was little possibility of an easy lead. Nearly everybody in the county, hell, even the state, would have a hand saw in their truck. This was going to be a needle in a haystack, a massive haystack covered in snow.

Ah, hell. The M-E wanted us back in Snoqualmie on Monday. I can phone ahead if we're tied up out here. Wonder what he's gonna find with that microscope… damn smell was something else…

With enough petty cash to cover a week of room and board, Shay wasn't really *concerned*. In fact, he was feeling confident now… pleased to sit back as his two friends discussed baseball history in the front seat. John made a quick stop at a little café with a sweet pink sign shaped like a 4-foot-tall cupcake. Pete quickly returned with three cups of hot coffee and a pastry for each of them; John thanked him for skipping the milk.

Spectating from the back seat, Shay's attention turned to tiny downtown Tillamook as they passed a theater marquee, restaurants, a dime store, and a few boutique shops. The only busy spot seemed to be Woolworth's, with its bustling soda counter facing streetside through large holiday-decorated pane windows. The town was quiet today; the weather kept most folks inside. Parked on the curbs were a peppering of older and newer vehicles; a Model A Ford with pumpkins piled in the bed and the tailgate down made him smile. He even spotted a little black '49 Dodge sedan that could be a twin to theirs, if it weren't for the fact that Chrysler loved to restyle taillights and grilles every other year. For a moment, he pondered how, if he someday had to leave Portland, he might enjoy relocating to somewhere like Tillamook. The cozy streets were a pleasant contrast to his overwhelming experience visiting New York City some years earlier. They had already passed the west end of town and now headed South back toward sparsely populated woods.

Hell, even that hayseed nowhere in Montana where Gabe came up… could be nice. Christ, I wonder how he's faring in Chicago. I should write him. They'd love it here. Lindy could make jellies in tiny jars. Pretty lass… damn feisty.

Shay shook loose the thoughts of past days and returned to the present, interrupting John and Pete discussing the '48 Dodgers roster. Pete was enthused about some Robinson fellow.

"Boys, we'll make a few stops and get a lay of the land, poke around a bit under the snowdrifts. If nothing jumps out at us, we'll come back here tonight and get a good night's rest. Only hunker down there if we strike gold *and* we can find accommodations. Deal?"

He received two nods of agreement in return, both men cradling their coffee and watching the road unfold ahead while they talked baseball. Apparently, the White Sox were getting their arses handed to them lately. "But *next* year, I tell ya!" Pete insisted.

Off the beaten path

The boys had been cruising for half an hour, shifting the idle chat back to the case files while Shay marked on a little road map of the area. He circled potential points of interest for each case, primarily nearby towns and logging routes. The main highway passed through a couple of small towns and communities south of Tillamook, and there was a chance each would warrant a visit. Beside each note, he ranked their importance based on population and locality. These local road maps were chock-full of helpful information.

"We'll be looking for something remote, and the smaller the population, the better the likelihood somebody would notice anything out of place. Should have worn a flannel, perhaps..." he joked with John and Pete.

Pete snorted at the idea. "That's a silly thought, boys... suppose we should've worn black suits like your boss and his Fed friends, huh? John's the only one here who looks like he might be somebody! Shay, you look like a dandy. You look like you sell houses. Fancy tailoring and all! John, you look like a banker or a city councilman." His teasing was met with snickering.

John slapped the steering wheel and retorted, "Ah, we're all *some*body. Just doing my best to look like somebody *useful!*"

Shay diverted the conversation. "Well, I may be a dandy, but I'm a *useful* dandy. Let's find ourselves up the road, chip away at this, and try to find something evidentiary. Talking through anything we find interesting."

"Sounds like a lot of talking!" John grunted.

"Maybe so, Johnny-boy. Think of it as a sweeping method when you're searching an area. Concentric circles, drawing tighter every revolution. Multiple eyes on the same footpath. Every man makes a pass, and nothing gets missed. Worked well in the war. It worked with those files already! Not so easy with poking around small towns and few leads, but we need a working pattern regardless."

It was a simple method, one Shay's unit had put to use on occasion, searching for Nazi stragglers and small detachments. Cameron Mason had taught Shay by drawing with empty shell casings in the dirt in the woods. Putting it to use in investigations? It was some of the most fun he'd ever had, regardless of the often depressing context. Though, to be fair, most of his workload for Billy Bigsby was sitting in a car with a telephoto lens for long enough that your legs would take to feeling like needles and radio static. John usually took the follow-on-foot cases as he was much more forgettable.

Dammit, Mason. Miss you, old boy.

He wondered how Cam was doing now, after the debacle with Gabe in New York. It had been almost five years, though Billy had recently shared that Gabe was in no shape for this work, not after what they had done to him in that institution. Lindy insisted he was getting better every day.

No hard feelings, Cam, we know ye meant well.

John and Pete had turned back to chatting about baseball. It seems there was a particular rivalry between the fans that had Pete poking John in the shoulder, something about stolen home runs. John had simply put up his hand and said, "I don't really watch the game that much, pal. I'm not going to argue about something I don't care about." Pete took the hint and dropped the subject. He turned to his left and put his broad arm across the back of the bench seat so he could face both John and Shay.

"You boys see all of those hills? Stretching back to Portland, all around here. They had some hellacious fires here back in '45. It was really a sight; you could hardly breathe in Portland. That massive glow in the sky. In fact, I know a couple of guys who lost their cabins out here. Damn shame, somebody said it was the Japanese dropping some sort of fire balloon. Depressing stuff really changed the area. The third fire we've had like that!"

Peyte used his right hand to motion out toward the hillsides, where swaths of sparsely grown vegetation lay under a soft blanket of white powder. He patted John on the shoulder.

"Sorry about the scores and all that, Talbot. You're all right. I don't really care who you root for, even nobody. Me and my old man... I used to play baseball. He'd take me out for a catch every day before I grew up, before he took to the bottle. Guess nothing lasts forever."

John was distracted, only half paying attention, adjusting his mirror as well. Someone driving behind them was using their high-beam headlights, quite an annoyance on a road like this. Turning the mirror away didn't help, so John cracked the window down and reached his arm out, signaling for the driver to pass. It was a long, straight stretch; the other driver could pass safely.

Passing is precisely what the other driver did. Bright lights still blazing, reflections in the side view mirrors, the other driver was nearly on their bumper before swooping left and pulling up next to the sedan to pass. Shay watched his shadow draw across Pete's face.

Pete offered his opinion, "damn fools hardly need high beams. It's the middle of the day."

John agreed, "I say they should have some damn consideration. I'm already snow-blind here!"

John glanced to his left just as the car passed.

"Say, isn't that the panel wagon we saw back-"

Just as the men had turned to look and see the brown Chevrolet delivery wagon with its broad flat sides passing by, the other driver grasped the steering wheel with both hands and yanked it hard to the right, slamming the broadside of the wagon into the driver's fender of their sedan.

The steel squealed and collided with a **CRUNCHHH.**

John had no time to compensate; the Chevy's impact forced the Dodge off the road and directly into the ditch. They were moving at more than 50 miles an hour, and the soft snow under the tire treads offered no grip. The Dodge blasted through the ditch and launched into a pine tree not far from the roadside; in that split second, none of the men had been able to let out the word save Pete's guttural "shit!" as an explosion of snow, steel, and steam obliterated the front end of the Dodge.

The dashboard earned its namesake as Pete's head dashed against it. Now, he was hunched over in the seat, half-shoved into the footwell by the sheer impact. John had gone face-first into the steering wheel; he was collapsed, slumped in his seat.

Shay had no time to react physically as the car crumpled against the thick tree trunk. Still, the fleeting image of the unbuckled seatbelt lying on the bench seat next to him had crossed his mind as his body was thrown forward between his friends and fully out through the windshield. His lanky body contorted as it landed half on top of the warped metal folds of the hood.

With quiet effort, the panel wagon corrected its course after the impact, rolling to a smooth and calm stop some fifty yards past the Dodge. The brake lights went dim, and the wagon shifted gears. Then, slowly, it idled in reverse toward the men in their sedan. Narrow bias-ply tires rolled over the soft snow drifts and roadside gravel, coming to a stop adjacent to the Dodge some twenty feet up on the shoulder of the road.

Slowly and calmly, the driver's door opened as a man in gray coveralls stepped out. A black-booted foot aggressively extinguished a cigarette dropped into the snow, snowflakes collecting on a bald head, as the man slipped on a pair of leather gloves that fit his hands and bony knuckles snugly. The leather creaked in the muted winter air.

The only sounds now were the man's slow, heavy footsteps and the steady pat-pat-pat of blood dripping onto the floor mats of the Dodge.

Sweltering

The first thing Shay felt was the heat. It was permeating, drenching him in sweat. Then he became aware of the stiff, uncomfortable rope binding his right wrist to the wooden arm of a chair. The third thing he felt was a weight around his neck. It was not heavy, more of a tugging. It was as though something was draped over his neck, and its heft was cutting into his collarbone. His eyesight was blurred, so he naturally tried to reach up with his free hand to clear his eyes. That's when he felt the actual pain. A sharp, vicious pain shot through his arm and up into his neck. He paused and relaxed his left arm, and simultaneously, the shooting pain began to subside. Squeezing his eyes tightly shut and wincing in pain, he started blinking away some of the sweat and crust that was blurring his eyes.

He was unsure how long he had been unconscious, but his entire body ached; he felt like a freight train had run him down. As his eyes adjusted to the meager light in the room, beads of sweat rolled down his face. Still a bit disoriented, he dropped his chin and took a good look at himself. His coat was gone, and his shirt was soaked through with sweat and blood. His left arm was clearly fractured and had sustained some lacerations, which were crudely wrapped in cotton cloth. Whoever had patched him up and likely tied him down had used his Shay's leather belt as a makeshift sling for his busted arm.

The air's humidity was giving him short breaths. He took in a couple of significant lungfuls of air, and again, a cacophony of pain shot through his left side, causing him to cry out and curse bluer than a sailor. Wiggling a bit, he could feel the crackling and wet sensation of the busted ribs on his left side, one of them protruding slightly through his shirt enough to poke into the bicep of his arm that was strung across his chest. Fear-borne adrenaline began coursing through his veins as he realized the severity of the situation. Shay had not taken such a hit in years; he had almost forgotten about this level of pain. *Almost.* His mind brought back flashes of the war, the trauma he had received, yet miraculously survived.

Adrenaline is a hell of a drug. He felt his ankles tightly bound to the chair's legs. His right hand was tied to the arm of the chair, but trembling slightly, and a cool flush passed over him as he resolved to get himself out of that chair no matter the cost.

Just then, a voice came from behind.

"Irisssh…"

The voice was familiar, but the speech was wrong, soft like a hiss.

"Talbot?"

The tired-sounding voice replied.

"Yeah, issme."

Shay wiggled his feet to turn the chair, but was not successful. Slowly, he turned his head to the left and leaned as far back as he could without tugging on the muscles connected to his busted ribs and arm.

"Talbot, ye sound off, lad. You okay back there?"

There was a pause as though John was looking for the words.

"Iss fine, Irissssh. I'm… I'm all here, but there's… they doped me up, I think… You look like shit from here."

Confusion in his voice, John's words trailed off. Shay took a very shallow, but relieved, breath. As the panic left his veins, the adrenaline washed a strangely calm sensation, and Shay settled a bit into his chair. He looked at the ceiling; it was poured-cement and stained, musty— the sort of place they laid underground. Pipes and ducts ran this way and that; he felt like he was looking at the belly of a warship or trapped somewhere in a sewer. One dim red light bulb hung from the ceiling in the corner he was facing.

No, he realized, *those are steam pipes. We're in a boiler room.*

"Johnny boy, it's damn hot. Can you see anything? Where's Petey?"

John let out an exasperated breath.

"I got one eye, Irisssh. Mmouth is mush… cotton balls."

His voice was still confused, now with a dash of scared. Shay knew he'd need to keep John talking. With his toes, he rocked the chair back. It was a dusty wood floor, and he felt moist grit under his shoes. Turning his ankles, he was able to shove the chair to the left a bit.

"Hurrkkk…" he grunted. He braced with his hand, knowing he dared not try to contort himself with the broken ribs lest he feel that pain again. He shuffled with his feet, slowly turning the chair around.

The wood legs let out a croaking as they scooted on the cement until Shay had turned enough to see John.

John was tied to a similar chair; he was lolling his head, and his hands were tied behind him. His ankles were bound just the same. His head was bandaged up and slanted across his face, his eye covered, and a half-dollar-sized bloodstain coming through the white bandage where his eye should be. It was an awful sight. Worse, Pete was nowhere to be seen. Behind John was an ancient oil-burning boiler leaking around its rusted cradle mounts, making the room unbearably hot.

"Johnny boy, *hey!*"

The urgent and loud whisper caught John's attention. John raised his head slowly, clearly drugged.

"Irisssh your arm… You okay, buddy?"

John smiled halfheartedly but wide enough for Shay to see in the dim light that John had broken several teeth on the right side of his mouth upon the steering wheel of the Dodge during the wreck.

"Oh, Talbot, ye look a bit worse off than I. Stay with me, lad. Please, keep yer head up, yeh?"

John nodded and spat out some blood, but missed the floor. His leg was a red mess from what must have been several failed attempts to spit out the blood from his shattered teeth.

"Okayyy Shay, I'm sorry… I'll… I dunno. So tired…"

He trailed off but held one-eye contact with Shay. In the red light, the blood and sweat ran into a sickening slick on the faces and necks of both men.

"Pete is gone. Do… do you remember anything from the wreck, John? Have you seen Pete since?"

John shook his head, 'No,' and dropped his chin to his chest. In a wet murmur, he replied, "I jusss woke up here, no Pete."

Shay wagered they would be in trouble if they attempted to flee. John was in no state to mount an escape, and Shay was sure that even if he could brave the pain of getting free with all his injuries, he couldn't help John get away without risking both their lives.

You're too fucked to run, boyo. Better rest and recon… These bastards. How long were they following us?

He sat in silence, waiting. Breathing. Hoping for a good idea.

The boiler made a few bubbling blurps, and a few drops of condensation from steam pipes broke the monotonous tone. No sound came from outside the room, and Shay couldn't see any doors. His eyes were still hazy.

Shay knew they were in a bad way, and he would have to wait and see what might come next before he made any moves. He supposed if John wasn't too badly injured, any drugs that were slowing him down should wear off in a few hours. Shay also knew he could use those few hours to rest and heal a bit. He'd been in worse positions than this, and he'd be damned if he would let the captors prevail.

Lifting his chair once again with his feet and bracing himself into it again, he scooted it further left. Now, the red bulb shone dimly from behind him, casting his shadow onto the floor next to John. At the end of the shadow, he could see tufts of dust rising in the red light, perhaps from a draft. It seemed as though there was a door there in the darkness, but it was still too hard to see.

Shay needed a bit of time to consider his options. Some of that would be deciding just how much pain he could take in an escape attempt. Worse, they'd need to find Pete before they went anywhere. Right now, even breathing was hard for him. Shay was impatient, but they were stuck for now.

"Johnny boy, rest up. I'll think of something to get us free, but ye need to sober up. Can you do me a favor?"

John grunted, 'mhhmm,' and his head nodded a bit.

"If there's dope in you, you'll sweat it out quick. Quicker still if you're respirating. Just take deep breaths, squeeze your hands and feet, and move your muscles, okay? Just try and keep moving. Clench your thighs."

"Sure, okayy… I can try…" he murmured before spitting down his leg toward the floor once more.

John then began squirming in his seat, breathing a bit harder. Shay knew this might wear the man out and put him out again from sheer exhaustion, but it might also get them free faster. It was worth the chance. Shay himself closed his eyes to formulate a plan and perhaps say a short prayer, atheistic as he was.

There, in the wet red room, the two men existed. Resting. Squirming. Sweating. Bleeding.

Trapped.

Introductions

Hours had passed. Nobody could say how many. Shay had awakened first and roused John with a few stomps of his foot. The darkness still loomed in most of the room, the red bulb still casting its hue across the two men, giving them just enough light to see their desperate situation.

"How you doin', Irish? Your arm looks busted..."

Shay was relieved to hear John's voice sound a bit more like it should, less slurred and wavery.

"Talbot, you don't concern yourself with my arm. I'm sure I'll be fine in good time; I worry about your head. How's that eye?"

John shook his head back and forth in a futile attempt to remove the sweat-soaked bandage covering his eye.

"I was worried, I was real worried about it before. I can feel myself blinking; I don't know how bad it is, but the pain I can live with. I'm just hoping for the best, pal."

Shay had a bit of a chuckle at that, shooting back, "You and me both, lad. It couldn't get much worse!"

John snorted a cynical laugh.

At that moment, there was a resounding click coming from the darkness on the far side of the boiler. After that, the slow creak of a heavy door opening. Both men hushed their voices and peered toward the sound, and now the breaching light from the hallway. It was a yellow light, industrial and dirty. Something akin to cheap light bulbs, buzzing and flickering just faster than the eye can catch. The mingling of the amber and red hues on the floor was sickening. It looked unearthly to their maladjusted eyes. For a moment, there was no sound. Not even a breath; the bound prisoners held theirs.

A rhythmic squeak began to echo in the room. The grinding of coarse dirt under the squeaky wheels of a rolling cart was slow and deliberate. The cart appeared first around the side of the boiler, followed shortly by a man who could only be described as looking morose. In the dimness, his gaunt facial expression and pronounced cheekbones were offset by his bald head to the extent that he looked something like a graveyard ghoul. Almost immediately, Shay recognized the man as being the same traveler he had seen at the gas station that morning near that brown Chevrolet panel wagon.

The man's heavy boots and coveralls indicated he was a laborer of some kind. His lurching steps with the cart took him to the side of the room, where he left the cart in place against the wall and stood up straight. He said nothing and simply stood there in stillness and silence for what felt like ages. Not wanting to tempt fate, Shay held his multitude of questions about the man and simply waited for something to happen. John squirmed a bit in his seat but understood the need for silence, so he kept his mouth shut.

After a number of minutes, footsteps could be heard approaching in the hallway. They were slower and had a much lighter foot than the silent sentry lurking in the corner. As their echoes reached the outside of the door, there was a pause, and then what sounded like a turn on the heel. The otherwise quiet environment naturally lent emphasis to any of the sounds the men were hearing now.

After a beat, into the room walked a late-middle-aged man in a tattered white lab coat. He was wearing dark slacks and shoes, the frayed and dirty edges of the lab coat looking much like grimy fingers reaching down to meet the floor. The glint of spectacles flashed as he turned in the light, and his round stomach was testing the buttons on the front of the coat. He had a crown of dark hair around the sides of his head and a shadow on his face, indicating he had not shaved in recent days.

The man had walked over to his silent compatriot, placing his hand on the bald man's shoulder and whispering something into his ear. Without a word, the bald man stepped forward and turned, practically marching directly out of the door and into the hallway. From the Doppler effect, he could be heard walking away for quite some time. In the meantime, this potbellied and bespectacled man standing there in the room simply interlaced his fingers and twiddled his thumbs in front of him. It was unsettling, and Shay thought he could see the hint of a smile on the man's lips.

Finally, the man stepped forward from the shadow near the wall into the red glow, sharply cut by the shade over the crimson bulb.

"You have been *naughty* boys, you know."

The words seethed out, with a thick Eastern European accent. It was something akin to Russian, perhaps Bulgarian. Shay found it to be fading, a bit like his own washed-out Irish accent.

"We're good lads, honest. We'll *continue* to be good lads if you tell us where my big friend is," Shay replied sarcastically. His tongue couldn't be held.

The captor stepped toward him, clasped his hands behind his back, and leaned down toward his prisoner.

"I think now is a poor time for joking, young man. You do not appear to be in a position of any power. Do you wish to know *why*?"

Shay counted his words, recognizing this man was a serious type and should be handled as such. Just then, footsteps could be heard in the hallway yet again. The bald Mr. Boots was returning.

"I'll bite. You could have left us or ended us there in that wreck. You brought us here. I'm *dyin'* t'know why, sir."

Mr. Boots walked into the room with a cardboard box, which he dropped on the ground next to Mr. Labcoat. Shay gave them silly names in his head to help himself stay emotionally above the grave reality of the situation. The box was filled with reports and case files from the back seat of the Dodge. Some of them were wet, and some were stained with blood and what looked like motor fluids.

"You have been... searching for me and my *work*, you see. I do not appreciate that, not one bit, young man. Not. One. Bit."

His tone is sharp and clearly perturbed. Following the old man's chastising, Mr. Labcoat leaned further toward Shay, now only a foot away, nose-to-nose. He peered over his small and greasy glasses lenses at Shay' tired face.

"I apologize for that. I could nae have been looking for you as I've no morsel who you are, sir. We were simply following some clues, earning a paycheck. That's all, sir."

Mr. Labcoat huffed at the statement, standing up and pointing toward the box.

"And this *verk*, this paycheck, it is worth... your life?"

He raised an eyebrow. It was a serious question, and he was waiting for a serious answer. Shay considered a response that might be a bit more of a chess move or maneuver than his usual off-the-cuff responses, but the pain in his ribs and his utter exhaustion clouded his usually sharp mind. With luck, John cleared his throat and raised his head. He spoke through broken teeth, his tongue finding their edges between words.

"You seem like an educated man. I hope you'll agree that each man has gotta make his way in the world, and it can't always be something every other man will agree with. Sounds like we just hit an impasse, is all."

Shay let him talk and remained quiet, watching the sentry.

"You are very correct, boy. That is the nature of strong-willed men, I suppose."

Mr. Labcoat squatted down to meet John's eye, his filthy coat edges landing on the damp floor. It was as though he'd ruined his coattails doing this same thing a thousand times. John's breathing intensified, but he held a cycloptic gaze firmly on Mr. Labcoat, who tutted about the situation as he shone a small flashlight in John's uncovered eye before speaking.

"Of course, when I say you are not in a position of power, I simply mean you must *know your place*. I am not a cruel man; in fact, I have already given you a gift, young man. I am a benevolent man, a man of science if nothing else."

He took John's hand, still taped to the armchair, and clasped it with his right hand in an affirming and very friendly gesture. With his left hand, he tapped John on the forehead just over the bandaged eye.

John swallowed the lump of fear in his throat and spoke up, "We're worker bees, sir. That's all. What can we do to, uh… I suppose maybe get outta here?"

John was serious, but Mr. Labcoat laughed at his question. From the side of the room and cast in shadow, Mr. Boots simply stood there, arms limp at his sides.

"You are quite brave to ask that, Mister Talbot. With all of the information you possessed? It was only a matter of time before you found my little facility,' The man adjusted his dirty glasses and stood up again before continuing, 'and I have no intention of letting you hounds back out into the wild so you may *sniff* me out once again. No, that is not acceptable."

He turned and marched over to the little cart, lifting the cloth draped over it. Underneath were a good dozen glass jars, each with some liquid and some with an object inside. The dim light gave away no secrets here. Mr. Labcoat removed two lidded jars from the cart and turned back toward the boys. He held each jar out in front of him, allowing some of the hallway light to shine through its murky contents.

"I must inform you, both of you men *shall* individually be answering my questions. I have no ill intention toward you *personally*, and as such, I will be making use of this delightful concoction I possess. It is not dangerous to either of you. Each of you will imbibe what you are given, and then we will discuss... shall we say, reality and opportunity."

Through his accent, his enunciation was impressive to Shay. It was clear he was a highly educated man despite his relatively humble, even off-putting appearance. Shay supposed he should try to steer what might happen next.

"Ye've plenty of options here, sir. My friend and I are happy to cooperate; there's nary a thing we can do but cooperate. Is there any hope we could turn on the light and have a conversation? Make introductions? It's awful poor in here. I'm in a bit of pain, and I think we'd be happy to cooperate freely if you'd be willing to improve our conditions... just a bit?"

He had repeated the word 'cooperate' several times. It was an old subliminal trick that often helped sway minds. In this case, it was a Hail Mary pass, as he had little recourse and not a single other idea in his rattled mind.

"I think *not*, young man. I am pleased you've survived this far, and I look forward to what they say in the Westerns. 'Test your mettle,' yes, that's the saying. I'm going to test your mettle, and then we shall *talk*."

Shay offered, "Well, get on with it, old boy. We've little choice being tied up and such, and I'm in no mood to bicker about it. John, let's do as the man says?"

John gave a knowing nod and grunted, 'mm-hmm,' and they braced for whatever came next.

Mr. Labcoat handed one of the jars to Mr. Boots. They removed the lids of the jars and forced both Shay and John to drink the contents to the bottom. It was not a particularly unpleasant taste, but Shay could tell that hidden in the sweetness of the cloudy concoction was something very chemical, something very foreign and unnatural. His palate felt odd, very cottony. Within moments, and by the time the captors had returned the jars to the cart, his head began to swim.

There was no fight left in him now, and his body felt weak. Frail. Yet, at the same time, he could feel the blood in his veins pumping warm, like his heart was churning... shunting more blood than usual. It was an odd sensation, very inwardly sensitive. He felt like he was becoming a warm river of blood carving through a landscape of damaged meat and bone. Taking a deep breath, he let his head back limp and prayed for the potent drugs to run their course.

Mr. Labcoat and Mr. Boots left the room, returning the boys to near darkness.

"Irish? I don't feel right. This ain't what they gave me before, not… so…" John's voice trailed off. He had slipped unconscious. Shay lifted his head to see, but it fell chin-to-chest as his vision faded to an oily black.

Interrogatory

Shay awoke, feeling alert, and looked for the red light. The room was pitch dark. No, not just dark. He realized he could not open his eyes. They felt glued shut, and his head was too heavy to hold high correctly. Despite this, his mind felt sharp, and his hearing was fine. It was as though the drugs were only weighing down his body now, leaving his mind clear.

In the blackness, he heard what had woken him. It was the sound of heavy boots yet again, but, upsettingly, he also heard a chair being dragged across that gritty floor. It was not his own; it must be John's. He opened his mouth to protest what he assumed was occurring, but at that moment, his throat felt white and cottony, just as his palate had before. No words escaped his mouth, only a bit of breathy gargling from the saliva that had collected in his throat while he was unconscious. His mind screamed, but his body whispered.

He awaited a response, any response, but the dragging sounds continued, and nothing interacted with Shay now: the clatter of a closing door, the muted sounds of footsteps heading away, the creak of a chair dragging in tow. This moment was the first that Shay was truly and genuinely *scared*. He was blinded, physically broken, and bound in what may as well be no place at all. If he could scream, he wouldn't bother now. There was no light in the room and no hope in his heart at the moment, so he swallowed through the dryness of his throat and relaxed his heavy head.

He could feel his arm healing; the fracture in his forearm was beginning to cement. He remembered breaking that arm as a child, having fallen off a brick garden wall trying to catch a butterfly that was fluttering about. His mind swirled back home now, around the imagery of the bright sun and blue sky over lush, green meadows. The forefront of his mind was a quaint memory about the last time he took a walk to the sea, the last day he saw home. He tried desperately to hold onto that memory, but it was to no avail.

From the back of his consciousness sprang the notion that he had never been in a worse situation, a darker place. He had never smelled so much of his blood and pus, and he had never experienced a situation where he couldn't see a way out. The dread of hopelessness had set in, and it was weighing heavily on his heart, sedated as his body was. In the darkness there, all he felt now was the binding on his ankles and wrist. That, and the sputtering tears rolling down his cheeks as the severity of his situation sank in.

In silence, he wished for a clock. He imagined the ticking for a while, trying to keep time, trying to count the minutes. It nearly drove him mad, as he reached well over an hour without a sight or a sound breaking the monotony. It was like being trapped in a well where nobody might come for water. The only echoing thought left now was, would they bring John back? He lay his head back and forced himself to sleep.

Sometime later, he was rocked awake. He could see again, though blurry. He felt a hand on his shoulder, and another rock his chair back. As he leaned back, he looked up and saw the sallow and serious face of Mr. Boots. The face was upside down. Boots began dragging Shay out of the room. He paused and set Shay's chair to rest, and John was next to him, regaining consciousness and writhing in his chair.

"Hey! Wake up, Shay, they're gonna…" The voice was cut off with a wet thump.

Boots had knocked John out cold, probably a blackjack to the noggin or some other nasty device. Shay's body was still too doped up to speak, merely grunting his disapproval.

He was dragged what felt like a hundred yards down several hallways lined with random doors and narrow, unmarked hallways leading off in directions he could not see. Every so often, they would pass underneath an old ceiling light, and Shay noticed that the bulbs were archaic. They looked like they might be 50 years old, some of them almost looking like handblown glass, like an old Edison bulb. This place was *old*.

After dragging Shay into a room near the end of one of these hallways, Mr. Boots set him down and turned on the light; it was blinding. The ceiling was lined with fluorescent tubes, and there was a sickening blue tinge, the irksome buzz they put off. He looked around, and his vision nearly returned. What he could see clear enough to identify was a row of steel examination tables, or perhaps they were just workbenches. There were large objects in the corner of the room, covered in a drop cloth —a heavy green canvas that smelled like machine oil or heavy grease. Immediately, Shay was reminded of the smell of the Army canvas tents that he had resided in on several occasions during the last war. It was a familiar smell, and he realized that those might be surplus materials.

The last thing he could identify across the right side of the room was a glassware chemistry rig. It was sprawled across about 20 feet of countertop, and the lighting gleamed off the tubes.

Look at this Vincent Price movie set Hollywoodland fookin' shite...

With a huff, Mr. Boots dragged him to the direct center of the room, facing the wall furthest from the door and toward the draped objects that loomed near the corner of the room. Here, he was left in silence for several minutes as he took stock of the room.

A voice came from just behind, startling him.

"You're prepared now, I see.' It was Mr. Labcoat, with his tongue-sharp accent, 'You should be ready for our testing of the mettle, mister Irish. Your friend truly cares for you. Your papers say Séamus, but no, I think I will also call you *Irish*."

"Fookin' hell, old man! You spooked me half to death with all these theatrics!"

The words came out raspy, but his voice was returning. Still, the words he used felt odd. It was as though his response was not as measured as he intended. The drugs were clouding his judgment. Mr. Labcoat put his hand on Shay's bad shoulder over the sling arm. Shay winced but did not cry out.

"You're strong, I see. You must have a tolerance for pain. I admire that. Your friend, Mr. Talbot, does not. He did not seem to possess much mettle, it seems. Sad."

The words seethed out of his mouth. He was grinning, excited. Shay could hear it, though the man still stood behind him.

"I know who you are and why you are here. I wonder, do you know who I am?"

Shay shook his head, biting his lip as Mr. Labcoat released the grip on his shoulder.

"No, but I've known men like you," he offered.

"I'm curious, how so?" Mr. Labcoat walked around him and now squatted in front of him, making eye contact. The man's face was a mess of dry skin, rashes, and minor scars. His ears were large and dark inside, with untrimmed hair, and his eyebrows were thin from age and lousy skin. The smiling continued, and the teeth in this man's head were a shade between piss-yellow and concrete-grey. Shay almost had to look away.

"You're a genius and probably a mad science type like in the films. And now you've got me and my friends in your house of horrors, I'd say. Where are ye holding my boy Pete, ya daft fucking mad Russkie *cunt*?"

Shay felt almost embarrassed at his accusation. He had no intention of pissing off his captor, but the words simply came out of him bluntly. His mind whispered, *'It was the drugs they fed ya, must have been….'*

"No, no, young man. I am simply a Doctor, so you may call me a Doctor, and I am here to practice medicine. Perhaps it is medicine you simply do not understand. Is that mad?"

"If you're the sick bastard who gutted those bodies and set them walking again, yeh, you're mad. I *should* call you Doctor Frankenstein. Now, *where* is my pal Pete?"

He was testing his captor. The smile never broke. This man was broken inside, and it was coming out of every crack and crevice in his face—an ugly, determined madness. Shay could feel it in the air between them.

"Irish, we can't be friends if you continue to insult. I am not your enemy, though you may think so. I will likely employ methods you do not appreciate, but in this, we must… agree to disagree. And your friend is indisposed. You mustn't worry yourself about the large man."

The Doctor stood up and adjusted his glasses with his index finger. The nail was thick, calcified, and yellowed.

"I know John's alive, so for that, I'll say ye may not be all bad. Doesn't make us pals, old boy. Never will. Now, get on with it."

He was furious at being shrugged off over his missing partner, but couldn't let his emotions take over. He fought the drugs that were making him so talkative.

The Doctor put his hands on his hips, looking disappointed.

"Get on with what, young man? What do you think I brought you here to accomplish?"

"I suspect that you're gonna cut us up, hurt us, try to get us to talk."

The doctor chuckled and walked away toward the examination tables. He sat against them, folding his arms, his ankles now crossed nonchalantly.

"Your kind always feel so special, believing you hold some knowledge that I do not possess. I am smarter than you, young man. I have no questions, and I seek no answers from you. I am conversing with you as... let us call it, a bedside manner. You are here because I find your bodies useful. That is the extent of it all."

Shay was worried. The man seemed relaxed and not threatening now.

"Then what the devil do you *want* from me?" Shay demanded.

"Your *guts*, mister Irish. I just want to test your guts! Like in the cinemas!" He clenched his fists, thrusting them toward Shay's abdomen comically, throwing shadow-boxing punches as his glasses slid down his greasy nose. He was grinning widely, and his eyes gave away his amusement even moreso.

Shay shot back, "Oh, so we're simply laboratory rats? Here for your amusement?"

"No, Mister Irish. I will find many practical uses for two living bodies. The amusement is... tertiary, at best. Now let us proceed."

Sick sonofabitch. He's using us like he used the dead. He's graduating from stiffs to living men. If I don't get us out of here...

With that, the Doctor walked over to the draped objects on the far side of the room. Shay braced as the doctor unceremoniously slipped one of the heavy green canvas tarps to the floor. The smell, which struck Shay like a slap in the face, was putrid but very chemical. His eyes still hadn't become clear, so he squinted.

Shay could see some movement and something that looked like glass. It was a tall object, about six feet. Its shape was difficult to discern, but it was pyramid-like. There was movement at the top of the tower of shapes.

"You've made a gaffe, old boy; I can hardly see shite. Art project?" he asked; Shay's sarcasm was speaking for him. The drugs gave him little self-control.

The Doctor walked over to Shay, leaning forward again and peering into his eyes.

"Ah, I see. We will need to rectify the serum—too much numbing agent, not enough stimulant. Your vision shall not be so blurred in the future. Come, let's get a closer look, shall we?"

Mr. Boots was behind Shay, who had not noticed. His chair was shoved aggressively toward the pyramid of shapes in the corner. Shay looked up at Mr. Boots as he was shoved. Shay memorized this man's face well, in anger. He turned his head back to the mass of shapes just in front of him. A drop cloth remained on most of this heap, but the upper glassy-looking portion he'd made out before was uncovered.

Turning his gaze upward, Shay's vision was met with a damned odd sight. The top of this object was a glass-like tubule, like a jar, and in it was the head of a large dog. The rest of this towering shape could not be seen; it was under another drop cloth.

Shay grunted. "You mad bastard…"

The murky brown liquid sloshed around a bit as the head of this dog turned to make eye contact with Shay. Its neck must have been attached to its body through the bottom of the container. The poor submerged animal opened its mouth to reveal teeth and a tongue, which jostled clumps of floating debris and sloughed rotten tissue floating through the liquid, which filled the container nearly to the brim. Its eyes looked down and met Shay's gaze, and through the convex glass, this poor creature conveyed fear.

This creature was itself afraid. It moved its lips and jaw but made no sound. As it moved and blinked at them, more bits of rotten flesh from its lips and eyelids fell away into the viscous liquid.

Shay vomited across his stomach and lap. Bile, blood, a bit of the sick concoction which he had been forced to drink. It soaked into his clothes, and he spat up as his eyes welled up with disgust and sadness.

"You *made* this poor thing? Great fookin' work, you sick demented clown! Damned mad science. I stand by my reasoning, *Doctor*."

His captor beamed with pride at the horrifying scene.

"You're bothered? It's strange, yes, but the science of replacing a gaseous environment with a liquid composition has allowed us great strides in adapting the environment in which a living thing may survive. Is it not interesting? Think of the *implications...*" the doctor trailed off, taking off his glasses so he could peer closer into the container himself.

Shay was scowling, staring daggers through this cruel man who clearly had no empathy for that decrepit creature. The Doctor took no notice.

"Let me show you something even more surprising, Mister Irish. May I?"

Shay sneered, glancing down at his bound hand and remarking, "As though I've got a choice?"

The doctor chuckled and patted Shay on his good shoulder. He held his gaze with Shay, reaching back and grasping a furl of the second drop cloth underneath the glass vessel. With the wicked smile still on his face, he leaned closer to Shay yet again. This time, he whispered into Shay's ear with hot, foul breath.

"You are going to *understand* my work, my new friend."

With a tug, the second drop cloth fell away and gathered in a pile on the floor. The smell hit Shay in the face like a closed hand—it was a copper smell, sulfurous and rotting. As he looked up at this tower of shapes, the edges fell away, and his eyes refocused toward the center.

In front of him was the greasy and half-rotted body of an obese man. Metal barrel straps held the body to a wooden crate framework and dug into the fat, slick skin. There were black cable-like stitches running up a jagged line in the chest like an autopsy was performed via hatchet. Fetid, blood-and-pus-soaked rags lay across open incisions. The left leg and right arm were gone altogether; the skin flaps edged in gangrenous shades where they had been sewn up after the limbs were eviscerated from the body. The neck was stippled in a lattice of sutures, but the worst of it was peeking out from under a wrap of putrid old gauze.

Just in view, underneath and covered in vaseline or some other greasy muck, could be seen the specific place where this human torso had been joined to the head of that dog who was peering down at Shay through the thick and contaminated fluid.

Shay was speechless for a moment, his emotions of disgust and horror mingling with sheer awe. A rock of sheer revulsion set in the bottom of his stomach, and he dry heaved, but no more vomit came forth despite the stench. Shay's jaw was agape, and his body was flush and sweating, his brain screaming with all the rage and shock and terror he'd ever felt, magnified by ten times.

He felt a firm pair of hands on his shoulders as the Doctor stood behind him, nodding and admiring his work. Shay could now see the slight twitches in the body, the dog's head moving unclearly in the sloshing bin. The leg of the thing shifted a bit; its flesh gouged deeply where it had been fighting those restraint straps for long enough to ruin the tissue nearly to the bone.

"Yes, yes. You see, the *extent* of my research goes beyond what most would ever dream."

The Doctor walked around the chair where he stood in front of Shay, taking to one knee and now grasping Shay's legs with his chilly grip. He dug his thumbs into Shay's thighs, hard and deep, sliding them up toward Shay's crotch. He was looking for a reaction.

His hand moved until his thumb pressed against Shay's testicles, and the Doctor was breathing heavily.

"This is what I can do with *ruined* flesh. Imagine what I can do with tissues that are... Vigorous..."

Shay shut his eyes tightly and fought the drugs. He felt this almost surreal drive to shout, scream and vomit, and curse the gods. His jailor was reprehensible and monstrous, but Shay clenched his jaw now to retain the roiling stew of vitriol his mind crafted. He firmly squeezed the arm of the chair with his right hand and took one deep breath. He knew what he had to do.

Exhaling sharp and fast, Shay slid his broken left arm out of its makeshift sling and thrust it dead forward, latching his hand onto the neck of the Doctor in front of him. His grip was weaker than usual but still fierce, and the surprise caught the Doctor entirely off guard.

Shay could feel an Adam's apple in his hand, giving way under the pressure of his furious grip. He would *crush* this man's goddamned throat.

My arm, it feels... Shay's eyes widened as his blood ran ice cold.

The Doctor let out a wet, strained gurgle as his hands flailed and tried to pry away Shay's hand.

Just then, Mr. Boots came out of nowhere once again and punched Shay in his still-broken ribs. The explosion of pain caused Shay's body to recoil; his grip dropped as he curled his arm into his ribs, instinctively, trying to protect the weak spot. He let out a bloody scream, and the massive mutant strapped down in front of him snapped its head toward him as it began convulsing in its liquid prison.

Excitement. Terror. Pain. The air of the room was drenched in all of it.

The Doctor sat on the floor, off balance and in a state of surprise. Mr. Boots said no words, merely poised between the Doctor and Shay. The restless, pathetic sounds of the creature in the jar, wriggling its well-fastened limbs, could be heard over the doctor's efforts to catch his breath.

"You... your ARM! Do you SEE? This is... *cough* This is my *work*! The effects are faster than I have ever seen... You will believe, mister Irish!" the Doctor gasped the words out.

Shay was nearly doubled over and wincing at his broken and battered ribs, but through his tears of pain, he sneered at the Doctor, whose throat was already showing a shade of purple.

Christ... my arm... he gave me... I should still be crippled... confusion wracked Shay's mind as he realized he'd been experimented upon already.

Even my chest, my ribs... I should be blacked out from that hit. I've healed so much... what did they do to me? What have they done to John?

The Doctor regained his feet and stormed out of the room, coughing and sputtering. Mr. Boots dutifully tied Shay' left arm down at the wrist, taking away all his freedom. Mr. Boots then walked away, stone-faced and saying nothing.

Shay was left there in the chair, with this wriggling fat corpse and the sad-eyed dog, for far too long. It took him a while, but his body found Shay something else to vomit up. All he could do was shut his eyes and heave until he passed out from the pain in his ribs and utter exhaustion.

They left him there, sitting in this filth, for hours.

Weakness

John was tipped over in his chair, lying on his side. His head was sore from where it was struck, but moreso from where it hit the ground. He hardly noticed, as bad as his mouth still ached. Half awake, he dragged his tongue across the viciously sharp, shattered teeth, counting them as he went. He kept losing track of one nasty gap where a tooth had been uprooted instead of shattered. *It could have been worse, I suppose. Maybe I'll lose a couple of pounds. Janine said I look heavyish.*

Janine was a sweet-faced girl he'd met at the dive bar near Smith Tower on one night he'd been too couch-sore to fall asleep in Billy's office. She was just a sight, a Rubenesque little gal with half-Indian blood and a tongue as sharp as Shay's. She worked as a ticketer for Greyhound, and boy, was she fun after a couple of highballs. "Shoulda kissed 'er goddammit," John grumbled to himself, spitting out a clod of dirt from the floor as he spoke. His thoughts of hourglass waistlines faded as Mr. Boots dragged a still-chairbound Shay into the room, plopping Shay in the same place his seat had been before.

"Talbot, ye still alive?"

John, face still pressed to the floor and chair still bound to his body, replied with a gravely, tired voice.

"Pissed m'self."

"Me too, Johnny boy, me too. *Hours* ago."

A dead silence followed their banter in the room. Mr. Boots stood there between the men. John coughed a bit, then looked up sideways with his one eye toward Shay.

"See any potted plants around?"

"Ha! You fooking dolt. No ficus or ferns for you. Just the floor."

Mr. Boots looked to John, then back to Shay. He stood pensively, almost looking as though he didn't know what to do. Shay had an idea.

"Hey, pal. I wonder could ye roust up a bucket? We've been here a day, and I've got to use the loo again."

John piped up, "Yeah, for sitting. Not standing. Get the picture?"

The bald, silent man glanced over his shoulder at the door and left the room without a word.

John and Shay chuckled at the stupidity of it all. Shay was trying hard not to think about the hours he'd just spent sitting in a room alone with a crime against nature. It was the last horror Shay wished to see or think about for the rest of his days.

"Did you see the dog?" John asked toward the floor.

"Oh, can we not talk about the fuh-*huck*-ing dog... please. This is a shite show, and I'd rather not discuss that monstrosity, yeh?"

"Sorry, Irish."

Silence for a moment.

"...But it *was* a fuckin' mess, wasn't it?"

"God-DAMMIT, John Talbot, just lie there and shut up while I think."

"...Sorry."

"...Aye, it was a mess..." Shay sighed.

Shay was exhausted, and John was right. There was a showmanship about it. The Doctor wanted to display his creation, his genius. It smacked of pride, which was nearly the stereotypical 'mad scientist' of lore, something a bit Mary Shelley. In truth, that beast in the last room was more frightening than any fabled monster.

Defeated, he decided to open up a bit to John. After all, this might be their final hours. "I think it took me about an hour."

John lifted his head, engaged. "An hour for what, Shay?"

"Took me about an hour before I wasn't scared o' the thing anymore. Never seen, never *imagined* such a fucking sight. That thing is like an eldritch other, an unspeakable thing. An obscenity, it's... It's against nature. An affront."

"But after an hour?"

"Chrissakes, man. I just... I felt *sorry* for the thing. I wept, John. I wept for all of this. We make light of things to keep our feet moving; we harden our hearts against the horrors of mankind's war machine and the way society chews up and spits out the weak... but that thing? I saw it, John.

"I saw it too. Real up-close, the doc-"

"No, John. I... I *saw* it. I connected with the thing. The eyes of a dog, of a mammal... that was somebody's pet once. A tame thing, a loved one. A house dog. I could see the pain in its eyes… it was a plea, John. Suffering there, hurting, unimaginably hurt. I fookin' *wept* like a baby. I don't think I can bear to see that pitiful thing again. It broke my heart."

John was taken aback. In his years of knowing this man, he couldn't have predicted such softness. He had always looked to his friends as a source of strength, and seeing this weakness in Shay now broke something in John as well. He felt beaten and deflated.

"Shay, you... You're a tough sonofabitch. I might seem like... well, I'm not. I'm a wreck, I'm a drunkard, and you boys are better than I deserve. If you don't stay strong, how are we ever gonna find Pete? Who's going to take that Miss Fisher out and tell her he's in love with her?"

Shay snorted. "Ah, Christ. Yeh, maybe I'm sweet on her. Can't say the thought hasn't occurred to me…"

"I could tell, Irish. So what? She's a little older. She's one in a million, and from what I could see, she's yours if you just *ask*. Gotta live through this crap if you want the chance, though, you skinny delirious sonofabitch." John was smiling, which was an odd sight, considering he was beaten to hell and lying on a filthy floor.

"Heh. I'll think of something, Talbot. Just rest up and be ready for *any*thing."

Mr. Boots broke the silence with his heavy steps in the hall. Stomping into the room, he dropped an old metal pail on the floor between the duo. He hastily cut the ties to the chair from John's ankles, binding his ankles together. He then uprighted John, cutting his wrist ties.

John needed no instruction; he grabbed the pail and hopped around behind the boiler. He took a few minutes, then hopped back around without the pail. Mr. Boots repeated his unbinding/binding ritual with Shay, still without a word. John waved his friend to the 'loo.'

"Your turn, Irish. I dumped it behind that scrap pile near the steam pipes. You might do the same."

Shay took the opportunity while Mr. Boots reattached John to that damn filthy chair with the baling twine he carried. Within minutes, Shay was finished and tied right back down. Again, both of his hands were bound to the chair.

"I could use somethin' for the ribs, old boy. Think the doc can script me for a Paracetamol?" He received a blank stare in return.

Mr. Boots departed, but not before Shay grasped his hand and implored him for water and food. Boots left without comment but returned shortly later with a loaf of stale bread and one thermos of water. It wasn't much, but the men appreciated it nonetheless.

There was something in the man's eyes. The man never really looked at anything, but more toward it. It was eerie, but in this little fact, Shay could see that this man wasn't 'all there,' wasn't right in the head. He'd file that idea away for future use.

For a while, the duo sat and whispered. They shared their ideas about the place, the long hallways, and the old equipment. John thought it looked like an industrial complex, which was out of place in the area. Shay had a few guesses but wanted to discuss John's eye.

"Does it still itch?"

"I guess. Not as much now. I can still feel myself blinking, sure. It's sorta... crusty under there. Scabbed or whatnot. I can't see shit, but I don't think I lost the eye."

"Guess we'll give it a peek when we cut loose of this madhouse."

The heat in the room wasn't as bad now, which meant the boiler was cycling and someone was controlling the temperature in the building. Their conversation turned back to the building. The floor plan meant the building must be at least a half-block long, and it was also rather old construction. The place reminded Shay of a barracks and armory he'd visited once in San Francisco a few years prior. It was cement over brick, tarred corners, and a weighty, poorly-poured foundation. Narrow doorways with wooden doors, no fanciful molding or decoration to be seen. It felt very drab and utilitarian, like an old prison, but without the iron bars.

In their limited observations, neither John nor Shay had seen nor heard any indication of 'outside.' No windows, sounds, or voices. Just the Doctor and his bald friend, and a musty smell that permeated every breath of air.

"S'gotta be underground, man. I think we're underground. There is no air in here. It's... stale."

They talked about Pete for a moment, but only for that long. Neither man wanted to guess why their friend had been kept separate, but they agreed to search for him first if they were able to free themselves. It was a hardship not to know anything about the big guy.

Mr. Boots came around sometime later, dragging Shay out into the hallway and to the middle of a small room not so far away as the last time. It was a cell of a room, some ten by fifteen feet, and nothing but the doorway and a bulb in the ceiling. The grey, dirty walls made Shay uncomfortable, but he refused to complain to this mute drone in the coveralls. He stared at the wall for a little while.

A familiar voice joined him from behind.

"Your effort earlier was in vain, though I hold no ill will. A caged animal will inevitably rattle the bars... futile as it may be. Are you feeling better?"

The Doctor's voice was a bit hoarse but still firm and willful.

"I'm fine, you old *sod*. Don't worry about me, just sitting here in my stink thinking about leaving soon."

The Doctor laughed at the statement as he put on some exam gloves.

"You'll be here for some time, young man. I've got much research to do with you. When my compatriot here brought your group in off the road, I had much fixing to do. Your arm was out of its socket, your ribs protruding far worse. I see they're healing well. Your friend in there, he's got a special gift of mine. You will *see* in time."

Shay leaned forward a bit and caught his eye to ask yet again, "...Pete? What about him?"

"Oh, you'll see your sizable friend again soon, I can promise you. Now, let's focus on you, my special new project. Let's have a look at your hand there and see what we can see. Yes?"

The Doctor cut the rope, securing Shay' injured arm. Although the doctor's dragging a stool out for Shay to sit on in front of him was unsettling, it was far more troubling when the man performed a gentle, careful, and comprehensive medical examination of Shay's injuries. His touch was clinical but doting.

"I placed penicillin in the water to keep you from festering, as well as painkillers, so that you could function. Your ribs will heal; it's moreso a flesh wound you have here, mister Irish. I will set the protruding rib now."

Shay perked up, realizing what that meant. Simultaneously, Mr. Boots came from behind and pulled a leather strap into Shay's mouth to bite down. Shay knew the score and did so without question. In one quick and very succinct motion, the Doctor used his palm and thumb to set the rib back into place.

Click.

"AUUGGHHHHHOOOOOOooooooohhhhh ye cunt!"

Shay howled through the leather chew, and his body tensed up while the agonizing pain shot through his body, subsiding into a dull, stabbing pressure that was far more bearable. While Shay was in tears from the pain of the rib being forced back into place, the doctor took that distraction as a chance to draw a vial of blood from Shay' bound arm. It did not go unnoticed, but Shay held his tongue. The doctor replaced his gloves and returned to inspecting Shay's injuries.

"My new friend, you have quite a tolerance for pain. You are very familiar with pain. I wonder if this has any connection to the fact that you are healing at a rate I have rarely seen outside of theoretical projections?"

The Doctor held Shay's arm out straight, an arm that should still be broken. A fracture like that should take weeks to heal, and there was little left of it now but bruising.

"I'm keen on vitamins, don't ya know!" Shay joked. He was met with an icy, humorless gaze.

"Do you think my work here is *interesting*? While you and your friends have met my brilliant creations, you have no *idea* how we are making such strides! I may tell you in time."

He took the rope and re-tied Shay's arm to the chair; Shay was fully bound once more. The Doctor reached down with a scalpel he'd deftly produced from his pocket and cut a deep incision into the meat of Shay's leg.

"Jeezus, FOOK, man. What are ye doin' that for? I'm cooperating!" Shay cried.

"Yes, and this is a good opportunity for me to observe your body cooperating with my experimentation, Mister Irish. I will return in a matter of hours to check on your... *progress.*

Doctor Labcoat took a small ruler from his other pocket, placing it next to the wound after dabbing some gauze to reduce the blood. Mr. Boots handed him a camera, which he used to photograph the incision. It was all so very clinical, and Shay was gritting his jaw, focusing on feeling the metallic tinge of blood mixing with the chill of adrenaline as his captors stood up and left the room, abandoning him once again to watch a bare wall. He squirmed as he watched the wound in his leg run red, the exposed muscle fiber shifting around in the pooling blood.

This loon is going to cut, poke, and prod until we're dead or too diminished to experiment on. It has to stop.

Over the next few hours, working through the pain, he devised a plan. It was a simple plan, but possibly his only chance to escape with John. The last thought on his mind now was seeking the answers that had brought him and his friends so much calamity. He knew he'd need to spring the escape soon, maybe shortly after he was once again returned to the boiler room with John.

Cooperation

What felt like ages had passed; Shay was thirsty and famished. His leg hurt, but not as much as his ribs. He looked down at the wound that the doctor had created; it had been a two-inch incision, and now it was a puckered 3/4" wink of a cut. He knew this would fare poorly for him if the madman decided to make him another experiment, like those walking corpses, or perhaps... he shuddered at the thought of that poor dog and its terrible fate. Sounds returned to the room behind him.

Whatever this cus made us drink has affected how I'm healing. My arm is nearly back to good, and my leg should still be bleeding out, but... oh god. I hope Pete's faring better than us...

"Mister Irish, we are back to check on your well-being!"

The Doctor was in fine spirits. The man walked around his chair. Shay could immediately smell the gore and blood spattered across his lab coat. The cuffs and smock were stained a ghastly black-red. The coat smelled like something else, too—something like tar or epoxy. It smelled toxic. The Doctor squatted in front of Shay and took a good look at the wound.

"Why, my friend, we are in such great luck! My theory is proving correct, and you are quite the specimen, aren't you?"

His accent was heavy on the word *specimen*; it was grotesque. Shay said nothing.

"You'll need to explain, Doc. I'm a simple-minded sort."

"Our serum is more compatible with your... *makeup*... than the others. Now, I'm tasked with finding the reason. Is it genetic? Is it your diet or something environmental? Oh, I wish I could speak to your mother. This is quite the encouraging finding!"

The Doctor took another photograph with the little ruler, and his face was beaming. He was nearly giddy.

"Mister Irish, my new best friend! Come, come. We are going to get you cleaned up! This is wonderful news!"

Mr. Boots came and cut the bindings on Shay's wrists and feet. Shay was worried this situation might be a trap; it was too easy. He knew the men should be more worried about him fighting back.

"Oh, I can read your mind, mister Irish. You will not be acting out, no. You're going to be a *good* boy. Do you know why?' and without waiting for a response, he answered his question, 'Because you do not know where your *little* friends are, and you do not know where my *big* friends are. You won't do anything foolish because you know if you do, they might be subject to punishment in your stead. Isn't that right?"

Shay stood up slowly and rubbed his raw wrists, nodding his head.

"May I just go back in with John? I'm not really interested in… whatever you've got planned, Doc."

"Oh no, my friend. We have so much to learn from each other! Come, follow me. We must begin at *once!*"

Hurriedly, the Doctor strode out of the room, beckoning Shay to follow. Shay did just that, with Mr. Boots immediately behind. Their path took them down a baffling number of corridors. Shay realized that this was no simple building; there was some sort of large complex. There were no markings on any doors nor any signs on the walls, so he paid close attention to the floor layout and listened for any hints that might help him navigate if he was able to get free with John and Pete. In one particularly well-lit corridor, there was one single white door on a pale gray wall. The door looked newer than the rest, but perhaps only because it was a metal door of far sturdier construction.

The three men entered the room, and the doctor put his hand on Shay's shoulder to guide him through it. Much to Shay's dismay, it was another grim scene of examination tables and medical equipment. More worrisome, most of the tables appeared to be occupied.

As the madman strode with Shay toward the far end of the sizeable room, he pointed out some of his work. It was unsettling, and Shay simply listened, making no remarks or asking any questions.

"That is where I am taking new specimens and cleaning them, and over that way is where I work with the 'parts and pieces.' Some of the bodies, you know… they do not arrive in good condition, you see?" He gestured his hand in a scattering motion, flippant considering the subject.

"One subject arrived without legs. LEGS, mister Irish! How silly is that? I'd almost prefer no specimen at all! *Almost."*

Shay looked where the doctor was pointing and saw a very flaccid corpse of a white man, partly draped in white linen, but you could clearly see where the arm and leg of a similarly proportioned colored man had been stitched on and somehow fused. It looked almost as though there was scar tissue at the separation lines; Shay thought about what Doc Lowell had shown them some days prior.

"Nice work, Doc. Ye should be tailoring tuxedos with that stitch work!"

"You see, there are so very many preparations to make when I am building another of my friends. From what Mister John Talbot told me when I interrogated him, you had not only found one of my creations far north of here, but I understand you had a bit of an altercation! Isn't that exquisite? The kismet of how you were destined to come to me. While I have found some success with the fresh —I should say, the recently deceased —my future lies in making use of the living. One could call it... repurposing."

He was patting Shay on the back, almost in a friendly manner. It was damn awkward, but Shay held his ground. It seemed that somehow, through simply the ownership of his abilities, he might have ingratiated himself with this lunatic.

"Like ye done to mister boots?"

"Boots? Ah, I see you refer to my silent colleague. He... is another matter entirely."

They came upon that table with the multi-colored body splayed open from groin to throat. They stood there, and the doctor seemed to be waiting for Shay to ask a question. Shay peered over the body and saw something quite amiss. There was a substance in the body, something drastically unfamiliar. It was black and viscous, clinging to tissue and the edges of bone. There was no grit to it; it was almost translucent in the few places it had been spread thin. Shay was disgusted but curious. And with a man like Shay, curiosity always wins.

Swallowing the feeling of green in his stomach and throat, the detective took a light breath and lifted his chin. In an almost chipper tone, he asked the question that would come quickly to anybody, but few would have the courage to ask.

"What's the story with all the black muck in there, Doc?"

He nodded his head toward the chasm in the cold vessel, trying to hide his unsteadiness by leaning on the edge of the table. It was piss-poor acting, but the Doc was smiling widely.

He had struck the right cord. The doctor clasped his hands together excitedly and stepped over to the table to explain. Before he spoke a word, it became clear that he was something of a hand-talker. He offered a palm, stretching it outward toward the monstrosity, as his heels met in a pose that was almost theatrical. It was clear he had been waiting for an opportunity to get up on a soapbox, so to speak.

"Young man, in my work, there is a simple saying that, when extrapolated, would give you all the answers you seek. They say that all answers lie under the surface. You must simply... make your incision —sometimes literally —and ask your question. In fact, that was something a colleague of mine had told me on more than one occasion. He was the best Oxford offered, but in the end, he was never able to cut deeply enough to answer all the questions I brought. Instead, when I returned to my home country, I stopped asking questions of other men of science. I was ostracized by my peers almost immediately. Those timid fools were afraid of the future, you see."

"But you weren't the type to stop asking, were ye?" Shay prodded.

"Never. I simply asked for permission to find my answers from those in power. It's funny to me; it amuses me the way people are so afraid to ask questions the way I do. So, without my colleagues, I persisted. And I found my believers in the men who funded my work. True visionaries, all."

He withdrew a gleaming scalpel from his pocket. It was slender, with a knurled handle and a blade half as long as the handle itself. Looking down his filthy glasses into the void of the torso, the doctor reached in and used the scalpel to remove a bit of fatty tissue from the inside of the rib cage. Pink mixed with black, settling on the blade as the doctor lifted the sample for Shay to inspect more closely.

The smell was burning Shay's nostrils, but he played along and swallowed his disgust. He had no intention to offend his host, so he did his best to withhold the bile churning in his gut as he leaned forward toward the sample held in front of him as though it were a soup spoon.

"Just what are we looking at?"

The Doctor's gaze turned from the sample up toward the wincing eyes of his guest.

"As I said, I began asking questions. From my education, I received knowledge of the body, its composition, and its inner workings. I was never curious as to the state of things as they were. As God made them. Instead, the questions I asked were intended to understand what the body *could* be. Understanding what could be done to the body, perhaps to make our natural form something more."

He was still grinning; pride shone in this old man's eyes.

"What did ye find, then?"

"Mister Irish, I found God himself. I cut so deep that I found God."

Shay could no longer hold his tongue, and his sense of humor took the stage as he sneered, "That shite looks like caviar, not a bearded sandal-clad deity…"

A stifled laugh from the madman answered his ridicule. The doctor rested the scalpel and its wet sample on the patient's lap, then walked around the table to the other side.

"You have faith, but not in me. I understand. Let me show you my ways, if only that you might understand better the mechanics of what makes man. Of what makes you, young man, so interesting to me."

He knelt behind the table and returned moments later, holding up a silver instrument. It looked like a hypodermic needle, but it had three syringe tips protruding, each glinting in the fluorescent light. Each tip led up into one of three chambers that made up the complex plunger assembly. Each of the three round sides had a glass viewing port, and three distinctly different shades of liquid could be seen within. This was no medicinal device; it looked like an instrument of torture— precise torture, *surgical* torture.

"Mister Irish, you are going to participate in this experiment. I want you to see the…." He paused and thoughtfully gazed into his palm, rolling the syringe over as he inspected its contents before continuing, "I want you to see the magic."

Before he could protest, Mr. Boots led Shay by the shoulders to the head of the table. He handed him one end of a leather strap, stretched it across the forehead of the corpse, and tugged down firmly on his end. Shay took the hint and did as he was shown; the strap ends pulled taut, and the pressure discolored the deceased man's brow.

The doctor stood at the absolute head of the table between the men. He raised the syringe into the air and expelled the air bubbles, flicking the syringe body to help. Turning to his guest, he used his index finger to slide his glasses up the bridge of his nose while he planted his feet.

"You see, my new friend, God is not here today. God is not the only one who creates…," and he drove the trio of needles down through the tear duct of the body's left eye.

With his index finger again, the doctor depressed the chrome plunger and sent the contents surging into the skull of this lifeless mound. *Skish.* In the quiet room, the wet sound was gut-twisting.

Mr. Boots held his end of the strap firmly, his attention fixed on the table. For a moment, Shay could see an expression where there had previously been none. Mr. Boots was stalwart, his grim expression the same as Shay had seen for several days now, but in his eyes, there was fear—genuine fear. At that moment, Shay understood that this man might not be as complicit as one would assume from his hand in their captivity.

The doctor stepped away and began humming. It was some unknown tune, but it sounded militant. Some old anthem or regale of a fallen eastern nation. He set the syringe down nearby and returned, wheeling a tall, bright-red metal cabinet. It looked almost like an automotive mechanic's toolbox, replete with a chrome lever at the foot that looked as though it might open the lid or serve some other mechanical purpose.

Shay held his strap tight and returned his gaze to the flayed-open flesh of the experiment on the table. He saw that, in the eye socket where the injection had been made moments prior, some of the fluid was leaking out. A few off-color blue, yellow, and white drops rose through the skin and formed a small puddle next to the bridge of the nose. After a few moments, the colors began to blend, and when the fluids mingled, they emitted a small but putrid puff of acrid smoke. It was a sizzling chemical reaction, and Shay could only wonder what might be going on inside the brain tissues of that poor bastard on the slab.

The smell of ozone caught his attention. He turned back and saw that the doctor was holding cables protruding from the back of that red box. On the ends were metal paddles about the size of a silver dollar each. The doctor stepped between Mr. Boots and Shay once more, leaning toward that open chest cavity. Holding the paddles in the air, the doctor turned back to Shay and spoke.

"When I was a surgeon, they trained me well and set me upon fixing the living. The day I showed them how to fix the dead, they cast me out. Perhaps you will not be so shortsighted."

He turned back toward the body and used the paddles to spread the soft lungs apart. Pushing them aside, he shoved the paddles deep into the pink and black mess underneath. Under the table's edge with his foot, he pressed that lever on the base of the red box. A low hum resounded, and the doctor released the pedal. He depressed it again and began rhythmically stomping the pedal. Shay understood that he was sending an electrical current with that machine across the cold heart of this body. Those paddles in that black muck made a sludgy, sickening noise, and the smell of ozone was tinny in Shay's nose. Mr. Boots was clutching his leather strap, but his eyes were now squinting pensively.

Shay's mind raced with what was to come. Memories of that lurching bastard under the streetlamp flashed as he held fast.

Baby Jesus, I ain't in yer fan club, but this... just give me one of those miracles of yours and let me survive this. I swear, I'll stop knockin' ye down a peg when someone mentions you or your da'...

Shay was no stranger to unusual situations, but this one topped the list. He stood there, waiting for some response, waiting for another one of these mutilated bodies to spring to life. He watched as coagulated blood began to slowly shunt out of the severed arteries in the chest cavity. At first, he thought he might vomit into the open cavity. After a moment, adrenaline once again found its way into his veins, and an incredible wave of calm came over him. He knew that his only chance to survive this ordeal would be to play along.

The heart was pumping, not in a living way but in a mechanical, forced way. It was like a cheap prop at a Halloween party, something twisted from a Frankenstein film. Those severed veins and arteries unclogged as those chemicals in the skull began to circulate. In no time, a black and bubbly ooze began to pour out, collecting in the bottom of the open rib cage, where the entrails and digestive system appeared to have been completely removed. Shay felt a strong urge to look away, but his fight or flight response had kicked in, and he chose to fight his sickness. With tired hands, he wrenched his end of the leather strap down just as the body began to writhe.

The fingers twitched, and the shoulders spasmed. The neck muscles of this beast tightened, and Shay could feel brute strength attempting to lift the head off the table. The doctor stepped back from the table, raising the paddles. Shay glanced over his shoulder at the man and saw that he was wide-eyed and panting heavily. Teeth glistening in that dull blue light; it was pure excitement.

The Doctor's sneer absolutely terrified Shay, who was now using all of his body weight to hold that strap. The arms began flailing off the sides of the table: the white arm clenched its fist, and the colored arm, with fingers outstretched, reached for nothing. Sinew and muscle came to life; burly legs went taught, the body arching its back like a dying cat.

As both powerful legs lifted the hips of the body into the air, the pale stomach fat shifted back and lolled to the side as the entire body seemed to scream in silent agony, recoiling at the poisons and toxins within. The chest cavity was leaned so far back that the congealing blood and black liquids sloshed back, over the heart and past the lungs, running in a stream over the edge of the massive autopsy incision and splashing onto the table, some onto the floor.

Mr. Boots said nothing, but he turned his head back to the doctor and, with clenched teeth, made a frantic nod toward the undulating body. Shay looked back as well and could see the doctor's wild eyes peering over the rim of his glasses.

"Oh, I suppose that's enough demonstration. I have had my fun for now."

From the shelf under the table, he reached and withdrew a long wooden handle. Shay and Mr. Boots were now struggling to hold that strap, and Shay could feel his grip slipping. The nervous sweat of his hands made the leather feel greasy. Three feet of wooden handle were withdrawn by the doctor, when the end of the implement slid off the table's lower shelf and thumped to the ground. It was a 10-pound hammer, the type railroad workers used to drive iron spikes that held railroad tracks in place.

Stepping one heel back and swinging the hammer with both of his hands, the Doctor brought the iron head of the hammer crashing down onto the forehead of this horrific creature. An explosion of bone, brain, and tissue spattered across the three men as Mr. Boots lurched back, falling onto his hindquarters.

Shay reeled back as well and stood there in stunned silence. Before he could speak, his stomach churned violently, and he fell to his hands and knees, where he dry heaved on the floor. He hadn't had enough food for anything to come up. In sheer horror, tears clouded his vision, and his hands began shaking from the adrenaline leaving him.

The Doctor dropped the hammer to the floor and wiped his hands off the front of his lab coat, which now looked like a canvas painted by death itself. He then walked to Shay and stood over him.

"As I expected, you have little to say. I will give you time to clean and steady yourself, and then we must confer. My associate will assist you, but please do not become lost in what you see. This is merely science, young man. Science is *everything*."

The Doctor walked out of the room, once again humming that

insufferable march.

Testing, Testing

The quiet Mr. Boots had led Shay into a dingy and forlorn bathroom, where he gave Shay a few minutes of privacy in the stall. There was little need for it; Shay had not eaten or drank enough in the last day to warrant using the toilet again. Instead, he took off his shirt and shoes and simply sat on the toilet for a while, letting the room's cool air dry his sweat and cool his skin. The stench of Ajax and ammonia hung in the air, but the floor tiles were stained and chipped in some places, while the grout molding was chipped in others.

He sat there with his elbows on his knees, head in his palms. He thought about the simple plan he had earlier. He mulled over how easily he might overpower Mr. Boots, a man who was undoubtedly a threat, but of what level nobody could say. Shay also knew that John was a survivor, and even in a bad state with one good eye, he would be able to leg it out of the building if Shay could stay untied long enough to overpower their captor.

We can't leave as it is, and more of these little tests are sure t' come. Who's going to wear down first? We can't leave with just two men. It's not right.

He considered their friend Pete, good old Pete. He thought about that poor man being tied up in some unknown room, forbidding himself from thinking about what tortures his friend might have undergone so far. What tortures might he be subject to if they left him behind? There was no easy choice here. Still, Shay knew that he could wait for an opportunity to take a crack at Mr. Boots and, in the meantime, possibly learn enough about the madman's work to discern what the endgame was or, with any luck, get the man to detail it himself.

Is it an invasion of some kind? Are the Reds behind this... a military program perhaps? Or maybe just causing panic? It can't be military, no.

There's no way this whole operation of two loony bastards is some sort of government plot, even if it was the Reds. There would be soldiers, workers... more than this, anyway. We're captive, and he's holding our pal over our heads. What would Billy do? Christ, he must be worried. He's got no idea where we are...

It struck him that he had not seen any more walking experiments since they arrived. All of the dozen or so unwilling participants were simply corpses or grotesque unfinished work, but no threats on two feet. His head was finally feeling clear of the brew they force-fed into him and John, and he could only assume John's recovery wouldn't be far behind. With Mr. Boots over his shoulder, so to speak, he knew that John was probably not being harmed just now. It seemed that the doctor liked his protector in the room or otherwise sent this silent man to complete the task.

He's got a crutch in that, t'be sure. He's not strong enough alone to take on two men, not brave enough to take on one. I'd wager it, anyway.

After some time, Mr. Boots tapped on the metal stall door with his knuckles, signifying that Shay had taken enough time. His legs were half pins and needles, but he did not care. *Anything* but that damn chair was a godsend. Not ready to confront his captor just yet, Shay acquiesced and came out, spending a few minutes at the sink to rinse his hands, face, and neck in the sink. He used the bar of soap to scrub his shirt free of dried vomit. Under his cotton plain shirt, he could see that his ribs were nicely healing, which gave him a bit of confidence in the face of what he would have to do to get out of here. It would be a brawl, and looking in the mirror over his shoulder at this stoic, hairless man, he offered a nod as he wrung his shirt out and put it back on.

I'm going to tan your hide, baldy. Just wait.

He was then led at a hurried pace by the scruff of his neck to a new room that he had not seen before. This one was smallish with bare walls; in the middle, a heavy wooden chair sat waiting for his duff. Across from the chair, perhaps 6 feet, was a small 8 mm camera, poised and waiting to record what Shay could only dread might be another scalpel test or similar torture. The thought of being vivisected again sent a cold shudder down his spine. Keeping his cool, he sat casually and crossed his legs as though he were at a fancy Café waiting for his libation.

Bring it on, you daft cunts. I'm not exceptional, but I'm stone compared to you lot. I'll let ye believe whatever you want.

He smirked and set his resolve, taking long, steady breaths to cool his nerves.

Much to the captive detective's displeasure, Mr. Boots then fed him a small jar of the cloudy concoction, wiping his chin with a soft cotton cloth like an infant. This time, it was different—more viscous, more chemical. He recalled the first time they made him drink.

Ah, shite. At least I'll get some sleep.

His stomach churned from the liquid; it felt cold, moving down through him. Then it felt absent... numb.

After a few minutes, as Shay expected, the Doctor came into the room with a rickety cart that clattered loudly, a tray of metal instruments on top. The old man rolled the cart right up next to the chair, and Shay could count at least a dozen various prodding and cutting instruments laid there on a sheet of butcher paper.

"Mr. Irish, you see, I have made preparations for our interview. I have questions, some of which you may answer with your tongue and some of which you must answer with your body. I believe you are a smart enough man to understand the difference, and perhaps you can be helpful; in that case, we can rely more on the former. You understand that, yes?"

Shay nodded in understanding but said nothing. The doctor waved toward Mr. Boots, who came around the other side of the chair and produced a matching pair of padded brown leather cuffs, the sort they use to bind somebody's wrists or ankles on a hospital bed. The man quietly bound each of Shay's wrists to the thick, oaken arms of the chair. The doctor took to writing a few scribbles in a small red notebook he had produced from his coat pocket, scratching away with the short pencil as he scowled. Then, peering over his glasses, the old man set a switch on the camera, and it began to whirr as it recorded the scene. The doctor then produced a cassette reel tape recorder from underneath the cart, pressing a couple of buttons and starting an audio recording to join the silent video of the small amateur camera.

Turning to Shay with his arms folded, the doctor rocked back and forth on his heels as he began asking questions. The blood and fluids on his lab coat had started to dry, and it crinkled stiffly with his movements.

"Mr. Hayes, you are a fine specimen. Your response to my serum has been... *promising*. That is why we must spend much time together. Have you questions for me?"

He seemed affable, but Shay chose to show some resistance.

"I want to see Pete. Wait, no... *may* I see Pete?"

The doctor smirked and shook his head negative. He reached for the tray and, in one swift motion, picked up a scalpel and swiped it across Shay's chest inside his shirt, where it had been left unbuttoned. Shay clenched his teeth and ignored the pain, a gash on his sternum now running red and trickling down his stomach inside his shirt.

"Tut tut, always joking. I will ask again, but I prefer this to be a more serious discussion. Do you think that is too much to ask? I think not."

There was frustration underlying the man's words. He was clearly maintaining his professionalism during the recording.

"It's my body, I'm healing fast. That's why you're focused on me, I understand. But… why? What's the difference between me and John?" Shay asked, looking into the doctor's eyes, not the camera.

The doctor reached into Shay's shirt and held a ruler near the incision that had just been made for witness by the camera.

"Very quickly, yes. You have impressive durability, perhaps twofold faster than previous subjects. I want to learn more about your life and health to refine my serum further. We are inspecting the blood we collected, though other factors may be influencing the process. Your time here has been eye-opening."

"You and me both, old boy."

"Aha! Yes, well. I may have a… *surprise* for you, but that can wait." He flashed a gray, toothy grin to his patient.

"Doc, I'm at your service."

"Then we shall proceed. Smoking?"

"Often."

"Drinking?"

"Yeh. Same."

"Exercise?"

"I do the routine our drill sergeants taught us, maybe three times a week. I walk a good bit, too, when I'm workin'…"

"Excellent. History of illness?"

"Typical, couple colds a year, flu now and then. Nothing worse."

"Do you take medications?"

"None but the occasional headache cure."

"Are you accustomed to healing quickly when injured?"

"Couldn't tell you, Doc."

"And your family?"

"I don't ever recall strapping me mum to a chair and cutting away at her, t'be honest."

He couldn't hold his tongue. Smiling up at the doctor, he expected the worst. The doctor did not strike him, nor did Mr. Boots. Instead, the Doctor had let out a bit of a laugh and shrugged.

"It seems that you probably did not. Perhaps someday, I will extend my research far beyond these walls, young man. For today, we have *you.*"

Reached forward again with the scalpel and made a dashing cut down Shay's right cheek. In an instant, blood found its way out of the wound and quickly mixed with the sweat that had been beading up on his skin. Mr. Boots reached over and grabbed Shay by the jaw and the top of the head, turning his wound toward the camera. The doctor briefly wiped the incision with a rag and held up the small metal ruler next to it once again.

Grunting but complying, Shay realized that his humor (as he had been told on more than one occasion) had bit him in the ass. Now, a searing pain in his face had him wincing, and his heart was racing like never before. He realized what was happening now.

Where's the fuzzy head? That shite they fed me, it's different. It's keeping me clear-headed. Doc said he was aiming to refine it... sonofabitch. This feels like an airman's pills. Maybe the stuff they give boys in the trench. They want me... awake. Alert. Pish.

In considerable pain and fighting off panic as the drugs set his teeth clenching, he blinked sweat out of his eyes. Wondering if stalling might be a viable tactic, Shay decided to ask a question of his own.

"I've seen your creations, Doc. I already know that you can fix things; you can put flesh back together. What could you need me for?"

"Very simple. I have perfected the art of fixing dead flesh, waking dead flesh. My techniques are effective, but on the living, they are a bit... what is that idiom? Heavy-handed. The living body is inherently weak, and, as yet, my techniques often do more harm than good. The serum has not been usefully effective in many living subjects, which is why I am so curious as to why your body is repairing itself so efficiently."

He leaned forward again, using the rag to wipe away some of the blood from the wounds he had made on Shay, and again, Mr. Boots held Shay's head steady while the Doctor placed that ruler next to each healing incision. Shay wondered how many questions he could ask before this experiment returned to that damn scalpel.

"Doc, you told me that where you're from, they let you do what you want. You can run amok; you could go home and conduct your experiments there. What are ye doin' in America?"

The doctor set down the ruler, and a thoughtful look overtook his visage. He adjusted his glasses, then folded his arms across his chest again with a sigh.

"It's elementary. My work is valuable to people who wish to see me succeed, as they have plans for my big friends whom I have assembled."

"I fought one of those friends of yours; there's no soul in that thing. You're building soldiers, that's it, isn't it? Figured you'd bring the Cold War stateside, yeh?"

The doctor shrugged his shoulders again and paused the tape recorder.

"Mr. Irish, if you choose to delay my research, I will continue without your cooperation. Is that what you wish?"

Hands shaking, breath short, Shay looked down at his bound wrists, seeing that the blood had soaked through the front of his shirt entirely; he felt very defeated at that moment.

"My curiosity gets the best of me, Doc. You can switch your machine back on, and I'll hold my tongue."

With a nod and a smile, the doctor did just that. The tape recorder started again, and the mad scientist stepped into the camera's frame to ask his next question. It was not fortuitous.

"I have seen your bones heal and your flesh mend, and in a surprising time. Tell me, have you ever lost a limb?"

His cold stare through those scuffed and oily spectacles was unnerving. Shay knew that his following answer might be his most important. Biting back a motion, he did his best to weigh his options and give an answer that might lead the villain standing before him not to do anything drastic. He looked down at his legs, his feet, then at his hands.

"I think you can count fine, Doc. I've never lost a piece."

He looked from his hand back up toward the doctor and saw that a deep and satisfied smile had grown across the man's face. A sheen of saliva had collected at the edges of the man's mouth; he was excited. When he spoke, it spread in stringy bands and writhed in the gale of his breath.

"I don't believe you are going to enjoy this, Mister Irish."

Still smiling, the Doctor retrieved a pair of talon-shaped surgical shears. They looked like small pruning shears, but polished and gleaming. In cutting roots, the curved blade provided greater surface contact and increased pressure. The doctor picked them up and squeezed their sprung grip a few times, the way people play with mechanical ice cream scoops. It was childlike. Shay squeezed his eyes shut tight and braced for the pain that was sure to come. For a few moments, he felt nothing but his pounding heartbeat. Then, he felt the firm hands of Mr. Boots on his shoulders, holding him in the chair. Eyes still shut tight, Shay felt the doctor interlace his fingers with his own and pull his left pinky finger straight out. The surgeon had quite a grip. His legs twitched in anticipation of the pain.

Come on, you old bastard, I'm ready. ComeoncomeoncomeonCOMEONNN

He felt the cold steel blades graze the knuckle, and one side of the shears slipped between his fingers. He could feel it slicing the webbing between as it passed. He experienced a brief bit of pressure at the knuckle, and then the pain followed. The intense, shooting pain of severed nerve endings. Shay held his eyes tightly closed as he heard blood splattering to the ground, and then there was a sickening *plunk* as the lost digit was collected in a steel basin. Shay knew damn well he would never regrow that finger. His breath heaved as his body recoiled from the pain, and he reminded himself silently through streaming tears that it was a small sacrifice and one that he could live with, one that he could still *fight* with.

Without opening his eyes, he spoke to distract himself from the pain. His voice was trembling with adrenaline.

"Doc, how do you do it?"

A voice came back from a few yards away, where the Doctor was cleaning his tools in a running sink.

"And what are we referring to, mister Irish? How do I do *what*?" he continued as he cleaned his implements.

"The bodies. I know how ye patch them together and get their hearts pumping again, sure, but... how to control them... after?" His voice wavered a bit as he felt faint.

"We will show you that marvel soon, young man. Yes, yes, we will. I like to say... I believe you will find it *enlightening*. A-heh. Yes."

Shay's vision spun, exhaustion and shock now taking their toll. He tried to reply to the voice of that madman behind him, but his tongue forgot the words as he fell unconscious.

No Good Deed

When he awoke, Shay had no sense of how much time had passed as he blinked away the crust in his eyes. His wrists were bound, shackled this time, and his hand had been bandaged where the littlest finger was now missing. Some part of him wanted to see how bad the damage was or maybe use how it had healed as a gauge of how much time had passed. He tried wiggling it; the pain was bearable… almost dull. That told him that he was either on some decent painkillers or a fair bit of time had passed. In his right arm, at the crook of his elbow, hung the plugged end of an intravenous line. It had been inserted while he was out cold.

As he regained his wits, he observed something like a care station beside him. He recalled getting IVs back in the service, but not often. His eyes followed the line until it went over his shoulder, out of view. He wondered what it might be… medicine? A transfusion? Something likely adulterated? His mouth was dry again, and his vision was soft.

He then noticed that his shirt and pants had been changed. Now, he had a tired but clean button-down shirt and some green trousers that looked like they might have survived a war. Considering the stink and crust on his previous garments, he was thankful for them.

I hope they burn that fucking suit. Did they… did they fucking sponge-bathe me?

Across from him was the camera, and nearby on the floor was the tape recorder. These were the preparations for further experimentation and the scientifically necessary documentation—for efficacy or perhaps posterity. The Doctor was clearly unhinged, so anything was possible.

At least the bugger is thorough, his inner monologue retorted.

He took a few deep breaths and looked around, finding nothing of note in the room but a few chairs and what looked like a thin plywood closet door. This would not be the place of his uprising, no. He would have to endure whatever happened next until he could be taken back to John. He wasn't going to leave to friends behind, and he probably couldn't escape without the help of one. Again, his mind shifted to Pete; his stomach churned as he considered the possibility that big Pete might himself be subjected to the sort of experiments that Shay had witnessed. The doc certainly had a propensity for sizable projects.

He sat there in the near-silence of the room, tugging a bit on his bindings, trying to scratch an itch. It occurred to him that he was, at this moment, almost bored. Just then, as if a wish had been granted, his company returned to the room.

Boots and Labcoat, what a surprise.

The tape recorder was ceremoniously clicked on, but no 8mm camera was present. This time, the doctor was more talkative than usual. Shay held his tongue while his captor removed the bandages from his hand and subsequently took a couple of photos after cleaning the wound area. The Doctor droned on about the state of things, noting the condition of tissues in clinical terms: abrasion, contusion, vascularity, and such.

Not keen to look but unable to resist, Shay glanced and could tell that the wound was closing where his pinky finger once had resided. He chuckled.

"Do I know anyone who tailors gloves?"

"My friend, you're healing splendidly. You are quickly becoming one of my favorite subjects. In fact, I was just telling my associate that your case has taken me away from my work to a notable degree. I am convinced there is much to learn inside you, yes."

He tapped Shay on the sternum, where the doctor's deep incision had almost fully healed. The old man had let out an audible gasp when he saw the wound, and his breath was fouled with tobacco and some kind of canned meat.

"If I had my way, I would not be in such a rush to find my answers; no, I would not. I am a patient man, you see?"

"Are you asking for my opinion, then? It doesn't matter. Just get it over with. I want to get back to John."

The doctor nodded and shrugged, then beckoned Mr. Boots over to assist before retrieving the camera and placing it a mere foot from Shay's face, off to the side.

"Cooperate with me for a short while, and I will return you to your friend. He is in better spirits today, from what I hear. Now, turn your head and show your cheek to the camera, yes?"

The Doctor turned Shay's head with his thumbs, then Boots came behind and held Shay's head steady. Doc turned the camera focus dial as he peered through the viewfinder, then clasped his hands together. He pressed a couple of buttons on the camera; it whirred and hummed as it filmed. The Doc's tone of voice changed, a bit deeper now and more insistent than ever. With his enunciation, his accent wore sharply on the words.

"We are now practicing a dermal incision, two centimeters in length, with a depth of one-half centimeter. This incision should heal in real time, providing irrefutable evidence that this serum is causing rapid healing, unlike any documented case. Observe."

His instructions to potential viewers of the film were unnecessary. The only thing in the frame was Shay's cheek and perhaps his eye. With a swift swipe of his hand, as precise as could be, the Doctor made exactly the incision he prescribed down Shay's right cheekbone through a bit of stubbled red beard.

"You will remain still and silent for the camera," the Doctor implored.

It was a pin-prick, a minor inconvenience to Shay. He was more annoyed than pained by this ordeal, so he played along and sat still for the camera.

The process was slow, and the silence in the room hung heavy. Boots held on tight, clenching Shay's head with dirty hands. The fingernails were grey and grit and muck underneath the cuticles of most. A small stream of blood collected and ran down Shay's cheek onto his sweaty, oily neck. A minute passed, and the small trickle stemmed into a drop collecting at the edge of the wound. The doctor leaned in and took a close-up photograph. Another minute passed, and the drop fell alone down into his beard as the slice was already closing. Another flashbulb fired another crisp picture. Five minutes passed, and the wound had closed itself fully—yet another flashbulb.

Ten minutes later, the doctor leaned in with a small cotton ball. He wiped the wound; it was now a streak of scar tissue. The camera shone its light once more. Twenty minutes passed, and the doctor withdrew a small flashlight from his pocket. He shone it closely and could not find the scar. The skin was smooth and pink; a clean streak from the cotton ball swiped down a dirty face. The thin lines of blood dried in the beard were now the only testament to what was once a stitch-worthy wound in less time than it takes to drink a cold bottle of sarsaparilla on a hot August night. A final flashbulb was expended, and the doctor clapped as though it were the end of a concerto opus before switching off the video camera.

"Ah! I am so *proud* of you, my friend. You are giving me much to be pleased about! My associate will return you to your compatriot and feed you both. We have much to look forward to, my young friend. We shall see. Yes, we shall see!"

The old man rushed out of the room with his flash camera, lab coat trailing behind him like the cape of the Phantom of the Opera. Shay shot his head loose from Boots' grip.

"Come on then, mute. Let's get back. I'm starving!"

Shay rattled his wrist restraints. Boots acknowledged, released Shay's wrists, and nodded toward the door. Shay stood up, and Boots grabbed him at the elbow before walking him out the door and down the hallway. On the walk, Shay barely noticed the steel-trap grip of the man leading him like a child.

He knew he would need to stop this circus before it went any further.

As they reached the room where the men had been held captive, a voice rang out from down the hallway. Boots paused there, holding Shay.

"Oh, Mister Irish? You lost consciousness last time we spoke before I told you that surprise about yourself. In your bloodwork, we found perhaps the answer to all of it."

"Yeh? And what might that be, Doc?" Shay's voice echoed down the corridor.

"You have the *cancer*, mister Irish. It is in your blood. Most likely originating in one of your major organs. That we will need to ascertain as we probe further. Quite the surprise, no?"

A chill sank into Shay's soul. Mister Boots yanked him by the shoulder and dragged him away toward that dingy boiler room. Shay went along quickly; he had no fight in him just now.

…

"You back, Shay? It's been a while. Figured you'd run off without me…" John joked.

Boots sat Shay in his chair near John's. The light was dim. John sat there, appearing unharmed. His clothes were soaked through with sweat, and it looked as though he had been strapped to that chair for days. Shay wondered how badly the man needed a shower.

"You okay? Still doped up?" John asked. Shay was reeling from what the Doc had told him out in the hall.

"Just... I'm okay, John. I'm here." Shay took a deep breath and settled into his chair.

His jailor removed one side of the shackle and clamped it to the chair arm. Boots then poked Shay in the shoulder, motioning toward a box on the floor—a wooden fruit crate. Shay peered inside and saw half a dozen sandwiches wrapped in paper next to a dented thermos. He stood up and nodded back to his silent Guardian, but Mr. Boots was already walking out the door. Once the door shut, the lock rattled on the outside.

"Looks like our babysitter is gone, John. How are you holding up, you filthy bastard?"

He dragged his chair to John and untied the ropes that his friend had been trussed up with. John gave him the biggest grin.

"Fuck's sake, Shay. I wasn't sure they would ever bring you back. Hey, get my legs loose? I haven't stood up in a while except to use the bucket."

Shay untied his feet, and John stood up, straightening his back and letting out a groan.

"They left us here to eat. I think you should, uh... perhaps wash your hands with that hose faucet on the wall by the boiler?"

John chuckled and rubbed his temples. His bandage was filthy, and his eye was still covered.

"Yeah, sure. Good idea. Head feels better... I wanna see what this looks like; help me get these bandages off. Have you got a lighter or something?"

Shay took to getting the wrappings off without much effort.

"No such luck."

John sighed and patted himself down.

"Same here, damn. I could use a smoke. I'm hard up for a good smoke. How's the eye look? Can you see anything?"

Shay lifted the recently dressed cotton bandage off his friend's face; John was winking the bandaged eye, trying to blink.

"John, I can't see so well. Let's get over to the lamp."

They went to the corner under the little red bulb, and Shay held John's face gently with his free hand.

"Can you... Can you see out of it?" Shay asked.

"It's adjusting, but, yeah. I can see. It's a little fuzzy. The light is a funny color."

Shay pursed his lips at what he saw there, unmistakable despite the dim light.

"Sure, it's healing. Just gonna need some time, yeh."

He wasn't lying to John, but he wasn't going to tell him the truth either. His pal's eye socket was a patchwork of stitches and bruising, and the eyelid was puffy from irritation. More critical was the eye itself. John had bright blue eyes. *Had.*

Now, the eye John was wounded in was a rich and authentic brown. This wasn't John's eye. Somehow, the Doc had found a way to use his sludge to bond what was likely some wretched carcass' eyeball into John's head, and it dully stared at him like it hadn't taken fully yet. Shay silently hoped to the powers above that it would, then hoped in a small way that it wouldn't.

Good Christ. Suppose it's better than the alternative, but...

He decided against saying anything to John just yet.

"Sandwiches, man. Sandwiches! That mute bastard finally brought us some food. Let's make do, go scrub your hands, and we'll get at 'em!"

Shay had changed the subject with speed, patting John on the back and directing him toward the water spigot he'd seen behind the furnace on a bucket trip.

After a brief wash-up, they sat down on the cool cement floor and devoured the offerings. Shay put what he'd been told firmly out of his head.

One crisis at a time, Sonny. You need to save your friends.

Ham sandwiches and lukewarm tea—it was a feast for the weary. The sandwiches were dry, nothing special, but several days' hunger had racked up quite an appetite. They didn't speak while they ate and drank. Shortly later, with full stomachs and an empty thermos, they dragged the chairs together and sat close, their knees touching. Shay gave John a good look from head to toe. He seemed to be in better condition than he had been a few days prior.

"I see they gave you fresh clothes as well."

"Probably sick of the smell' John chortled, 'say you look all right yourself, pal. Better than the other day. Was I drugged up, or did you have a busted arm?"

Shay leaned in a bit closer and thought of the best way to explain.

"They've been... John, we're here as lab rats. I've been through the wringer, as they say. How about you, lad?"

"Nothing but interrogation after they showed me that horror under the tarp. I've mostly just been trying to rest, waiting for you. They sure seem keen on you, Shay."

"I'd prefer they weren't. Not that I have much say in the matter, but… I don't think we're going to like where this is headed for either of us. I don't think the Doc is going to let you kick back and rest for long. Seems like we've got a few minutes to ourselves, shall we figure out a way out of this place?"

John nodded, gently rubbing his sore eye and looking around the room.

"Shay, I'm with ya. No matter the cost. That stuff they were showing us, they… this place is sick. Evil. I don't want to stick around and see what else…" he trailed off.

"I've got a bit of a plan, John. It could get messy, but I think it's worth the risk. Of course, we try and find Pete on our way out. And some coats, definitely some coats. If we are still anywhere near Tillamook, there's bound to be a biting cold waiting for us outside.

John nodded his head emphatically as he hushed his voice a bit to retort.

"Find Pete, that goes without sayin'. Listen… I'm not keen on the idea that we need to go out in a blaze of glory, Shay. I don't know what you had planned, but I think that damn mute is under some sort of… control, like a spell. When he gave me a change of duds, I asked him for a damp rag so I could scrub up, and do you know what? He brought me a bucket of warm water and some soap. I'm not convinced he's all bad. He's just not playin' with a full deck."

"*Soap*? Christ, I got three minutes in a moldy bathroom stall. What I wouldn't give for a hot shower… I'm with you, let's try and get out of here swiftly and quietly. Had I known the old sod was so soft-brained, I'd have asked for a whisky!"

"Heh. You call *me* a lush. Quietly, yeah." John was pursing his lips.

"Well, quietly after we make a bit of a ruckus. Do you need to do anything before we make our play? I could use a little rest."

John stood up and jokingly flexed his arms.

"I'm stoked, Shay! These scoundrels don't know what's about to hit 'em!"

"Pipe down, John! It's simple. When the time comes, I need you to be rowdy; we need a distraction—something to get the attention of Baldy out there."

"Easy, right? Say, before we go at this… be honest with me. I saw how you grimaced. How bad is it?"

John pointed to his eye, his face still swollen.

"I don't think the wife will take me back sober if I look like roadkill!"

The two men shared a little laugh, his sarcastic tone masking his fear poorly.

"Johnny boy, you're going to be fine; truth be told, I think you shed a few pounds. You're looking dapper."

John playfully socked him in the arm, chiding him, "...but not a dandy!"

"Never a dandy. You're too slouchy and American for that. Enough pitter-patter… let's get some rest, just half an hour, perhaps. Then, it's time to go."

John sat down in his chair and stretched his arms wide. "I'm with you, Shay."

Shay slouched onto his chair, folded his arms, and let his head loll as he chortled, "Roadkill. Heh."

Without another word, the men sat in silence with satisfied stomachs for just a little while.

Hail Mary

With a yawn and a stretch of his legs, Shay rubbed his face as he awoke.

"John... you awake?"

Groaning, John came to and grunted. "Sure, sure. That was more than half an hour, Shay."

"I figured you for needin' some beauty rest, Talbot. You ready to tussle?"

"Only if I get to slap you once or twice!" John teased, standing up.

Stretching like a cat, Shay stood up with John, thumbed toward the chair, and stepped clear, rolling up the sleeves on his scrappy duds.

Shrugging, John took a good grasp of his chair while Shay took to acting out.

"TALBOT, You ate my food! I should beat the piss outta ye!"

John picked up his chair and swung it wildly. He released it just so, and it sailed in an arc, shattering against the door frame as it struck. Stifling a wild grin, he balled up his fists and began shouting hysterically.

"You damn dirty RAT! You dragged me into this! We're gonna die here, but I might just kill you before they get the chance!"

Shay raised his fists like a traditional boxer, knuckles out, whilst circling John with long strides. He screamed back, "Shut your pisser, ye drunken fool! I'll be damned if your mangy-mutt face is the last I'm going to see!" He kicked over his chair as he circled.

As the latch on the metal door clanked, they took to wild sparring. In the dark, it would look plenty real. Shay led with a haymaker over John's head. John ducked it and half-shoved him away.

"C'mere, you lanky cocksucker!" John growled, Shay, teasing right back, "...oh, you sound just like yer ma!"

John bit his lip and swung low; Shay danced around his right hook and gave him two taps in the flanks just above the hips. John's pudge padded the blows.

The hallway light flooded into the room as Mr. Boots swung the door open in haste, breathing heavily from his hurried arrival.

Shay rabbited a gut punch at John, pulling it so perfectly that John barely noticed as it made a *pap* sound. John grabbed his friend by the shoulder and slapped him backhanded across the face, Shay spinning on his heel and prat-falling dramatically to the floor.

"I'm gonna punt my size nine up your Irish ass!" John shouted. Shay was writhing on the ground, shielding his face but peeking to watch their captor.

The scuffle was the perfect trap; simple-minded Mr. Boots had fallen for the ruse, and he ran over in a huff, shoving John to the ground. He turned back toward Shay, who was rolling on the floor, still cradling his face and groaning like a constipated farm animal.

Boots snatched Shay by the shoulders and lifted him in a poor effort to get him seated back in his still-overturned chair. John leaped up behind their captor and swung his right arm underneath the silent man's armpit, up and across his chest. It was almost a choke-hold; the bald man's right arm was crooked up and useless.

Standing up and lunging with his left hand, Shay grabbed Boots' throat. When he found Adam's apple, he squeezed harder than he had ever before. Boots' eyes went wide in panic. Shay used his right hand to hold Boots' flailing left arm while John held him firm.

"Grab your wrist, John. Grab your right wrist and crush him!" Shay barked, John doing just that.

"This bastard is STRONG, Shay!" John grunted.

Shay was sneering, staring this man down as he choked the life out of him. Yet, for all their strength, Mr. Boots still stood tall and stiff.

John kicked the back of Boots' knees and buckled his right leg, then his left. Shay leaned in, and all three men landed in a pile, Shay still squeezing the consciousness out of this man. After what seemed like forever, a final twitch shivered through Boots' body as he succumbed to the assault. John felt him go limp and let him loose, sliding the crumpled man off himself.

"Shay… Shay!"

His friend continued to squeeze, his eyes ablaze.

"SHAY!" He shouted, and Shay's grip finally released from the throat. A gurgle escaped as he let go.

He fell back onto his duff and sprawled out across the floor flat as he caught his breath.

John kneeled over Boots, taking off the man's belt to secure his hands. What he saw in the dim, yellow fluorescent light from the hallway churned his stomach.

"Ah, Christ… that's…"

Mr. Boots lay there unconscious, half-snoring as is usually the case for someone whose lights were put out. The glistening lips flapped with each short breath. Yet this man had no tongue or teeth. His mouth looked like it had been clear-cut, like a forest. The cores and roots of his teeth showed like little tree stumps; they had been mechanically filed down.

"This is just all sorts of fucked up, Shay. I can't… what happened to this man?"

"Worse than we got, if there's any justice. I have no time for zealots or jailors, John."

Shrugging, John replied softly, "Well, how about slaves…"

John helped Shay to his feet and dusted his friend off a bit. Shay clenched his hands and released them rhythmically, trying to work out some of the stiffness from their little skirmish.

"I've only choked him unconscious; he's not dead… yet… what should we do?"

In the hallway light, he could see John's off-colored eyes flash toward the one unbroken chair, where their shackles hung off the arms and legs limply. Shay nodded; it was so obvious.

Minutes later, with Mr. Boots battened down, John and Shay crept out into the hallway. They moved slowly, hoping not to arouse any further attention. They both knew that the madman must be lurking around somewhere, and they had no desire to say goodbye.

They whispered to each other to figure out the best path of escape as they came to a four-way split.

"John… this hall to the left is where they took me the last couple of days, so shall we go right?"

John nodded his head and again sneaked in that direction. Every door they came to, they checked underneath for light and listened for signs of life. Shay gingerly checked the knobs of each door with two fingertips; most were locked. They found a few supply closets with barren shelves and empty supply crates. They found one well-lit room with a sizable oily stain on the floor, which neither of them had any inclination to inspect closely. There were two mops in a bucket there;

John snagged Shay by the sleeve and nodded toward them, whispering, "Let's arm ourselves!"

John spun the wooden handles from their bases and handed one to Shay. John held his stick in front of him and across his body like a shield; Shay held his loosely, parallel to the floor. He had never had much luck with combat weapons; he was into boxing as a lad.

They continued down the hall but found nothing but glass-windowed lab doors. There was no light, no sign of life inside, and the hallway ended in front of them.

"Pete has got t'be here somewhere, John..." he implored, his friend nodding and doubling back toward the four-way split.

A dead-end hall behind, having come from the left hall and having been down the adjacent hall during their "testing," the only sensible choice was to turn right. They walked about 20 yards down a hall without doors (though some rough walls looked to have been sealed up a long time ago), and around a left corner, they found only one door there, which was otherwise a dead end.

"Ah shit, Shay... we gotta go back past those goddamn experiments."

Shay put his hand on John's shoulder and pointed to the door.

"Hey, not so fast, John... see that? I don't think that's a closet, mate. Thicker frame. Let's give it a peek, yeh?"

John shrugged, sighed, and slowly paced toward the door. Underneath it, they could see a flickering light. It was akin to a dying bulb, flickering very quickly and intense... almost vibrating—a shimmer.

"That's a bit queer, I'd say," Shay offered. John grunted back a midwestern "ayuh" as Shay stepped around him.

Standing there, he tried to figure out what he was looking at. The light nearly danced across the floor through that narrow gap. First, in patterns like Morse code, faster than the eye could really decode. Then it swept across in waves of rich blue and purple hues. Shay tried the knob, but it was locked. John pulled his arm as though to say, 'Hold on,' but Shay jiggled the knob.

Almost in response to the sound, they heard a sigh emanate from the room. It was a heavy breath, a bit wet and raspy... almost asthmatic. Shay froze in his tracks, and he saw that John had paused as well.

In the softest of whispers, Shay leaned into John's ear and said, "Sounds like a big man in there."

John cupped his hand and replied, "You hope it's a man."

Shay shot back, "I'm praying it's Pete."

They both knew that there was significant danger in opening that door, but Shay was willing to take the risk for his big pal. They surrounded the door an arm's length away from it, now holding the broomsticks in front of them.

tak tak tak

Shay used the tip of his stick to lightly tap on the door, to which there was no response.

He leaned forward a bit and used his knuckles to knock on the doorframe, to which there was a slight response. A muffled grunt came from within the room. Shay's eyes flashed open wide as hope took hold of his heart.

Shay turned to John and whispered as quietly as he was able, "I may not know what's in there, but I don't believe it's one of those things. The one I took down never made a noise. Are you ready to leg it?"

He leaned back and watched John analyze the situation. His scowl made it clear that he didn't love the options. Still, John nodded and thumbed toward the door, giving Shay the 'go-ahead.'

Shay took a step back, took two deep breaths, and with all his strength, he kicked the door, just adjacent to the handle. The thump echoed through the hallway, but the door didn't budge. From inside the room, they heard a tired groan. It sounded pained, and worry caused Shay to break his silence. He leaned toward the door and said softly, "Pete? You in there?"

"Mmmuuuuhhh…"

Another groan emanated inside the room. It wasn't a sure sign, but it was worth the risk. Shay stepped back and kicked the door again. He heard wood crackling, and he knew he was almost there. John put his hands on Shay's back to support him. Shay switched his stance and kicked the door with his other foot with the last drops of his strength. The doorframe split, and the door swung open, bouncing against the wall behind the door and closing again. It was so swift, he hadn't gotten a peek inside aside from a fanning of rich green light flashing across the door.

John gripped his friend's shoulder now, whispering, "Right behind you, but be ready to run!"

Shay used his stick to push the door on its bent hinges the rest of the way open with a slow creak. Near the door, they could see a table. On it, a contraption looked like the projector they use in classrooms, though it made a subtle tick-tick-click-tick noise in rhythm with the flashing of the attached light array.

"Pete?" Shay spoke softly.

The boys peered into the room in unison, leaning on the doorframe. Around the door and a few feet away, in the beam of the light, they could see the desperate and sweaty face of their friend Peter, his mouth bound with thick tape. He appeared cuffed behind his back, strapped to a heavy, high-backed chair. Shay's whole body felt a flush of chill as he stepped into the room.

"Pete! Peter, you tough bastard, are you okay?"

Pete gurgled past the edge of the tape but did not turn his head or move his eyes to look at Shay. The light transfixed him as it flashed and waved incessantly into his red and bleary eyes. Shay took a couple of steps toward Pete while John moved over to the machine; he found the cord running from the back of it, wrapped his hand around it, and gave it a stiff yank. The machine's clicking stopped instantly. The last flash of light faded across their faces before leaving the room black.

Shay could no longer see his friend. John fumbled around for a light switch on the wall but found none. Shay stepped a little bit closer to Pete, who was now beginning to shuffle and rock in the seat. Shay could hear Pete fighting his restraints.

"Pete, old boy, we came to cut you loose. You're okay, you're going to be okay. Can you move? Are you hurt?"

All of Shay's questions were met with nothing but pained groaning.

With his hands outstretched, Shay fumbled his way toward the chair. He placed his hands on his friend, feeling Pete's shirt on his shoulder and then his collar. He patted his way up to Pete's face, where he could feel the tape. Pete trembled and quaked at the slightest touch, so Shay supposed his friend was beginning to panic.

"Don't worry, pal, don't worry. It's me, it's Shay. You're saved. You're coming with us. I'm going to snatch this tape; quit yer wiggling, would you?"

Pete was now shaking his head back and forth, and the restraints behind him were audibly strained. It sounded like a heavy rope. Shay finally got a finger under the tape, and he was able to pull it off and away from Pete's mouth.

"Pete, relax, man. You're coming with John and me."

Pete wrenched his head to the side and gnashed his teeth. He almost caught Shay in the hand.

Shay stepped back in the darkness, "John, I'm not..."

"One second, Shay."

John had been fumbling around with the machine, having seen some dials and switches before he had pulled the plug. He felt around and found those controls again. Not sure what good it would do, he shrugged and leaned down to plug the machine back in. The light began flashing again, directly at Pete's face.

Shay gasped and lurched backward. "Oh God, oh my God. Christ in heaven. Pete, he's…"

He couldn't quite find the words to explain it. In a pink and red flurry of light, he could see that Pete's head was nearly shaved; heavy stitches were zigzagging his scalp. His jaw was offset and looked broken; there were massive gashes stitched back together on his neck and leading down his collar.

John found the control knob and, as he dialed it down, the flashing reduced to a slow pulsing and eventually to a steady pink wash of light. He reached for Shay and clasped his friend's hand.

"Irish, I don't think we got here in time…"

Now, they could see that Pete was an absolute wreck. His skin was blue and purple, and while his arms were bound behind him, one shoulder was fully dislocated, sitting about 6 inches lower than the other. Shay reached forward and grabbed Pete's shirt, catching the button line and ripping it open. A massive Y-shaped and stapled-up wound traversed the broad chest of his old friend. Pete's head swiveled again, and he tried to bite at Shay's hands, only missing by a hair. Shay and John both lunged back toward the doorway, where they stood silent for a moment. John put his arm around Shay's shoulder, gave him a comforting squeeze, and consoled him.

"I'm so sorry, this is… this is too much. We've got to get out of here." Shay was speechless, but he acquiesced, and they stepped into the hall.

Just as they had turned away, the creak of wood on concrete could be heard.

"John-"

Pete had fought his restraint so hard that he was able to stand up from the heavy chair he'd been tied to. As he did, the chair split apart. One could hear the dull squeak of nails being pulled from the boards.

The duo spun around, and, to their horror, Pete was now shuffling toward them. His massive body was leaning forward, and his cold, dead eyes were searching for something. This was no longer Peter; this was just a corpse: a motivated corpse, 400 pounds of mangled, oozing death and ill intent.

Despite his arms tied behind him and his feet loosely bound, there was no sense in sticking around to see if this thing that was once their friend might relent. The boys dropped their wooden handles and scrambled down the hallway as quickly as they could. Shay turned back as he sprinted, seeing Pete slam into the doorframe and tumble into the hallway, splayed out on the floor for a moment before lurching back up to his knees.

"Oh God, he's loose!" Shay wheezed. The cheap bindings on Pete's hands had come loose in the fall, and now Pete was fumbling to step out of the ropes dangling around his ankle. It was like watching a bear tangled in tent ropes. This was now a large, angry animal.

John was in the lead, beckoning Shay to hurry. Shay sprinted after him, instinctively looking back over his shoulder every few seconds toward their pursuer. As they neared the end of the long hallway that led them to such calamity, Shay saw Pete barrel around the corner and into view at the end of the hall.

"John, which way?" He pleaded as John reached the intersection once again.

Pete's stitches on his neck had split open; now, a wretched dark fluid was pouring out of the wound down his chest as he got his feet free of their entanglement.

"JOHN!" He implored as their old friend trudged toward them with heavy steps.

"This way!" John shouted, legging it down the hallway toward those labs full of horrors.

John paused to test the doors frantically and found one unlocked. He swung the door wide, and he and Shay leaped inside just as Pete lumbered around the corner into view; he was perhaps two dozen paces behind them. John spun around and slammed the door shut, locking the pitiful deadbolt and planting his foot under the edge of the door.

"This isn't gonna hold!"

He turned to Shay, who was wheezing and pointing to the far end of the room. John's gaze followed Shay's finger, and he saw a mound of tarps in the corner. He froze, realizing that he'd led them directly into the room where that canine-headed monstrosity had been so horribly demonstrated for them.

"Can't catch a BREAK!" John blurted out; he turned back to Shay, who pressed his finger to his lips, insisting that they be quiet.

Footsteps in the hallway grew closer, and then a heavy thud rattled John through the door as Pete tried to gain entry. John held the knob tight and leaned his shoulder into the door as Pete again bounced off the door outside.

There was no being quiet now.

Shay's attention turned back to the creature strapped to that metal chair. It sloshed and writhed in that basin of fluid, splashing out enough of the murky liquid that its snout was now in the air. The dog howled a croaking, wet cry of distress.

Shay's stomach turned. "Christ almighty…"

Pete slammed the door again, gurgling and grunting outside the door.

"Shay, shut that fucking thing up!" John pleaded, praying that silence might dissuade their friend outside the door.

There was a low wail at first, but the dog's cries became more shrill as it writhed and whimpered. It was becoming perturbed by the noise of Pete's body breaking the door off its hinges.

"I'll try, John, just let me, ah…"

Shay peered around the room but saw only the collection of jars and tubes and the various colorful containers along the other wall. He knew that in a room with no exit, they wouldn't last long against Pete… but perhaps there was a way he could use that creature under the dropcloth to his advantage. He ran over to the assortment of chemicals and checked the labels as fast as his exhaustion and panic would allow.

John hissed at him, "What are you doing? I can't hold this!"

Shay put a finger in the air for John to *wait*. He stood there, heels together, his left arm folded across, and his right thumb and forefinger on his chin.

"I have the plan, John. Hold that door a few moments longer; I'll be quick."

"Fuck you. Hurry!" John wheezed.

John squatted down and leaned as hard as he could into the door, his right foot planted under the bottom, and his left foot sliding and kicking as he tried to keep traction. Pete was now rattling the door handle, which spun free from John's grasp. Luckily, the deadbolt lock on the door held… for now. John could feel Pete's full weight against the wooden door, which bowed under the pressure.

He looked back over his shoulder and saw that Shay had selected one of the jars. His friend was now gingerly stepping toward that mutant in the far corner of the room.

"I don't know what you're doing, but hurry it up. No time to play scientist!" John was serious, but Shay let out a bit of a chuckle.

"John, it's exactly the right time to play scientist. Trust me."

Shay spun the lid of the jar off and splashed the liquid across the cloth tarp, filling the room with the creature's gurgling cries. He picked up another canvas cloth that had been crumpled on the ground and ran it back toward the laboratory equipment. John felt panic set in, and he could feel Pete pushing harder than ever.

John cried a bit, mainly from the exertion but also from the sheer panic of the situation.

"Here we go, Johnny boy. Get ready to join me behind that table!" Shay pointed it out to John.

"Ready… when… you are," John strained.

As Shay struck up a small Bunsen burner on the lab table, John realized exactly what his friend had planned. In a flash, his panic turned to sheer excitement at the idea of escaping this nightmare.

WHUMP

Pete collided with the door again.

Shay held the rag over the burner, and in a flash, it was up in flames; he went back toward that howling Colossus and tossed the burning rag toward the chemical-soaked tarp. Both men watched in what felt like slow motion as the cloth unfurled in the air, flames licking the ceiling and streaming behind it in a glorious flourish.

"You're a good boy, and I'm so sorry." Shay offered, tears welling in his eyes.

What happened next was undoubtedly the most insane moment either of these poor souls has ever experienced. In a flash of light and the hiss of combustion, that soaked tarp took to flame most violently. There was an audible whoosh as this hellfire stoked up and immediately charred the ceiling above it.

John leaped away from the door and grabbed Shay by the arm, the men ducking behind the furthest table adjacent to the door. The creature let out a shrill, prolonged burbling scream of pain and fear from its liquid prison; it was the last sound they heard before the crash of wood as Pete finally broke through the door, which slammed to the ground.

"Ghuuuurgh…" The beast at the doorway grunted in a manner that belied confusion. A shuffling sound came as it stepped to one side, then the other. Whatever creature was living in the body of what was once their good-natured friend now roared as it ran toward the flaming mound of horror.

John was entirely exhausted, barely able to crouch there behind the table.

Shay peered around the table, and what he saw was the most confusing sight. The brute had clenched his fists... and was violently hammering the body of this thing with blows. Each blow sent a croaking gurgle out of the throat of that dog's head, though it appeared to have stopped wriggling. Shay was unsure if this was an attempt to put out the fire in the name of self-preservation or to kill the offending creature out of sheer confusion, but it didn't matter. This bought them time.

Shay supported John by the arm, and they hunched over, sneaking out from behind the table and across the back of the room. The beast paid no mind; it was merrily engaged in its havoc now. They made their way out the door without being spotted and hurried down the hall away from that thing. They went to the end of this familiar hallway and found an unlit corridor. John turned back to Shay and whispered, "I'm not opening another door that doesn't say stairs!"

Shay gave him a thumbs-up, offering, "Best idea you've had all day!"

As they practically tiptoed down the dark hall, they came upon a wide door opening in the wall with large metal horizontal doors inset.

"Even better, it's an elevator!" John yelped.

In the dim light, Shay ran his hands down the wall beside it and found the panel with two large buttons. He rested his fingers against them, but before he dared press them, he stopped and said a small prayer. It was a murmur but a genuine prayer to the patron saint of safe travels, Saint Christopher.

"We're almost there, Shay."

John reached out and placed his hand over Shay's, pressing his fingers into the top button. The doors slid upward into the wall, and the freight elevator inside opened its maw to them with a clunk. The thing even had its dim light bulb screwed into the wall!

"Oh, thank Christ... thank you, sweet, fat little baby Jesus. Here we are, John, our saving grace."

They jumped inside, and John smashed the most prominent button on the wall; the double steel doors clacked shut. "More luck like this, and I might be praying to your Saints, Shay!"

John studied the panel and saw a few buttons. "B3, B2, B, and G..."

He had previously surmised they were in a deep basement, judging by the lack of windows and outside sounds. Moreover, the fact that they had been tied up in a boiler room, which is often located in the lowest level of a building. He pressed the one button marked with the G, and they felt the old electro-hydraulic elevator hum into motion and shunt them upwards. They were both holding their breath while the elevator rose. Neither man could be sure what they might see on the other side of that door once it opened.

John looked back at the button panel and then at Shay. They kept rising. He looked at the panel and the doors. They continued to rise—the hum, the rattle of old metal. John coughed into his hand, finally catching his breath.

"Johnny boy, we've been moving too long."

"Whaddya mean?"

"That's not just a basement. What else is fifty feet underground and has no floors between? That was a bomb shelter!"

John whooshed a breath out, standing up straight and furrowing his brow. "What sort of building has a bomb shelter out here anyway?"

Shay put his palms up, exasperatedly retorting, "How would I know?"

Finally, the elevator lurched to a slow and very comfortable stop. Shay turned to John and said with confidence, "We've got to go, no clue what's on the other side. Get your dukes ready, Mister Talbot. This might be a scuffle."

John nodded and clenched his fists guardedly, signaling to Shay to press the door-opening button. Shay did just that, and the metal doors rolled vertically into the wall again. In front of them, it was pitch dark and dead quiet.

"You see anything, Irish?"

"Not a thing. Let your eyes adjust."

A few moments passed while both men squinted into the darkness, and slowly, a few shapes became discernible: boxes, racks, corrugated doors, stacks of pallets, and an old pallet jack not far from them. It looked like a freight depot. The Chevrolet panel Wagon sat in the center of the room.

Shay rested his fighting stance, turning to John, "Chilly in here… let's find some coats and get out of here, yeah?"

"You search; I'll check the wagon." John went to the Chevy and ran his hands over the fenders and tires.

"Sonofabitch."

Shay replied, "What's the problem?"

"Driver's tire gone flat, wheel's cocked to one side. I don't think we can drive this out of here, and I don't know how to hot-wire a car anyway."

"Suppose we leg it, then. Let's not dawdle; safety might be nearby!" Shay reminded him.

"Sure, just give me a minute," John replied, opening the wagon's hood and fumbling around for a few moments before rejoining Shay.

The temperature was low in the thirties. The fogging of their breath hung in the dim light cast from that little bulb in the freight elevator. As they got further away from it, they could see a bit better around the warehouse. It wasn't large, maybe 30 feet across on each side. Shay stood guard while John peeked into closed doors. One room contained shipping crates, nothing of use to someone without a crowbar. The next held just a stack of folding tables.

Shay reached the third door and slowly opened it. "Ah! Smells like a loo," he exclaimed.

"No light?" John Prodded.

Click, click.

"Not working"

"Shit," John murmured.

"Smells like it, yeh. That's what I said."

The final door was where they struck gold. They stepped into the dark room and felt their way around. It was an office. John stumbled over the desk, desk implements falling to the ground. "Stapler!" John mumbled.

Shay felt along the wall until he found some material. "I've got something," he said, fumbling around with their treasure: one light jacket and one rubber raincoat. In the darkness, he whispered over to John.

"Here, take the raincoat. Tuck it in your pants, trap your body heat."

They each put on their outer layer and continued like blind men, feeling their way along the wall until John felt a heavy door. "You ready? I think this goes outside…"

"Ready, old boy."

They were shoulder to shoulder, and each of them was equally anxious to get the hell out of that crazy place. John grabbed the door handle and wrenched it, kicking the door open. Moonlight breached into the room, and the ground was a crisp, silvery white.

"We're still in the woods, John. Damn cold out there."

John snickered and pushed Shay out the door as he said, "I'd rather freeze than piss off whatever is back down there."

As the men stepped out into the snow, the dry pack crunched underneath their feet. They could make out footprints leading away from the door—shallow, formless indentations—not fresh. The low wind howled through the branches of the trees surrounding the building, some 30 yards away. When they cleared the door, Shay turned around and shut it. There was no marking on the door or the building.

Shay took a deep breath of the air. "It's so fresh… I can't smell death out here. That place smelled like fucking death." He leaned against the wall of the building and gazed up at the sky for a beat.

"Let's focus, Shay. I say we should check around the perimeter and get our bearings. I don't know if we would last out here all night."

"Yeh, sure. Good call." Shay was still gazing, awestruck, at the bright moon and silvery clouds lazily drifting across that icy winter sky.

"Shay, we don't even know what time it is. It could be near dawn or dinner time. I'm not going to stop until we find shelter, but I'm damn sure not going back in there."

"You're right, pal. Let's reconnoiter and make our way to civilization!" Shay snapped back to the reality of the situation, springing away from the wall.

They paced the building's perimeter, finding little. There were no other buildings, just the single warehouse with its steel roll-up door large enough for a box truck to drive into. A road led up a short hill and out of sight. Not far from the building was a stack of a dozen drums of heavy bunker oil, most sounding nearly empty by a rap of the knuckle. Two sounded full and were too heavy to move, confirmed by a shove. The boys continued their lap of the structure.

"Whaddya think, John?" Shay asked when they finished circling the building.

"Your guess is as good as mine. We could be anywhere from Canada to Mount Shasta right now, and I think we might be pretty well fucked."

"No, no way… we've got to be somewhat close to Tillamook, yeh? They wouldn't be driving far from all the bodies that were going missing; we must still be in that region. Let's go back around and follow that road out into the woods, looking for tracks, prints, or anything we can follow. There's bound t'be something out here, John."

"It's fuckin' cold, but… anywhere else is an improvement!" John flipped up the hood of the raincoat and tucked his hands deep into his pockets. Shay snapped up the collar on the coat and stuffed his hands in his armpits as they walked.

The snow-covered road led away from the rollup door. They returned to it and surveyed the path ahead. The snow was crunchy underfoot, but in the trees around them, it was a delicate powder. It left a contoured, voluptuous white blanket over everything around them.

John squatted down and studied the ground, mumbling, "…some tracks under a light snow here, see the dips; there's no other trail, this is our way outta here."

Shay concurred, so they headed up the road away from the little building and away from the last bit of warmth they would feel for some time.

Cold Companion

They had trudged perhaps half a mile up the road, their teeth chattering and Shay vigorously rubbing his chest and shoulders.

"Bit o' friction keeps the blood moving. I should have let him cut me up a bit more, bargain for a better pair of pants." Shay chuckled at the thought.

John was watching the sky as they walked. "It's late at night; the moon is rising. Those bastards have my watch..."

A half-hour of walking in the frozen air was wearing them down when they came upon a crossroad. The left gravel path led further up a hill, while the right path disappeared down and around a bend. There were no signs or markings; it looked like a disused forestry service road.

Through chattering teeth, John had decided, "Come on, Shay, I think we'll be better off going up."

"Ye sure? I'm of two minds..." Shay asked as he tucked his pant cuffs into his socks, hoping to keep out the snow.

John waved him onward and started hustling up the trail. He shouted back, "I think this is a fire trail. If we didn't leave Tillamook forest, the mountains wouldn't be too tall. Even if we don't find shelter, we might get a vantage point! Downhill could be a gully or a dead end."

Shay relented and chased after his friend, huffing, "s'pose if you're wrong, we can always just go back to the Doc and apologize!"

"Ha! I think you m-miss their ho-hospitality..." John teased, his jaw chattering as he spoke.

They laughed, and their laughter echoed throughout the forest. With John in the lead, the men clambered up that hill for another mile. The chill permeated every part of their bodies, but hiking uphill helped just a bit. It was below freezing, and they were wearing rags.

Suddenly, John shouted, "Aha!" And began running up the hill. Praying his friend hadn't lost his mind to the frostbite, Shay ran after him despite his smooth-soled shoes slipping on the gravel under the snow.

Once they rounded a tight bend in the road, they came upon a small shed-type utility building cutting a very rigid outline against the white surrounding ground, its slanted roof jutting against the night sky. John jumped and shouted in excitement.

"Wahoo! This is our lucky day… I just knew it!"

Shay rattled the door handle; it was locked. "I don't feel saved quite yet, John."

"This is a maintenance station! Forestry service, they probably keep supplies!" John informed him.

"Well, let's get this damn door open and find out?"

They took turns shouldering and kicking at the door. After nearly breaking each of their shoulders, they relented. Shay stepped back from the door and sighed.

"S'pose we could build a battering ram…"

John laughed off the idea's stupidity and beckoned Shay to follow him. In the snow, they stumbled around the rear of the building, and just as John had hoped, there was a small window up near the roofline that was perhaps not good for much sunlight but would probably allow a particularly lean Irishman to crawl through.

"Get over here, you're going in!" John instructed as he clasped his hands together; Shay used that as a step, and John hoisted him up to window level.

"It's locked; let me down for a moment."

John did as instructed, and moments later, Shay returned holding a wrist-thick branch. Although it was covered in snow, it would do just fine.

"Up we go!" Shay insisted, and John gave him a boost just as before. He smashed the old glass pane out of the window, using the branch to break out all the shards before reaching inside to release the window latch.

"Hup!" John lifted his friend high with all his strength, with the last of it. His fingers could barely grip in this cold.

Shay scrambled up through the window, and John winced at the cacophony as his friend tumbled onto a table of tools below. From inside the building, a lilting voice groaned, "I'm all right! Go to the door."

John did so and was met at the open doorway by his smiling friend, who was holding his palm to his forehead as a bit of blood ran down. The moonlight seemed dim compared to the light Shay had flipped on inside.

"Sure you're okay, Shay?" John asked, reaching for his friend's head wound.

Shay brushed his hand away, imploring, "I'll be fine, old boy, just get your ass in here and shut that door!"

John stepped inside and assessed their surroundings, grinning widely at their spoils under the small bulb's light. "Hell, it's got utilities! We can't be too far from a town or the like. Look around; let's get some heat going!"

They surveyed the contents of the outbuilding, which was perhaps only slightly larger than a two-car garage. In the middle, a beat-up Jeep sat. Half a dozen cabinets and racks held simple supplies such as rope, climbing gear, and firefighting equipment. Tired canvas-edged smoke masks hung on the wall, and a few axes and shovels leaned in a corner. A small oil stove stood proudly in another corner, but no oil was found.

"I'll take a look at the Jeep, Shay." John lurched into the passenger seat and started wiggling knobs and poking around the map pockets.

"Oh, boy!" Shay gasped when he peered under the workbench. He snatched up a portable radiant gas heater, set it on the bench, and promptly ignited it. It was small but more than enough to stave off the frozen night air. John climbed out of the Jeep to join him.

Shay hugged John and, with tears in his eyes, said wistfully, "You brilliant, stupid cus! We coulda died snowmen, but ye saved us!"

John felt the same wave of relief his friend felt, and he hugged Shay back for a while as the warmth of the heater radiated across their faces and bodies.

"It was luck, Shay. Smart luck, but just luck. I'll seal up that window, and we can rest. You warm up those bird bones of yours and then find us some provisions if there are any."

John carried a stepladder to the window and stuffed a trash bag filled with wadded newspaper into the cavity where the glass had been broken out. Shay moved on to searching cabinets.

Both men were exhausted but relieved to know that they could survive the night. The only food found in the cabin was a dented can of pork and beans, which they shared using a flat pine paint stick as a spoon. In no time, they were asleep on the floor under a pile of blankets.

...

John woke up feeling a chill, though not freezing. He rubbed the sleep from his eyes and looked around. The two beds of old wool blankets they had found were still no match for the chilly cement floor. He turned to Shay, who was sitting up next to him about a dozen feet away, leaning against one of the cabinets. Shay was smoking a dry, hand-rolled cigar, which they had found the night before.

"Did you get any rest?" John inquired, taking the stogie and having a puff.

"I got enough. It's cold anyway, hard on the body…"

John interrupted, "Not too cold to sleep, pal. What's on your mind?"

"I hate to say, Mister Talbot, but… we've got to go back."

John sat straight up and looked at Shay like he was some sort of lunatic, like he had gone stark raving mad.

"Go back? For what? Please tell me you're joking, Irish."

"Not in the least, John, not in any way. We've got to go back."

John pressed his temples with his palms and let out a frustrated groan. "I need at least one good reason, maybe two. You know it's a suicide mission, right?"

Shay took a long, thoughtful puff of the cigar as the smoke swirled about the cold air of the room.

John's face was cast in a bit of light, and what Shay saw there and his friend's eyes saddened him. John was utterly defeated. The man looked bedraggled. Shay chewed on the end of the ancient cigar and spat a leaf of tobacco on the floor. It was like smoking a cardboard box. He didn't really mind.

"I'm sorry, John."

"Sorry for what?"

"For all of it. I'm sorry for dragging you into this; I'm sorry for what happened to Peter. I'm sorry for what's going to happen next."

John squinted his eyes, peering at Shay as though he could perhaps figure out what Shay meant without asking. They sat there in silence; Shay gave John time to ask. He didn't.

"I've got to go back, John. That cruel bastard is going to get away if we take the time to summon the cavalry."

"Shay, that's just asinine, that's crazy talk. We need to get the hell out of here and survive this cold to reach safety. That's what we need to do. We're 33% down on men, 60% if you count by the pound. You've been cut up and tortured, and you want to go back? I knew you were nuts, but this is just silly."

"I can't let him get away with what he did to Pete. I can't let him set up shop somewhere else and cause more chaos and death. It's not like I'm long for this world anyway…"

He handed John the smoke as John leaned in, asking, "What did… what did he do to you, Shay? You seem fine, you're just worn out, is all…"

"I've got cancer in me, John. The Doc told me as much."

"He put cancer in you?" John half-shouted, tensing up.

"Nae, it seems it was there on its own accord. Suppose I've lived a wee bit too rough." Shay sighed and pulled his blanket up to his chin.

"And now you're going kamikaze to take this bastard out, huh? It's your sole responsibility? Gotta play John Wayne? I won't let you do it, Shay. Sick or not, you have reasons to live. Hell, so do I."

"I think whatever he gave me, it's… it changed me a bit, John. I don't feel normal."

John leaned back and stared down his old friend. "Just what the hell does that mean?"

"Look at my head, John. Where I banged it falling through the window…"

John sat up on his knees and leaned in close, spitting on his thumb and wiping Shay's forehead.

"Jesus… it's… it's fully healed, man. It's nothing! Last night, you were…"

"…Proper gashed, yeh. It's all sealed up now, and it's got to have something to do with what the Doc put in me. I need to know. I need to ask him. I need answers, John. You can take the truck and get to safety, but I can't live without answers. Maybe he can… ah, forget it."

John chewed on his thoughts for a bit, relighting the cigar with a match and lying back into his blankets as he puffed on it.

"It won't play out like that, Shay. There are maybe two gallons of gas in the Jeep, and that's it. I don't know if I can make it anywhere but another snowdrift. At least the keys are in it… Fuck. You're crazy, but you're right. We gotta go back. Besides… might be some gas in that wagon of theirs."

Shay leaned his head back onto the Jeep door with a thud.

"Think they'll still be around?"

John chuckled, reached into his pocket, and mused, "Might have stalled them a little…" as he dangled a small metal barrel in the air by its wire. It was a distributor condenser from under the hood of the Chevy panel van.

"You sneaky, cheeky bastard. Hope they forgot to bring spare parts!" Shay laughed heartily.

John smiled as he tamped out the acrid cigar on the ground, then stood with a grunt, sighing, "Well, unless we want to dine on rubber hoses, we'd better get back there and get it over with."

Standing up and stretching his arms to the sky, Shay agreed, "Let's get this over with."

In no time, they ransacked that little maintenance shed and, along one wall, collected everything they thought might be of use in their impending infiltration of that horrible place. They piled their arsenal into the back of their Jeep.

Shay stood there observing their collection of odds and ends, fists on his hips. Two empty steel drums with band-clamping lids, several sections of rope good for a few dozen feet, some free climbing hooks, four axes, and a half-dozen road flares. On the floor was an empty red jerry can good for a few gallons. Both of the men had stuffed screwdrivers and wrenches in their pockets.

"I'm ready when you are, Shay."

"No better time than peak sun!" Shay exclaimed.

The boys had readied their chariot; it was silly, to say the least. The bumper was strapped with three bald truck tires, the winch having been unbolted from the front bumper and remounted to the bolt holes on the rear bumper. Excitedly, Shay hopped up into the Jeep and settled into the well-worn bucket seat. It reminded him of his short stint as a bomber gunner in the war. He hated the altitude, but he loved those stupid little seats. The way they bounced around and swiveled, he remembered scratching his initials into the aluminum frame on a mission once while they were flying high above the French countryside.

"All set, John, shall we?"

John nodded and rolled up the corrugated garage door, mockingly bowing and sweeping an open hand toward their freedom. Shay peered over the hazy windshield glass and turned the starter ignition.

Click.

He rattled the shifter in neutral, depressed the clutch once more, and tapped the gas. Holding a deep breath, he twisted the key once more in the hopes that there might be something left in the battery.

Nothing. The battery was dead. Shay threw his head back and groaned.

"Aaaaahhh… fuck me… suppose we could push-start the bastard?

With a sigh and a shrug, John went around behind and shouldered the Jeep out of the garage. The little shed was on a mild hill; as soon as the wheels touched gravel, the Jeep was rolling down the slope. Shay was laughing giddy as a child as he slammed the shifter into second gear and let out the clutch. The Jeep lurched as the driveline turned the engine. The ignition didn't fire. Still slowly rolling down the hill, with John running and chasing behind him, Shay shifted the Jeep into first gear and once again took his foot off the clutch pedal as he feathered the gas pedal.

Chuff chuff chuff chuffchuffchuffBANG!

Starting with a misfire, the Jeep's ignition fired up as the generator supplied just enough current to light those old spark plugs. The engine's friction slowed the Jeep; she was now running. The valves clattered because the oil had not yet reached all its pathways in the motor. Shay jammed the brakes, skidding the Jeep to a stop in the gravel before he reached the bottom of this little access road they had been rolling down.

Huffing from his run, John caught up to the back end of the Jeep and slapped the fender.

puppita-puppita-puppita

The jeep idled quiet but rough.

"I knew it! You can't kill these things, Shay!"

Grabbing the windshield frame, he leaped up onto the passenger seat of the Jeep.

"John, you'd better hold on tight. We have very little fuel, so I'm going to get us there as quick as a bunny."

Grasping the dashboard handle, John nodded toward the Road. Given the go-ahead, Shay released the clutch and feathered the gas. The little Jeep took off like a startled mule.

Down the road, they rumbled, the Jeep trouncing around and sliding in the light, icy snow. The little Jeep had taken them halfway down the road that they had used to escape; John's knuckles were white as he squeezed his coat collars tightly, and Shay observed the look on his face that belied his friend's feelings about their return. John looked pensive, to say the least. Hoping to lighten the mood, Shay began humming the tune of Flight of the Valkyries. His friend looked at him at first in confusion, then, with a chuckle, he gave Shay a thumbs up and joined him. "Onward, captain!" John joked.

Shay jiggled the steering wheel playfully, half-singing the tune.

"Bum-bum-ba-BAAAA-bum, Bum-bum-ba-BAAAAAAA-BUM!"

He didn't stop with that tune until they had nearly reached the warehouse. As they got close, he slowed down and directed John's gaze to the snow.

"No tracks… they must still be here!" Shay was shaking with adrenaline and hunger.

"Then let's go in quiet-like, Shay…" John implored.

Shay killed the ignition, slowing to a crawl road well before they could be seen. They silently coasted downhill the next few hundred yards until they were at the edge of the property, facing the building they had recently narrowly escaped.

"Okay, I'll wait here. You check around back, and then we go in!" Shay whispered.

John was sweating, more from nerves than effort. He hopped out of the Jeep and slowly walked around the building, careful not to make any noise. When he returned to the Jeep, he nodded and assured his friend, "Everything looks clear, Irish."

Setting the parking brake, Shay climbed out of the Jeep to meet John as they slowly circled the building back toward the barrels of bunker oil.

"You sure this is going to make a stink?" Shay asked.

"My old man worked in a steel mill. They had this one guy—a real lame duck—and he took to making the warehouse his ashtray. Apparently, one day, he put a cigarette down a barrel of this stuff, thinking it was machine oil. My old man said that barrel went off like you wouldn't believe, shot the lid to the ceiling, and black smoke filled the warehouse faster than anyone could run out of there, seeing as the place was closed up for winter weather. Seven men had to be carted off to the hospital, and two dozen of them needed weeks to recover. Pops was outta work for a while, but we built some nifty model cars during that time. Still, he was miffed, and rightly so. Nasty shit, and we are going to take advantage of that."

"Sounds like a plan, Talbot. It's a nasty plan. Risky, but worth it surely."

Within minutes, they had relocated two massive barrels into the back of the Jeep and one more on the passenger seat. Shay took his place in the driver's seat as John slipped inside through the side door where they'd emerged the night before.

Come on, old boy, get in there and get it done!

Shay was champing at the bit to receive the signal. He waited in that cold seat, fingers on the ignition key, listening. Birds were squawking, a little wind was blowing in the trees, and there was a light hum from the building in front of him. At this moment, he felt how deeply desperate their plan was, but he reminded himself that they had little alternative to speak of. He wasn't even sure the tired battery in the Jeep could fire it up again.

Can't risk letting this mad bastard do any more harm. Can't risk him getting away. Can't take the chance, can't do it. You've got to end this.

A small *rap rap rap* on the corrugated roll-up door broke his concentration. "Okay, we're up!" He murmured to himself as he cranked the ignition key. The little jeep rumbled to life, quietly idling and ready to work.

Oh, thank you, beautiful stupid little truck...

He put the Jeep in second gear and slowly idled toward the building, executing a J-turn. He came to rest with the Jeep's rear bumper mere feet from the roll-up door. At the same time, the door began to rattle as John pulled the chains from inside.

"Shay, back her inside real slow!" John whispered loudly, like a schoolchild telling secrets.

"Roger that, Talbot!" Shay replied as he crept that little truck backward into the building. He was feathering the clutch so it barely revved up off a quiet idle.

"Elevator locked open?" He inquired.

John pointed back and replied, "Jammed with a broom. We're good!"

He navigated the Jeep into position just behind the Chevy panel van, letting it idle in neutral. Then, hopping out of the seat, he helped John move the first of three barrels of bunker oil into the freight elevator.

"Shay, when we get these loaded, you get the gas outta the Chevy. I'll worry about the elevator."

"I've got the siphon ready!" He replied, producing a severed length of gardening hose from his pocket.

After moving the last two barrels into place, Shay stopped John and grasped him by the shoulders.

"You've got the lift rigged? Ready for this, yeh?"

John gave him a thumbs-up and assured him, "I'm ready. You get that gas, and I'll start the show!"

Shay took to siphoning fuel from the Chevy's tank. John chuckled as Shay spat out the gasoline as suck-started the siphon hose.

Now, it was his turn. John had no reputation as 'book smart,' but he was clever, and that counted more. In the few minutes he'd had with the freight elevator, he figured out three things: firstly, he used a flathead screwdriver to override the switch on the lift doors. Now, he could raise or lower the lift without closing the door on their level. Second, he removed the button box from its two-bolt mount in the elevator and pulled out the wires. Now, it could only be operated from above. Thirdly, he had opened the extruded steel access hatch of the freight elevator. It was like heavy chicken wire. It was just big enough for what he needed, and he placed two of the three barrels directly under the open hatch.

"Almost done with the first round, John. I'll empty this can into the truck and fill it once more if there's enough in the truck. You ready for your end of the mess?"

With a wicked grin, John kicked over the third barrel in the elevator and slapped the "down" button on the outer wall. It began its descent with a satisfying hum.

"FECK! Foul shite!" Shay cursed and complained behind him, suck-starting another round of siphoning the panel van's fuel into the jerry can.

John was transfixed; the foul, thick, and tarry stench of the bunker oil saturated the musty air of the elevator shaft even while it was departing downward. He could hear the slosh of gallons of the muck dripping down the sides of the elevator into the shaft, and the glisten of it from above was almost pretty.

He thought about the sallow feeling in his eye and the hazy vision. He'd almost forgotten about it in the tizzy of things, but he knew just now that Shay had almost certainly lied about how good it looked. He knew that there was something unnatural in his old friend, and he knew that they would either get answers or bring death here today.

Probably both.

Ka-clunk. The elevator settled into its springs a dozen or more yards below.

With a sneer, John peered over the edge, down the shaft, and through that open hatch. There, he could see those two black circles of open fifty-five-gallon drums resting there, a powder keg beckoning him like a cracked blind beckoning a voyeur. His heart was pounding.

Blowing a kiss to the bastards below, John struck a road flare.

204

Foxhole

A light snow fell gingerly now, dusting everything outside in brilliant white. The men sat huddled in their beat-up and frozen little Jeep parked just inside the building, facing out the open freight door. The old leather hide and the rusty-sprung seats creaked while their breath fogged in front of them. Shay scanned the horizon for signs of smoke, knowing there would likely be ventilation shafts away from the main building. He wondered who had undertaken such an effort to build this old bunker, whether it be some private entity or perhaps the Army Corps of Engineers.

"Smoke's coming up pretty foul now, Shay."

"We'll need the masks soon… but not yet. Can't hardly see shite through those old visors."

John had his hands shoved deep in his pockets, his right heel tapping and shaking his leg. It shook the Jeep a little bit as well. He turned to his friend as they waited for whatever came next.

"Think this is a sure thing? Smoking them out like a foxhole, think they won't be prepared?"

"John, I don't think anything in life is a sure thing. And I'm damn sure nothing in war is a sure thing, but I think this is our best move."

John shrugged and squeezed his hands tightly in his pockets. Shay had a sneer on his face.

"It's our only move, boyo. We don't know how many people are down there, no matter that we only met the mad doctor and his shiny-headed henchman. If they don't come up, we go down. That's about the extent of what I know."

John sighed and asked his friend, "How are you always so calm?"

Shay chewed on the question for a bit before answering, "Because I know that every decision I've made has brought me to this point.

Because I don't regret much in my life, and the things I do regret I'm hoping there's still time to fix. It's the least I can do for Pete. Try and right one last wrong."

John leaned forward and rested his head on the cold steel dashboard. "Say, you remember that dancer? The one with the veils."

"What a silly question!' Shay poked John in the ribs, chuckling. 'If I'd forgotten that lass, you might as well leave me down there with those creatures because I've got no heartbeat."

John was reminiscing about a particularly memorable night they spent in a watering hole in Italy, where a very exotic young lady performed an equally exotic dance for the men shortly before they returned after the war had ended. Their reconnaissance detachment was tasked with reclaiming equipment and supplies in the withdrawal, but their commander had been generous with leave. Generous enough that the boys had been laid back with brandy, pocket money, and a carton of hand-rolled cigarettes for two days before they stumbled into that little bar, and it was another two days of wine and dining there before they needed to return to their duties.

"I was thinking she had those beautiful silk scarves everywhere. The way she moved, it's like every inch of her was a secret. I couldn't even tell you if she was fair-skinned or sun-kissed. It's just... I was just thinking maybe I can get one of those scarves to cover my eye. Really lean into a dark and mysterious mood, you think?"

He joked through chattering teeth, and Shay appreciated the levity.

"I'm telling you, old boy, it's not that bad! No, if you cover it that assuredly draws more attention. What you need is a Banana-yellow suit and a missing tooth right up front. Hell, dress like that, and nobody would notice if you were lacking an eyebrow or even a hand... fook's sake, even a pinky!"

He held up his shivering hand with its little nub where his pinky should be. John guffawed over the idea.

"Ah, hell! If we come out of this in one piece, you can take me to the tailors. What do you say we get ourselves ready, Irish?"

"Just a moment, I want to check outside for signs of life. We know they can't take the van, but we don't know if they might be escaping just up the hill."

"Got you. I'll watch your back!" John assured him with a pat on the shoulder.

With that, they grabbed their masks and fire axes and paced to the open roll-up door. Shay walked a slow lap around the building, and

John stood silently, listening. Waiting. Hoping they wouldn't have to go back down into that labyrinth of horrors. But he knew, deep down, that they were destined for a fight.

Smoke had filled the ceiling of the freight room by the time Shay returned with a shake of his head.

"Nothing out there that I can see, John. Nasty smoke. You need some fresh air before we get to it?"

"I'll enjoy that when we're done." John's resolve was set; his hands gripped firmly on his axe, and his fireman's mask perched over his brow. Its smoke filter jutted down like a little elephant trunk.

Standing over the freight elevator shaft, Shay hit the call-up button. As it hummed to life and began to rise, moments felt like eons. The smoke billowing out of the shaft concealed whatever might be rising their way. Just before it reached the top, the men slid their masks down over their faces and stepped back.

KA-CHUNK

The lift settled into its place in front of them, and they could see that the bunker oil had burned off, leaving only a nasty residue and something on the corrugated steel floor of the elevator that had not been present before —a crumpled pile next to the overturned barrel.

John looked at Shay, who shrugged and stepped into the elevator. With the head of his axe, he poked the rumpled pile, but nothing moved.

"Is that-" John asked, but Shay was already lifting the blanket over whatever it was.

"Ah. It's Mister Boots! And he looks... he looks worse for wear."

The smoke had cleared a bit, and under that dim bulb, John could see the shiny head of their prior captor. The man's face was strained, frozen in a gasp. There was no life left in this sad thing.

Silent and solemn, Shay beckoned John inside the elevator and shut the cage. As the lift descended with a whirring hum, Shay replied, "Let's finish the job, then."

As the left reached the bottom, creaking into its springs, John extended an arm and prevented Shay from stepping out yet. "Listen!"

They stood there in the smoky haze, waiting. Nothing moved, but something down the hall was making a racket. It sounded like a bear knocking over trash bins.

"Be ready," John whispered through his mask as he hoisted the empty steel barrel and tossed it into the hallway. Sounding out a tinny ringing like a schoolyard bell, it bounced off the adjacent wall. They stood dead silent, waiting. Nothing moved, but the shuffling sounds from down the hall continued to echo through the smoke. He then dragged the bald man's husk out of the elevator by the pant cuff and left him there in the hallway with a pang of guilt over the man's fate— the tragedy he may have faced, which they'd never know.

Oh, piss off. You'd do the same to us, I'm sure of it.

Shay tapped John on the shoulder and held up his hand in a 'wait' motion. Using a pointed hand and a closed fist, he signaled John to step into the hallway and wait. He then signaled, with a bladed hand waving toward the hallway, that he would advance toward the noise. John nodded, acknowledging he would cover from behind.

As they stepped out of the lift, John blocked the doors with a chair that had been set in the hallway.

Treading slowly, the men took their positions, leading and flanking. Shay tiptoed forward. John paced behind him, about 10 feet away, matching his steps. He knew that if things went south, Shay would swing that axe, and he wanted to stay just out of the blade's arc.

As they advanced, they passed a few doors. At each doorway, they paused while John turned the knob and opened the door slightly; Shay stood outside the door with the ax held high, ready to bring it down on the head of whoever or whatever might be lurking inside.

The first door, nothing. Empty room. The second door creaked open, but the room was also quiet. A laboratory and tables, but nobody inside. All the while, shuffling and ominous racket continued down the hall, made near-invisible by the smoke that hung in the air.

Leaning in with a whisper, John advised his friend, "Any of these closed rooms wouldn't have been smoked out. We'd better be ready."

Nodding, Shay continued advancing. John's heart was in his throat; sweat poured down his brow. In his hard-sold shoes, he did his best to tread quietly just behind his brave friend. They were getting close; the ruckus was louder now. Something substantial was moving at the end of that hallway. It couldn't be more than 30 feet now, but the smoke was so thick in the corridor that he could barely see his cohort only five paces ahead.

"Shay!' John whispered, having a realization, 'Do you think that could be?"

Shay stopped dead, peering over his shoulder and putting up a flat palm to signal STOP... but it was too late.

"HRAAAAAAGHHHHH!" With a guttural shout, the monster that was once their friend Peter emerged from the smoke in a stooped rush and lunged at Shay, toppling him to the floor.

"Shite!" Shay shouted as he was knocked to the ground, the wind knocked out of him.

John leaped forward, shouting, "Shay!" He gripped his axe handle tightly and raised it in front of himself, hoping to knock Pete off balance. It was no use. The giant man swung wildly and struck the ax out of John's hands, grasping him by the arms and pinning him to the wall.

"PETE!" John gasped, hoping in vain to stop the assault. The big bastard lifted him clear off his feet and slammed him into the wall, a sickening *crack* as John's head bounced off the cement block. This thing was furious and confused. It lifted John once again and tossed him away to the floor like a rag doll, turning back toward Shay, who was now back on his feet and gasping for breath.

"Pe—" he tried to sound the words out, but he was wheezing under the mask and choking out, "Pete... It's SHAY!"

The words held no meaning to this wild thing, and with heavy steps, it advanced.

At this moment, Shay knew what must be done.

Dropping to his knees and springing forward in a tackle, Shay's shoulder caught the big man just below his left hip and sent the two of them tumbling to the ground.

"John! Get UP!" He shouted, scrambling to mount this behemoth. Pete writhed and struggled to gain footing, but to no avail. Shay straddled the small of his back and swung his right arm around that thick neck, using his toes to kick Pete's legs apart so he might not find footing again. He was practically riding this insane beast, but from the corner of his eye, he saw the handle of that axe.

Reaching out with his free left hand, he grabbed the handle and brought it up close to his body. The head of the axe scraped metallic along the concrete floor, Shay sliding his left hand up the handle until the cold iron head butted against his fist. Through the mask, he shouted with tears streaming down his face in a last attempt to save himself an awful task.

"Pete... PETE! Ye' got to STOP! I don't wanna do this!"

Grunting and writhing, whatever was left of his friend now struggled beneath him and, at any moment, would surely rise to its feet again to wreak havoc.

Still leg locked and attempting to choke the beast, Shay took a final look at his pal through smoke and tears. Pete's red eyes flashed at him wild and unfocused, like a deer caught in a trap. There was no saving this man.

"I'm sorry, big guy... I'll take care of Melly. She's a good lass."

Shay released his chokehold and reared back on his heels, sitting on the back of this mad thing. He raised the axe in his fist over his head and brought the blade down on the neck of his friend.

RUNTCH

The blade had embedded itself deeply, cutting and crushing as it plunged. The writhing ceased, the body fell flat—the cold, wet slap of a heavy head on hard ground. For a moment, everything was still.

"I'm sorry, Peter..." Shay offered through the lump in his throat, his breath heaving through dangling filter canisters in his mask. The visor was fogged, and he was reticent to lay eyes on the gore beneath him.

Softly, a hand rested upon his shoulder, rising and falling with Shay's still-heaving breath. Without turning his head, he uttered, "I *had* to. I... had to, John."

"You're okay, Shay. It's okay... You had to." John consoled his friend.

Shay dropped the handle of the axe, though it fell slowly to the ground with one end still stuck in that grisly mutant. He stood, wavering a bit, and grabbed John's arm for support.

"John, we... We've got t' find the madman... are you all right? Your noggin..." he huffed between breaths.

"I'm bleeding, but I'm all right, Shay. It winded me pretty good, but I was a footballer. I know how to manage."

Despite the smoke, Shay could see the glistening stain on John's collar and the pain in his eyes. "You're a stud, Johnny boy. We can finish this."

John nodded and pressed his forehead to Shay' in a gesture of camaraderie. Their masks clacked together.

"I'm ready. You can—"

BOOM!

John was cut off by the sound of an explosion, a blast that shook the building. It was muffled, muted.

"Up top?" John offered, and nodding in agreement, Shay grasped John's shoulder and motioned for them to head back to the freight elevator.

Now that the caustic smoke cleared to wisps, they found their way more manageable than before. John kicked the chair away from the freight elevator door, and they slammed the gate shut, punching the button to head for the surface. The slow pace of the lift and its reassuring hum gave them just enough time to steel their nerves and calm their breath.

Peering upward, they both knew they were headed into either carnage or a trap, and through the dread, they both found themselves ready.

As they arrived at the ground floor, John swung the steel elevator doors open.

"Dirty bastard…' Shay muttered, the flickering flames reflecting off his visor. He stepped forward, silent, toward the burning wreckage of their little jeep there in the large doorway of the building, 'he torched the gas tank!"

"Shay."

"Ah fuck it all to hell. The madman's gone off! We were too slow!"

"Shay…"

"No, no. I was foolish. We should have gotten the authorities or some such…"

"SHAY!"

"WHAT?" He shouted, throwing his hands up as he turned to face John, who had taken off his firefighting mask. John was holding something up in the smoky air.

"I have something he doesn't…' John offered with a chortle, and he slapped a small object into Shay's palm, '…and he's on foot."

Shay lifted his smoke mask and held up in his fingers the little distributor condenser and its little dangling grounding wire from the Chevy panel van's ignition distributor, which he'd pilfered the night prior.

"You clever bastard, Johnny fookin' Talbot…"

The Thrill

KERRRRUNTCH

"Again!"

CRUNNNCCHHH

"Once more, Shay!"

Shay threw the Chevrolet panel wagon into first gear, lurching forward a dozen feet, then shifting back into reverse. "You sure?" he shouted to John, who was in the back of the wagon eagerly peering out the dingy windows of the rear doors.

"Yeah! A little to the right, er, your left!"

"Aye!" Shay shouted back and slammed his foot on the accelerator pedal, dropping the clutch and gunning the engine. The wagon shunted back with great speed toward the little jeep.

With another bone-jarring collision, the Chevy's rear bumper finally shoved the burned-out Jeep out of the way and off to the side as Shay slammed the brakes and halted the Chevy there in the open snow.

John leaped into the front seat and swung the passenger door wide open. "Now we follow his footprints; I'll hang out on the running board so I can see better and direct you, okay?"

Shay twisted the wiper switch, and the little, paltry aluminum wiper arms began a slow, sweeping rhythm, clearing snowflakes off the windshield.

"Okay, but he can't be far as it is," Shay replied.

"Yeah, but I'm too damn cold and tired to chase him on foot, and I don't think he'll head into the woods. That's suicide."

"Fair enough, John. Off we go!"

He shunted the old transmission into second gear and slowly accelerated up the drive. For now, he could see the footprints of what they assumed were those of the mad doctor.

"Prescient, how I left a little gas in the wagon, yeh?"

Shay prodded John, who gave him a thumbs up and waved him on, replying, "I can see 'em leading up the hill. Just keep her rolling…"

They idled onward, the tires crunching and compressing the snow underneath. The woods were quiet, clear, and bright. A light breeze fluttered John's hair across his face as he peered out over the hood and scanned the adjacent woods for any sign of their prey.

Shay spoke softly and with a grimace, reassuring himself, "The old codger only had a ten-minute head start; there's no way he gets away from us." He hoped he was right, and even moreso, he prayed that they were following the right man—that sneering, torturous bastard.

They came upon the crossroad from the day of their escape. John slapped the roof of the truck and ducked back in, perturbed.

"The tracks ended. He ducked into the treeline, Shay. We have to follow." Shay slowed the truck to a stop, idling there.

"Talbot, take the wheel. I'll follow his tracks; you watch my six!"

John made a sour face. "You sure you want to take it to the ground? He could be doubling back, or…"

"Which is *why* I need t' move with urgency, John. Take the wheel!"

"Ah, hell. If you hear the horn beep, shout back. I ain't gonna let you get far…"

Clutching his axe, Shay grimaced at the cold and nodded to John before stepping off into the brush.

Got t' move quick. These prints won't last forever, though the canopy might stave off the snow a bit…

His leather shoes were packed around the ankle with snow almost immediately. The raincoat trapped just enough body heat to let him move quickly, to keep his blood pumping. That, and the furious flow of adrenaline when faced with a deadly hunt. Deftly, he stepped over jagged fallen limbs and around spindly growing trees as he trudged in the footsteps of the man who couldn't be far ahead. Each of the footsteps ahead of him made a clear, distinct impression in the snow, some of them oblong and broken; the man was slipping and moving with careless steps.

Ye may have better shoes, but you're old and fat, and I'm going to snatch you up like a bratty child.

He smirked at his juvenile monologue and chalked it up to perturbation, the idea that this leather-faced cur might go free after what he had done to John, after what he had done to Shay himself.

BEEP BEEP

John had sounded the horn. "CLEAR!" Shay shouted in retort, with a short *BEEP* from John to acknowledge he'd heard. Shay could hear John rev up the Chevrolet and move it further up the road adjacent to the treeline Shay was stalking.

Hear that, old man? We're going to eat you for supper, you mad cunt. I'll bet my wages on it. Come on, come ON!

He tread lightly now; the footprints became muddled as though the man were running for this stretch. Shay grasped his axe handle with both fists and bore it across his chest, ready to defend himself or attack as needed. His breath was heavy, stinging his lungs with the cold air.

You can't outpace us both, Doc. I've got a friend, and he's got a truck. YOUR truck... and I'll tie ye to the bumper for the trip into town!

CRAKKK

Behind Shay, a twig snapped, and immediately, a pit sank in his stomach. ...*Fucker.*

He spun on his heel and came face to face with the barrel of a revolver.

"Ah, Doc! Thought ye were run-in'... seems it was the doubling-back that had your... footer-"

With a furious sneer, the old man swung the pistol across Shay's face, and the world went black.

—

"Oh, my bleeding' *head...*" Shay professed as he blinked the blood out of his eyes.

He was slumped in the passenger seat of the Chevrolet.

"Shay, he's got us dead to rights." John's voice was calm but with a tinge of worry, as it should be.

Shay felt the engine idling softly. The heater box fan was spun up, and the men were collected in this tin wagon in some weird respite from the snow despite the imminent threat of death. From the back of the truck, the raspy voice of the mad doctor echoed.

"You *stupid* little fools. You have ruined my plans once again and for the last time. You held so much promise, do you not see? And you treat me with such... *contempt.*"

John chuckled and turned in his seat, resting his back against the steering wheel. He fumbled around a bit behind him but found the keys, twisting them to kill the ignition. The truck fell silent, and now it was just the three men there in the little wagon, pattering falling snow on the steel roof.

"You gave us plenty of reason to hate you, or did you forget what you did to my eye?" John asked with a growl in his throat that sounded like he was ready to kill. He pointed at his face, the unblinking eye in a sallow socket.

"You petulant boy, I saved what I could, and that was a grace. You should *thank* me."

John spat on the floor of the truck, his fists balled. "THANK you? You caused that goddamn wreck! You cost me an eye, you nearly killed us both, and Pete is… You turned our pal into some kind of *freak!*"

The old man shrugged and cocked the gun, aiming it at Shay. "Fair enough, but no matter. I will leave your righteous corpses slumped in the snowbanks and return to my work, and you will not bother me again.

Shay piped up in hopes of distracting the man.

"Oh, but you don't know? We burned that place to *dust*, mate. Your little hole in the ground is now a chimney. So where will you go from here?"

"Insolent FOOL!" The old man shouted, sneering and sweating at the brow. His gun rattled, still trained on Shay, just out of reach of either of the captives. The Doctor removed his fogging glasses and folded them into his breast pocket, hands trembling as he continued his vitriol.

"I should have left the two of you to die on a laboratory table. No, no… Mister Irish and his condition, I simply *had* to know more of its effects. Hubris, I am afraid, has led us all to this point. Well, no further, I assure you."

John sat up straight and leaned over in the sight line of the barrel. "You're gonna need the truck, ain't ya?"

A lifetime passed, that shaky barrel now aimed at John's head. Shay was still a bit woozy, but felt very much that John might be making some sort of last stand here.

"John, let's… let's go with some dignity then, yeh?" He patted his friend on the shoulder and swung open the door of the truck.

"SLOWLY!" The madman shouted as he weaved the gun back and forth from Shay to John. Shay obliged, moving slowly and stepping out just next to the passenger door. The Doctor slowly swung open his rear door, never breaking gaze with the men.

John reached behind him and fumbled around again, finding the keys and taking them out of the ignition before slowly stepping out of his driver's side door.

Shay saw John wince, flashing his broken teeth; it was masked but unmistakable to a friend. *Oh, you daft bastard…*

The Doc circled the truck and met the men in front of it. They stood back against the hood as the old man trained his gun on them, aiming back and forth like a grim bastardization of she-loves-me-not.

"You'll need these, but…' John held up the keys to the truck, 'I should warn you, I played football as a youngster. I was a quarterback, I could throw these keys into that tree line, and you'd never find 'em. Or…"

The old man, dragging his cold feet, stepped closer and asked, "Well, what do you wish for, a 'sporting chance'? I would consider that."

John stepped forward, keys in his left palm. "If you promise, yeah. It's a sporting chance. Twenty paces."

"As you wish, hand me the keys."

John took another step forward as the madman lowered his gun barrel toward John's gut.

"Here you go… *NOW SHAY!*"

Shay's reflexes twitched, and he lunged toward the gun, clutching it in his hand just as John snatched the Doctor's forearm and pulled him in tight. Shay gripped the gun and stuck his finger under the hammer while he wrestled the weapon, but the old man's steely grip wouldn't loosen.

"Eye for an EYE, you sonofabitch?" John screamed wildly and stuck the dashboard cigar lighter he'd palmed into the old man's eye. It hissed and seared, the audible sizzling of soft flesh.

"AaaAAAAAUUUUAAAGGHHH!!!!!!" The old man screamed in sheer agony as the red-hot steel coil melted into his eyeball.

BANG

"Ah! fuck!" Shay yelped. The gun had fired into his left leg just below the hip.

"SHAY!" John cried out as he balled up his fist and knocked the old man out cold.

"I'm… I'm fuckin' *shot*, Talbot. You fucking loon! You got me SHOT!" John grabbed the pistol from the snow and rushed to aid Shay.

"I'm sorry, I'm so sorry! It was all I could-"

"Ha!" Shay punched him in the arm and snickered, and John paused at the lunacy of it.

"You're not… you're messing with me? You're *fucking* with me…

Shay? Are you even shot?"

Shay sat up against the front of the truck in a cloud of steam as it escaped from the radiator. The bullet had exploded through his thigh and blasted a golf ball-sized hole through the copper radiator of the Chevy.

"Ah fuck, no, I'm shot t'be sure… but the shock, I can hardly feel it. The cold seems t'be aiding as well. Through-and-through, see?" He pointed to the radiator and smiled, his teeth chattering.

John stood tall and watched Shay bleed into the snow. He scooped up some fresh powder and was pressing it into his palm, where the red-hot cigar lighter had burned his hand as he baited the Doc.

"Well, shit. You're gonna need a doctor, Shay. I don't know if I can get you to a hospital in the Chevy with the radiator gone."

"No need, mate. We've got a doc right here, and rightly? He and I have unfinished business. It's just a short drive back; the Chevrolet will get us back."

Sighing, John offered a hand, and Shay took it to stand before leaning his weight on the hood.

"Hey, Johnny boy, hand me that pistol, would ya?"

John hugged Shay from the side, pressed the gun into Shay's hand, and clasped it there for a moment. "You're nuts. I'm with you… But you're nuts."

Shay smiled and shrugged, "You're the one that just saved our arses with a feckin' *lighter*, you absolute cockswain. Say, yank that fat old shite's belt off and make me a tourniquet, would ye?"

No Loose Ends

Sunday, December 24th, 1950
Christmas Eve

Billy sat there at his desk, cigarette half-smoked but having gone out long ago. He was gobsmacked, speechless. Well, speechless for Billy.

"All of it? It's all gone?" He asked, exasperation evident in his tone.

One hundred and seventy-six miles away, Shay and John huddled in a phone booth under a flickering streetlamp. They'd fought two feet of snow to get to that phone, but with the streets empty as a lawyer's morals, they had the privacy they needed.

"Every bit. Do you know how tedious it is to spend three weeks holding a gun trained on somebody?" John mused, rubbing his shoulder, which was still sore from the labor.

"So let me get this straight, when John called me two weeks ago saying you boys need more time, what you meant was you already had the whole damn thing solved… You just wanted to play it out a little longer?"

Shay took offense to the implication. "Billy boy, you old mountain goat, it's not about the pay. Consider the case closed as of the day we last spoke. No, we had some loose ends to tie up. Needed to make sure no other sorry sod ever went through that sort of ordeal behind us."

Billy let out a low whistle and leaned back into his chair. The creaking springs could be heard through the handset in the silent winter air. "So those G men I offered up, Harry Truman's boys, you were stalling?"

John took the handset and replied, "Could you imagine? What kind of mess would this cause if anyone ever got their hands on it? I know it all sounds like the plot of a Vincent Price film, but that's the point. It's morose, and it was evil. Every bit of it, top to bottom. So we made the right choice, damn the consequences."

"Not that it was your call to make, but I understand. How's the leg, Irish?"

"Oh, it's still a sore subject, t'be sure, but I'm getting there. Walking upright with a nice cane John had crafted from a tree branch while we were hunkered down in that basement."

Concern in his voice, Billy asked on, "...and that other thing? The man had diagnosed you..."

"Just been back to a *real* practitioner today, Billy. Clean slate, I'm fit as a fiddle. I don't kin if that dire prognosis in that pit might've been true, but it's not true now, and I'll take that for all it's worth."

Changing the subject felt like the right move, so Billy asked, "Ah, I see. Say, you're a whittler, John?"

"My old man taught me. Gave me somethin' to do after I broke my foot junior year."

Shay tapped John on his toes with the cane, teasing, and butted in, "Must've been hard on your football career, yeh?"

Billy chuckled over the phone as John came clean, "Shay, I was lying... I wasn't a linebacker, and I sure as hell wasn't a quarterback."

"But John, you said about the keys... You never played football?"

"I shattered my foot at tryouts, Shay. I took theater classes for the rest of grade school. Damn ankle still goes stiff in the rain. I wanted to be Charlie Chaplin!"

Shay chortled and playfully snatched the receiver.

"Well, as it goes, Billy, you won't have to send any help or any of those black suits. We took care of everything, and there's nothing left of the place. We made sure that madman cleaned up his mess and then gave that hell the burial it deserved."

"And just... and just *how* do you manage to bury an underground bunker?" Billy asked, staring at the pinholes in his ceiling tile.

John leaned in and offered, "If you have a client seeking the whereabouts of a number of stolen cement trucks, Billy, just... pass on that job, would ya?"

"Ha! Sounds good. Well, did you boys leave him down there to petrify?"

Shay shook his head. "Who, the crazy old cuss? Nae is sitting in a tranquil room at the Oregon State Penitentiary. Underground, just the way he likes it. Pete... Big Pete had friends there, y'see."

"How'd you get past due process?" Billy asked, regretting the question the moment his lips stopped moving.

Shay leaned his head on the cold glass pane of the phone booth, smiling broadly. "Oh, the whole lot was built in cowboy times, Billy. Rimfire rifles and ten-cent whiskey. That castle was built on bones and secrets, and I couldn't be happier to contribute. They get enough John Does through that place every year…"

John took the receiver back and raised his finger to Shay. Shay lit a cigarette and nodded.

"Billy, about that final business? The… that letter you were going to sign for?"

One could hear the paper fluttering over the handset as Billy grunted and replied, "Hmmph. I didn't think it would have been so quick, Talbot. But it's here; as of Thursday, everything is signed. I'll hand it to you when you report in. Does that work for you?"

"Thank you, sir. You won't regret it. Listen, me and the Irish are going to find some chow, but thank you for handling things. Guess we'll see you after the break?"

"*Break*? You boys get seventy-two hours *flat*, and then I want both of your narrow asses on my couch. We've got work to do. Something big is brewing in Chicago, and I can't leave Gabe to fend for himself."

John looked to Shay, who nodded in the affirmative.

"Okay, boss, see you Thursday, first thing. Need anything from the road?"

"You boys owe me a sedan, but we'll worry about that later. Just bring your wits!"

"Sounds good, boss. Merry Christmas." John had a crack in his voice, sincere but with a sadness behind it.

Shay took the handset and said his goodbyes and holiday wishes to Billy, hanging up gently and placing his hand on John's shoulder.

"You need a shoulder, John?"

"Oh, it's not all bad news, just bittersweet. I'm sorry for being a sap, Shay; I just… I gave the old lady the house. A fresh start and all."

"Ah, the paperwork…" Shay replied, tapping his ash out the cracked phone booth door.

"Clean break, time to move on. She's been saying… I needed a new story, Shay. We both did."

"Then can I buy you a whiskey, lad? Take your mind off the weight of it?"

John smiled warmly, sliding open the phone booth door.

"I'll take a cocoa, neat. Like I said, time for a fresh start."

Shay followed him into the snow and paused under the Christmas lights strung across the lampposts. "But I didn't get ye anything for Christmas!"

John spun on his heel, his colorful eyes glinting in the warm golden glow. "All I want for Christmas, Shay, is for *you* to ask out that dame across the hall in your building. Oh, and lend me your couch for a couple of nights."

Shay snorted and cupped his hands for warmth. "Oh, my dear boy, I'm going to buy a house, and you can live in the basement."

"Ha! I'm shopping for apartments in skyscrapers. I'm never setting foot in another Goddamned basement again. Now let's go find a hot meal."

Shay hurried behind John, the wood cane clacking dull on the snowy street between his steps.

"Hope you like Oriental food, Johnny fookin' Talbot!"

—

Forty-eight miles away and twenty feet down, the silence hung heavy in a cold room.

The rusty cast-iron bed frame sagged in the middle. The mattress was stained like the apron of a kitchen person, reds, browns, and yellows. There was no sheet, and the pillow looked like it had survived Custer's last stand.

Cinderblock walls surrounded; the only reprieve from the dull grey was a black riveted steel door. Half an inch crack under the door allowed light in from the hallway, just enough to mind yourself when you needed to squat over the tin piss pail in the corner. Mildew grew on the walls all around, but most significantly behind that piss bucket. Another small shaft of light entered through a gap the breadth of a horsehair in the door of the sliding cuff port, situated at waist height. It was as though it was designed, as with every other aspect of this prison, to hurt and inconvenience in every conceivable way. One had to hunch over to speak to somebody face-to-face, and indignity suffered by many unfortunate souls who had been confined there. It was used for sliding in a tray of slop or applying and removing shackles. These men didn't deserve windows.

In the middle of the room, on a pile of sweat-soiled garments, sat a husk of a man—a nude form, lumpy, pallid. The sort of body one acquires living in squalor or the conditions of a gulag somewhere in

Siberia.

A croaking voice broke the silence of the cold air.

"The hypocrites. Hypocrites! They leave me to fester here as though I will be defeated. But I am not defeated."

The man rocked back and forth on his laurels, in and out of the beam of light. It shone across his nose, his brow, and his one remaining eye. Back and forth, rhythmically, light cast across his face and back again. The voice grumbled and crackled like a record player with a dirty needle.

"They have merely removed my implements and my opportunity. They have not defeated my intellect, they do not know the depths of knowledge which I possess. But I will show them, I will triumph against this miserable place and I will *show* them. The breadth of my success will be the last thing they see before I remove *their* eyes! Yes… An eye for an eye, as that John Talbot had so eloquently stated. An eye… for an eye.

CLANGGG

A heavy oak baton struck that steel door squarely, sending terrible vibrations through the air and permeating the cell. The old man clutched his ears and reeled back, nearly falling over.

"Auuaagh!" he cried like a child.

The small cuff port slid open, revealing the dour lower face of a guard. The man was leaning over and straining.

"It's Christmas Eve, for Christssakes. Shut your mouth and go to sleep, you pile of filth. Or else I'm going to come in there and *give* you something to cry about!"

Rocking forward, still nude on his pile of soiled clothes, the old man smiled at the guard whose face he did not bother to look at.

"Your family is lucky they are not forced to spend it with you, mongrel!" the captive man hissed, baring his teeth.

The guard sneered, "Oh, it's Christmas all right. Time for me to open my goddamn *present*!"

The jangling of a key inserted in the steel door resounded through the hall and the cell.

Still nude, filthy, and staring with his furious eye, the madman rocked forward onto his knees. As the guard fumbled with the key in the cold and aged lock mechanism, the prisoner spit on his fingers and reached behind himself, *inside* himself. A momentary discomfort; now, he firmly grasped the handle of the makeshift shiv he had carved from a discarded toothbrush.

CLINK

The latch released, and that cell door swung open, clanging against the bed frame. The narrow shaft of light highlighted a festive red across the air in the form of arterial mist, and only for a moment. Shortly later, the same door swung softly closed in the otherwise quiet cell block hall.

It would not be a Merry Christmas to all.

~